For Jody and Ted:
With Friendship
and Affection.

June 7, 2001

Nick
the
Greek

Harry Mark Petrakis

AN AUTHORS GUILD BACKINPRINT.COM EDITION

Nick the Greek

AN AUTHORS GUILD BACKINPRINT.COM EDITION
Published by iUniverse.com, Inc.

For information address:
iUniverse.com, Inc.
620 North 48th Street, Suite 201
Lincoln, NE 68504-3467
www.iuniverse.com

Originally published by Doubleday

ISBN: 0-595-00761-9

Printed in the United States of America

For my beloved nephews, Leo, Frank and Steve Manta
In memory of Sarto.

NICK THE GREEK

PROLOGUE

December — 1966

The highroad between Los Angeles, City of the Angels, and Las Vegas, City Without Clocks, cuts through the mountains and across the desert for a distance of three hundred miles. From Los Angeles, the freeway tracks eight lanes beneath terraced hillsides ridged with houses and knobbed with palm trees. Beyond San Bernadino the city traffic thins out, the road winding up past Victorville to Barstow. In the distance, the mountains peaked into trails of mist and smog.

Back in the Middle West, the weather had been cold, snow and winter hitting in force. But I followed the glistening, golden hearse bearing Nick's body from Los Angeles to Las Vegas on what might have been an early autumn day, warm breezes carrying the scent of desert flowers into my car.

I had been working in Chicago when I heard Nick died. Friends in California told me a writer who had been collaborating with him on a book about his life had found him dead in his room. They told me too that some of the

wealthy casino owners in Las Vegas were making arrangements to transport Nick's body to their city for a funeral
befitting a king. They planned a flashy farewell for the
boldest high roller of them all.

I flew from Chicago that evening. The next morning I
rented a car and followed the hearse with Nick's body
north to Las Vegas. We made a strange funeral cortege, a
rented Ford trailing a golden Cadillac. People in other cars
craned their heads for a glimpse, while attendants at gas
station pumps paused to watch. Near the ghost town of
Calico, children clustered before an old farmhouse stopped
and stared. When the sun broke free of the clouds and
flashed across the roof of the hearse, I bet even skiers up
in the mountains could spot the glow.

The trip from Los Angeles to Las Vegas took about five
hours and I had that time to think about Nick's life. Between 1919 when he first came to America and his death,
there had been more than three decades of the most spec-
tacular gambling a man had ever done. Maybe generals and
kings gambled for bigger stakes when they put armies and
kingdoms to war, but no man risked higher wagers at a
table than Nick.

Many people thought him the greatest gambler that ever
lived. He was bold and courageous and had mastered the
games he played. Still, he wasn't the best. In some of the
high stakes games they played, Arnold Rosenberg had
beaten him. But there was something grand about Nick
that suggested he was touched by destiny. The men he
gambled with and the women who loved him felt that awe.
A lot of people he never met admired him and wrote him
letters asking help for operations or for the education of
their children. He helped many of them, I know, and belonged in a way to them all. He was every loser's winner.

Those big games he played during the twenties, thirties, and forties took place in Chicago, Detroit, Kansas City, New York, and Phoenix. By the time he got to play in Las Vegas, he was in his middle sixties, poised and proud as he had always been. But his eyesight had clouded and his hearing had dulled. His reflexes slowed only a little, but like a great athlete, a tiny margin of loss makes all the difference.

He played in Las Vegas for some years and then began having trouble mustering the stakes he once gathered with ease. He might have slipped down into smaller, shabbier games like other aging gamblers. But Nick was a national monument like Boulder Dam and Lookout Mountain and the owners in Las Vegas wouldn't let him fade away. They gave Nick a tab to play on so the pilgrims visiting the Strip could watch the legendary Greek in action. Whether he played craps, poker, or faro, a crowd would gather around him. His wagers were more modest than he had once made in the big games, but the stakes were still impressive enough to excite the spectators, send them to other tables fumbling for their wallets.

He had always been too proud to take part in any shell game but he accepted that deception. I think he still considered himself a king of players and that was the only way he could play.

Yet, that charade must have come to an end as well. By his middle seventies Nick was drifting between Las Vegas and a small apartment he kept in Los Angeles, always trying to raise a new stake. His lawyer, Murray, told me that in those last years Nick would spend hours sitting in his office, carrying worn lists with the names of gamblers who owed him money. He wanted Murray to collect from them but he had never asked anyone to sign a note. He had

given away hundreds of thousands of dollars, one gentleman making loans to other gentlemen, except that most
other gamblers weren't gentlemen.

Murray tried to explain to Nick they had no claim without signed notes but Nick pressed him to contact the debt-
ors anyway. He felt sure when they heard he needed the
money, they'd gladly come up with the dough. In the end,
Murray lacked the heart to tell Nick how people ignored
his letters and calls. How can you tell a king he's been
dethroned?

All that is past history now that Nick is gone. I had
met him in Chicago during his first year there. I was just
nineteen and had been a professional fighter for about a
year. My eye had been badly cut in a fight that ended my
boxing, and Nick had helped me. I became his friend, as
close to him, I suppose, as any other man. When he left
Chicago, after about five years I joined him again, traveling with him to the cities where he played. We stayed together for a long time until, in the end, I guess I betrayed
him too, unable or unwilling to watch the sadness of his de-
cline.

The last time I saw him was about four years ago when
Elias Korakas died. Nick came to Chicago for the funeral
and when it was over, I drove him back to the airport. We
had a sandwich together while waiting for his plane. The
tab was about seven bucks and Nick asked me for a twenty
and gave the waitress the remainder of that bill as a tip. To
the end he relished the grand gesture.

What is the meaning of his life? I don't have that answer
any more than I understand the sense of my own. There
are only memories, some good and some bad, which is all a

gambler has left in the end. Like the memories I have of Nick, driving this road from Los Angeles with him as I had done so many times.

We'd cross the Nevada state line, no speed limit on cars in those days, and see the signs beginning to advertise the casinos on the Strip. Flamingo, Stardust, Sahara, Sands. Nick would lean forward in the seat beside me, his cheeks flushed and his eyes sparkling, staring toward that fertile oasis in the desert like it was some fabled and wicked city in the Bible. Faster now, Joey, he'd tell me. Faster now . . .

Show me a gambler and I'll tell you a sad story. The years I've lived around gamblers have proved that true but I've also learned life is full of sad stories. As we travel from one milestone to another marker, there might be worse things than gambling in games where money really means nothing and noon and midnight pass unnoticed.

And now, following the hearse off the exit for the Strip, I remember Nick telling me once that whatever our prisons and our sufferings, they can last only a lifetime. In the end death frees us once again.

If that is true, then I feel better, because now Nick can rest in peace.

CHAPTER 1

September — 1919

Nick had traveled across expanses of water before, from Smyrna on the coast of Asia Minor to Crete, from Athens to several of the islands in the Aegean. They had been one- or two-day voyages and although there had been some storms, the caique or steamer on which he journeyed was rarely out of sight of some spur of land. But departing from Greece that autumn on the freighter *Ajax*, bound for America with a full cargo of olives, olive oil, and wine, was taking passage to the other end of the world.

The war in Europe had been over only about a year. The great liners which had carried immigrants before the war had been converted to troop carriers and were not back in passenger service yet. But the captain of the *Ajax*, a bold, swarthy Chiot with a voice like a bass horn, was a friend of Nick's godfather's and passage for Nick was arranged. In addition to the captain and his crew, there were about a half-dozen other passengers.

A few days after leaving the port of Piraeus, their ship entered a dominion bounded only by water, as far as the eye could see. Each morning afterward, in any direction he looked, the ocean stretched vast and limitless. By the end of their first week at sea, it seemed to him the earth had been flooded, no dry land remaining anywhere. Noah must have sailed such an endless watery waste after the deluge.

All of the other passengers were Greeks traveling to join relatives in America they had been separated from since the start of the war. They ate together with the crew in the mess presided over by the captain, his mouth flashing gold-capped teeth as he regaled them with thrilling tales of close escapes he had experienced while running munitions for the Allies. Nick wasn't certain the captain was telling the truth but he was a superb storyteller who helped the passengers conquer their fears.

There were two women and three other men besides Nick. The females were a handsome young girl traveling with her mother for a reunion with the mother's brothers. She wore a white headcloth, and shyly refrained from speaking to anyone on board except her mother, to whom she whispered in a low, sweet voice. Her mother was a somber harridan with skin like flaked bark and eyes like looped nooses that threatened any man who came within speaking distance of her daughter.

In addition to the farmer who shared Nick's cabin, there was a carpenter from Larissa and a well-dressed exporter who had a cabin to himself and who argued incessantly with the carpenter about the virtues of King Constantine's monarchy and the vices of the liberal premier Eleutherios Venizelos. Nick supported the great Cretan statesman but did not join the debate, which, at times, grew so heated only the captain's intervention prevented the two men from coming to blows.

At the beginning of their voyage, waking in his berth
early in the morning, hearing the snores of the farmer from
Kalamata, Nick stared up at the solitary porthole. The blue
sky forced a small circle of light into the dark, close cabin.
He dressed quietly and hurried out on deck.

He was fascinated by the surge and wash of waves. He
noticed the difference when the wind was blowing away
from them or toward them and how they crested into
whitecaps with a stately and rhythmic roll.

The ship entered some terrible days of gale and storm.
Confined beneath deck, in the messroom or in their cabins,
the passengers endured the wild rolling of the ship, violently tossed by wind and waves. The young woman wept,
her mother prayed, the exporter heaved, while the others,
including Nick, sat in numbed and silent despair. Once,
peering out of a porthole, Nick saw waves rising high as
mountains, peaking and falling with a thunderous roar. He
did not look out again but thought wretchedly about the
wrecks of ancient ships strewn on the ocean floor for cen-
turies. They had been joined by the freighters and troop-
ships the German U-boats had sent to the bottom, and all
of these awaiting their freighter loaded with olive oil,
olives, and wine.

In the worst of the storms that befell them, the captain
surrendered to the waves and heaved to. He turned the
ship's stern against the wind and waves, letting the propel-
ler run slowly backward so that the ship was kept against
the waves. During that storm, Nick joined the young
woman's mother at her prayers.

But when the storms had ended, the *Ajax* was still afloat,
confirming the captain's reassurances that a good ship with
able seamen never need fear strong winds and heavy seas.

At the end of their second week at sea, they sighted a cluster of icebergs drifting south on currents from Arctic waters. Those awesome mountains of frozen waste disturbed the captain more than any storm and he heaved to, dropping anchors, waiting for the icebergs to be carried past. He told the male passengers that what was visible of the iceberg was only a fraction of the immense range and size beneath the water, deadly as a mine to any ship hapless enough to ram it in the fog or at night.

That danger passed as well and as they neared the end of their voyage a lightness and gaiety swept both passengers and crew. During the last few nights several of the sailors played harmonicas and accordions and they sang songs of the islands. Adding to the festivities, the captain broke out a special ration of wine.

On the twentieth day of their voyage, they prepared to dock at the harbor of Ellis Island. Alerted by the captain, Nick joined the other passengers along the rail at dawn, each of them silent as they strained their eyes for the first sight of the famed Statue of Liberty. Murmurs of awe rose from their lips when the colossal woman with the upraised torch loomed eerily out of the water, her flowing garments shaded in trails of mist.

Look well on that sight, the captain had told them gravely the evening before. Hundreds of thousands of immigrants have passed this way before you, seeing in that divine woman the symbol of their dreams.

Swept by fervor at her majesty and grateful for the journey's end, Nick felt himself allied to that whole courageous host that had preceded him, explorers, adventurers, and dreamers who had survived the hazards of their voyages. He felt a jubilation and a buoyance, an eagerness to

meet the challenges that lay ahead. When the ship's whistle
blew a shrill warning that they would be docking soon, he
joined his exultant shout to its wail.

Before going on by train to Chicago, Nick was to
remain a week in New York with Theron Valtides, a
childhood classmate and friend of his godfather's. Valtides
had emigrated from Smyrna in 1905 and had grown
wealthy in America through land development. During the
war he had suffered a stroke that left him partially paralyzed and confined to a wheel chair. His fluttering, bespectacled secretary met Nick at the port of entry. He carried
letters of reference Valtides had obtained from a judge and
a city official. Nick was soon cleared through immigration
and as he followed the secretary through the reception hall
he caught a final glimpse of the handsome young woman
with her mother who had been his companions on the
Ajax. She saw him and raised her arm in a buoyant farewell. He was delighted and waved back, the two of them
continuing to wave vigorously to the dismay of the girl's
mother, who glared at Nick and tugged down her daughter's hand.

The secretary led Nick to a large touring car with a
chauffeur, who drove them along Park Avenue. Nick
stared up at the buildings, which were taller than any
he had ever seen, until they drove into an underground garage. They took an elevator to an upper floor and from
there into a large, quiet apartment. The secretary led Nick
down a long corridor to a conservatory, bright with sun
that glinted across the green petals of palms. Sitting in a
large wicker wheel chair was Valtides, a big-shouldered
bear of a man with thick eyebrows and bushy hair that was

streaked with gray. Nick hesitated, until Valtides raised his
arm and motioned Nick to come to him. When Nick
reached the wheel chair, Valtides raised his arms and drew
Nick down into an astonishingly strong embrace. An
aroma of cloves and lotion rose from the man's body.

"Welcome, Nicholas," Valtides said in a low, vibrant
voice, which rumbled from his broad chest. "I hold you
now as I once held your godfather, the last time I saw him,
fourteen years ago."

Nick remained with Valtides for a week, except for
some brief walks remaining inside the large, sumptuous
apartment. They took their meals together. During this
time Valtides gave Nick twenty-five thousand dollars for
his godfather, the money to set up a fig-importing warehouse and office in Chicago. Under the guidance of Valtides, Nick stored the cash in a leather money belt that he
bound tightly around his stomach.

"This is a huge sum to be entrusted to someone as young
as you are, Nicholas," Valtides told him gravely. "But
your godfather has boundless trust in your ability to establish the business. Do not fail him."

"In the years I worked for him in Smyrna, he treated me
as if I were his son," Nick said earnestly. "I know this business can allow him, my godmother, and my godsisters to
come to America, escape the danger under which they live
there. I have made it safely across the ocean. I will not fail
now."

Valtides nodded slowly, approvingly.

"Now that the Greek Army occupies Smyrna, there are
fools who think the danger is over," Valtides said. "But if
they pursue the folly of marching eastward to regain Con-
stantinople, I fear disaster. If that army is beaten, nothing

will prevent the Turks from taking vengeance for that invasion on your godfather's family and on a million other Greeks living in Anatolia." He paused and sighed heavily. "We have only to remember what the Turks did to the Armenians in 1915 to understand what the fate of our Greek brothers and sisters will be."

Valtides was almost as gloomy about the prospects for the future in America.

"Strikes and riots," he said dolefully. "The Bolsheviks plan world revolution to foment disorder and take from us those things we have acquired by our labor. President Wilson has fallen ill, his dream of world brotherhood skewered by Lloyd George, Clemenceau, and Orlando. Now there is no one here to lead us, to provide inspiration for the people to go on. They are weary of the sacrifices of war and, I fear, will react now by embracing sport, sin, and sex."

On the day Nick was to leave for Chicago, he lunched with Valtides for the last time in the apartment dining room. The long table was set with fine white linen and gleaming silver and crystal. Valtides sat in his wicker wheel chair at one end while Nick sat at the other end. Housemen moved about soundlessly serving them while Valtides briefed him about what awaited Nick in Chicago.

"This man, Elias Korakas, your godfather's cousin, is a bold and brash fellow, owner of a small, dismal café called the No-worry Club." Valtides snorted in disgust. "Can you imagine any business by such a name? Listen to me, Nicholas. Your godfather loves Korakas and feels him to be honest, which may be true, but which may not be enough to overcome his numerous vices. One point in his favor is that his wife has more sense than he has."

While Nick listened quietly and respectfully, Valtides paused.

"How old are you, Nicholas?"

"Twenty-eight, Uncle."

"Have you ever married?"

"No, Uncle."

Valtides nodded. "Then you do not yet understand that it is extremely rare for a wife to have more sense than her husband, but it is fortunately true of Korakas. Therefore, if he neglects his promises to your godfather or shirks his responsibilities to aid you, speak to her. If she can do nothing with him, write at once to me, and my legs paralyzed or not, I will come at once!"

The secretary entered the room, pulling his clock nervously from his vest pocket in a sign that it was time for them to leave for the railroad station. Nick rose and walked the length of the long table to bend and embrace Valtides for a final time.

"Good-by, my boy," Valtides said huskily. "Remember what I have told you. Be guarded in your associations, vigilant about your money, faithful in your bond to God. With that trinity to guide you, you should not fail."

"I will not fail!" Nick echoed him with fervor.

As he started with the secretary from the dining room, Valtides raised his arm in a final wave, so martial and passionate a farewell that Nick felt as if he were a soldier departing for war.

Traveling on the train for the following two days, looking out the window at the landscape of the vast country he was invading, Nick glowed with a sense of his mission. Numerous times he slipped his hand under his vest and into his shirt to pat the money belt. The rhythm of the iron wheels lulled him into reveries and he speculated how it might feel to become a wealthy importer of figs, a mer-

chant so successful and influential, President Wilson would
ask to meet him.

He ate in the dining car, sitting alone at a table in the
corner and afterward returning at once to his compartment. When darkness sealed the land outside the window,
a porter made up his bed and he lay down to sleep for a
few hours, making certain the door to the corridor was
locked.

On the third morning after leaving New York, wakened
by the porter who told him they were entering the bound-
aries of the city, he dressed and closed his suitcase and sat
by the window. He saw huge steel mills with furnaces that
spewed fire into the sky. Around the mills were neighborhoods with small, shabby houses jammed so close upon
one another they reminded him of poor districts in
Smyrna. Pulling into the center of the city, the train descended into a cavernous underground. On other tracks,
black locomotives, their wheels hissing clouds of steam,
pulled long lines of freight cars. At the switches and cross-
ings, lanterns flashed red and orange beams.

When their train came to a bell-ringing stop in the station, he left his compartment and walked down to the platform. He followed the other passengers up the ramp into a
huge domed station that reminded him of a cathedral.
When he located the large station clock where Valtides
had told him Korakas would meet him, he positioned himself beneath it and waited. For almost two hours he stared
anxiously into the faces of men who passed back and forth.
He came unhappily to understand no one was going to
meet him.

Determined to prove he was resourceful, he made his
way to an exit where taxis waited. Climbing into the back

seat of one of them, thankful for his knowledge of the
English language gained in the American school in Smyrna,
he studied the paper Valtides had given him and told the
driver he wanted to be taken to the No-worry Club on
500 South Halsted Street. As the taxi emerged into the
traffic outside the station, Nick felt grimly grateful to
Valtides for warning him about the fearful and unreliable
Korakas.

The taxi rattled and bumped over the streets of Chicago.
Departing the bustling, noisy downtown district, they
crossed a wooden bridge spanning a river, into an area of
warehouses and factories. Outside the barbed, metal fence
of one of the plants, a group of workers walked back and
forth carrying placards with the lettering ON STRIKE. A
cluster of blue-coated policemen confronted them across
the gates.

Leaving the factories and plants, the taxi entered a raucous, gaudy settlement of run-down hotels, poolrooms, and
saloons. Under the marquees of striptease theaters and
something called "museums of anatomy" were large posters of nude and deformed men and women. Shills and
barkers, costumed as doctors and nurses, shouted the at-
tractions inside. Passing the entrance to an alley, Nick saw
two ferret-faced men rolling a drunk, going through his
pockets swiftly.

"What kind of hell is this?" Nick asked in shock, and he
feared suddenly for the money in the belt around his waist.

"This is part of the Levee," the driver said. "Packed
with bums, whores, pickpockets, and muggers. Saloons
here serve cheap whiskey and there are basement whore-
cribs where a man can jump on some battered old crock for

fifty cents." He paused, enjoying Nick's distress, and added mockingly, "You interested?"

"Keep going!" Nick cried. "Don't stop!"

He was grateful when they left that district of the damned and drove into a street of small shops and stores. With relief he noticed they bore Greek names. A narrow office housed the Hellenic Free Press and beside that building the Zephyr Coffee Company. A curtained window with lettering on the glass designated the Icarian Steam Baths and a striped barber pole stood before Spiro's Barbershop. There was the Athens Wholesale Grocery, whose double windows held casks of olive oil, loaves of round bread, and bottles of wine. The Macedonian Apothecary had a pyramid of medicine bottles in the window and Drollas Funeral Parlor had its windows decorated with palm plants and a wreath of flowers. Then the taxi slowed as it reached the rough-hewn and unpainted exterior of a café whose battered wooden sign read:

> N WO RY CL B
> El as Kor kas
> Propryitor

"This is it!" Nick said. "Right here!"

He paid the driver, counting the money carefully from his purse and then stepped out of the taxi, carrying his bag. He entered the café, a large, dingy, bare-walled room holding a cluster of tables occupied by drab and austere old men. Some read Greek newspapers while drinking small tumblers of wine or sipping miniature cups of coffee. A few sat staring stolidly into space.

Unable to see any evidence of owner or employee, Nick asked one of the old men for Elias Korakas.

"Do you think I'm sitting here waiting to answer questions!" the old man snapped.

"Thank you anyway, grandpa," Nick said amiably, and getting a firmer grip on his bag he started toward the swinging doors at the rear of the café. Pushing through them, he entered a kitchen saturated by odors of coffee, spices, and cheese. He set down his bag and spoke to a wizened old dishwasher bent over a sink.

"Is Elias Korakas here?"

The dishwasher inclined his head toward the back of the kitchen where a small group of men stood bunched together, their attention turned to something that wasn't visible. Nick walked to them.

"Ten bucks more on Ali Pasha," a voice said.

"You'll have to give four to one."

"It was three to one a minute ago!" the first voice said in outrage.

An excited hissing swept the group and a short, stocky man pushed open the circle of men around him.

"Give them air!" he cried. "In God's name, boys, you're smothering them!"

His neck was sinewed thickly and his hairy, muscled arms were visible below his rolled-up sleeves. He wore a soiled apron tied around his waist. At the edge of the group, pausing to get his breath, he looked directly at Nick.

"Excuse me," Nick said. "I'm looking for . . ."

As if he had not heard him, the man turned and burrowed his way back to the center. As his passage split the group apart, Nick saw a small circular arena of wire mesh on the floor. A pair of cages were separated from the arena by grills. Nick was astonished to see that each of the cages

contained a turtle, toothless and horny-beaked creatures in
their bony, mottled shells.

"Any more money to go on Sultana?" the stocky man
asked.

The men grumbled.

"Call yourself gamblers!" the stocky man spit with dis-
dain. "Not one of you with guts enough to wager on Sultana!"

"Ali Pasha will just whip her ass again!" another man
said. "Everybody here knows that."

Nick spoke to a man beside him.

"Is Korakas here?"

The man motioned to the stocky figure in the apron.
Nick pushed a little closer and called to him.

"Mr. Korakas, I'm . . ."

"How about you, Benny?" Korakas asked a short, fat
man in a wide-brimmed hat. "Show us you got guts. Cover
some of these bets on Ali Pasha."

"Trouble with you, Korakas," Benny said, "is you think
everyone else is dumber than you. This is your stinkhole.
You cover the bets."

Irritated at being ignored by Korakas, who had been too
busy gambling with turtles to meet him at the train station,
Nick spoke in a sharp, loud voice.

"I'll bet on Sultana!"

The startled men turned to see who had spoken. Korakas
came closer to Nick.

"Who the hell are you, mister?"

"I offered to bet on Sultana," Nick said, refusing to be
cowed.

"The beanpole probably wants to bet a buck," a man
said.

Nick had considered only a small wager to get their attention, but the man's remark rankled his pride.

"How much you want to bet, mister?" Korakas asked in a softer, craftier voice.

Starting to say ten dollars, Nick looked at the smug, disdainful faces of the men around him.

"A hundred dollars," he said briskly.

He was almost as shocked at the amount that came from his lips as they were. At that moment, almost as if he had been surprised by the sum as well, the larger turtle poked his head against the grill of his cage.

"Ali Pasha is hot and ready!" a man cried.

Korakas stared grimly at Nick.

"Are you serious?"

Nick nodded, suppressing a tremor of fear. As the men stared at him in disbelief, the tremor passed and he felt a curious exhilaration, a keen and spirited surge of power.

"Okay, let's see your dough," Korakas said.

Nick reached for his purse. When he counted out the thirty dollars it contained, he fumbled into his trouser pocket for a cloth-wrapped wad from which he peeled off the remaining seventy dollars.

"Must be straight off the farm," a man snickered.

"I'll take ten of that hundred," Benny said.

"Give me ten too! Like finding a double fin on the street!"

"I'll take fifteen!"

"Wait a minute now!" Korakas cried. "Let's spread the bets around." He spoke to Nick. "Three to one odds good enough for you?"

"You said four to one."

Several men muttered objections but Korakas motioned them to silence. He smiled amiably at Nick.

"We'll give you four to one, friend," he said. "Sarris here will mark and hold the wagers. Everything fair and square and no squawks at the end."

The men crowded in around Sarris, pulling out their money, pressing to get a share of Nick's hundred dollars.

"I'll take twenty!"

"Ten for me!"

"Ten more!"

"Wait a minute, I told you!" Korakas shouted. "This is my club, my kitchen, my turtles, and you're going to close me out!" He spoke to Sarris. "How much you got bet against this young gent's hundred dollars?"

Sarris pondered the figures on his pad.

"Three hundred and twenty bucks," he said.

"At four to one, that covers eighty of his hundred," Korakas said, "and I'll fade the last twenty." Waving aside the protests of those players who had not gotten to bet, he pulled some crumpled soiled bills from his pocket and counted out eighty dollars, which he handed to Sarris. Then he motioned sternly for silence and knelt down behind the cages. He gripped the handles of the grills. The men crowded closer and Nick was jostled and shoved back.

"All right, make room there!" Korakas cried. "Let that fellow up close to watch his dough disappear!"

The men opened a path for Nick and he pushed through them to stand in a place above the arena. With a whipping motion, Korakas raised both grills at precisely the same instant. Nick felt a quiver assault his knees.

The bigger turtle emerged from his cage, an armored

and imposing gladiator. He swayed forward with a confident swagger.

"There goes Ali Pasha!"

"What a champion!"

With a series of bobbings and lurchings, Ali Pasha advanced toward another cage at the opposite side of the arena. The smaller turtle, Sultana, had not yet left her roost. Korakas grinned again at Nick.

"Like plucking candy from a baby," Benny said.

When Ali Pasha was a few scant inches from the goal of the exit cage, he wavered and then stopped. He raised his tiny head as if surveying the men hanging above him. Then he lowered his head and drew it back slowly into the sanctuary of his shell.

At that instant Sultana emerged from her cage. Extending her head, stretching her neck, she bobbed and swayed forward.

"Come on, Sultana," Nick said in a low, urgent voice.

"Too late, my friend," Korakas said.

Slowly, steadily, Sultana shuttled forward. Ali Pasha remained immobile, his head hidden. The men stirred uneasily.

"Maybe he's had a stroke," a man said. He looked around anxiously. "Can a turtle have a stroke?"

Korakas bent over the inert turtle.

"Come on, Ali Pasha," he pleaded. "Come on, old comrade, old campaigner . . . let's go!"

Sultana kept advancing, her shell tossing and pitching in an ungainly crawl, diminishing the distance between her and Ali Pasha. A foot separated them and then the two turtles were divided by only a few inches.

"Why don't he move?" a man asked in a stunned voice.

"Come on, Ali Pasha!" Korakas cried wrathfully. "You lazy, worthless chunk of turd! Move!"

Sultana reached Ali Pasha, turned her head slightly to scan the monument of his inert form. Without pausing or losing gait, she disappeared across the finish line into the cage.

A shocked silence bound the men in a knot of disaster. Then an eruption of groans, curses, and laments swept them all. Hardly believing he had really won, Nick tried to keep from shouting in sheer delight.

"Shall I pay him off?" Sarris asked Korakas timidly.

"No, give the dough to the bloody turtle, you boob!" Korakas vented his frustration. "Of course pay him off! He won, didn't he?"

Sarris handed the wad of bills to Nick, who took them gravely, concealing the jubilation he felt at their vexation.

"Who is this guy?" Benny muttered.

"Never seen him in here before," another man said resentfully.

"Just butts in and don't ask if he's wanted."

A scholarly looking man wearing pince-nez eyeglasses smiled at Nick.

"Never mind the whining, boys," he said. "You were quick enough to bet when you thought you had a pigeon. Let this be a lesson. Whoso diggeth a pit may fall therein."

The men dispersed, still grumbling as they left the kitchen, a few turning to glare at Nick one last time. Finally, only the man with the pince-nez eyeglasses and Korakas remained with Nick.

Korakas raised a long stick and slid it through the wire of the cage, prodding the still motionless form of Ali Pasha in the rump. The turtle leaped forward and scampered swiftly into the exit. Korakas shook his head in disgust.

"We will never know what really happened in that cage today," the man with the pince-nez eyeglasses said. "That mystery will remain encased forever within the osseous shell of that abominable turtle."

"All right now, fellow," Korakas said to Nick. "Maybe we deserved what we got but you took four hundred bucks of our dough. Now tell me just who you are? A city inspector? A salesman?"

"Perhaps a turtle trainer?" the other man smiled.

"I came in here looking for Elias Korakas," Nick said.

"You found him," Korakas said gruffly. "I hope to hell you're paying back money I loaned some deadbeat."

"I'm not bringing you any money!" Nick said in aggravation. "I'm Nick Dandolos from Smyrna, your cousin Avram Potamis' godson! He wrote you I was coming and I expected you would meet my train!"

Korakas looked at him in astonishment. Then he loosed a jubilant shout. "Nick!" he cried. "Nick!" He pulled Nick into his arms and hugged him so tightly Nick's ribs ached.

When he released him, Korakas' eyes were moist. "Forgive me, my boy," he said. "I thought the letter said next week. I would have been at the station with bells and a band!"

"You probably misread the letter," the other man said.

"This is Banopoulos, editor of our neighborhood paper." Korakas still clutched Nick's hands. "This is my dear cousin's godson!" he said to Banopoulos. "Can you believe he's here?"

"I saw him pocket our money," Banopoulos smiled. He

managed to free one of Nick's hands and shook it warmly. "Delighted to have you with us, Nick," he said. "Now I will leave you to your family celebration. I must go and write an editorial about the folly of putting one's faith in a turtle with the name of Ali Pasha."

"C'mon upstairs, Nick," Korakas said excitedly. "The old lady, Lambri, will go crazy when she sees you. She's been baking for weeks."

With Korakas holding firmly to Nick's arm, they ascended the narrow stairway at the rear of the kitchen, coming to an apartment door on the second floor. Korakas paused with his hand on the knob.

"Tell me something, Nick," he asked in a low, puzzled voice. "How did you have the guts to walk in and make that reckless play? Did you think if you had lost I would have taken you off the hook?"

"They were only turtles," Nick said. "You were all so positive which one would win, but how can anyone be sure what a turtle will do?"

Korakas stared at him and then laughed raucously. As he started to turn the knob, the door was jerked open from the other side. A strong-visaged woman with flashing black eyes and dark hair streaked with gray stood on the threshold.

"What is it, man?" she glared at Korakas. "Riot? Fire? Why have you left the barn untended?"

Without answering, Korakas grinned and pointed at Nick. Lambri stared at him for a moment and then uttered an exultant cry. She embraced Nick, so obviously delighted to see him that he was moved and hugged her back. He saw Korakas wiping still another vagrant tear from his eyes.

"Walked right in!" Korakas cried. "Never told us who he was! Took our four to one against Ali Pasha and won a cool four hundred before we knew what was happening! What lovely nerve!"

"Is that reason to stand there howling?" Lambri said brusquely. "Go down and look after the place or those bums and loafers will steal you blind." She shook her head in apology at Nick. "Did you see those slimy reptiles? I'll boil them for soup someday if the health inspectors don't close this dump first."

"I take care of the inspectors," Korakas said. He started reluctantly down the stairs. "Remember I want to talk to the boy too."

Lambri led Nick from the hallway into a small parlor. She lit several lamps, the beams glowing across a pair of mohair chairs and a lumpy-cushioned couch. There was a coal-burning fireplace below a mantel that held a row of photographs, old tintypes in ornate silver and gold frames.

Lambri looked closely at Nick and then nodded in approval.

"You're a handsome young man," she said. "Taller than most Greeks too. But you're too skinny, not enough meat on your bones."

"I'm strong and feel fine," Nick said.

"Living under the Turks must keep you all worried and lean," Lambri said. "We received Cousin Avram's letters and we tried to understand the things he did not say."

"He was afraid to write too much for fear the mail was being opened," Nick said. "They were suspicious anyway and stopped me leaving several times. The arrival of the Greek troops made my trip possible."

"What are your plans now?" Lambri asked. She mo-

tioned Nick to a chair and sat down on the couch across
from him.

"I'll establish an office and warehouse here," Nick said,
"and we'll begin by bringing in shiploads of figs. Godfather has signed agreements with the biggest growers for
their best crops of Brown Ischias and Brunswicks. We'll
start with figs and expand to include olive oil, cheese, and
wine. With the business prospering, we'll be able to bring
Godfather and his family here."

"God make that come true!" Lambri crossed herself.
"Korakas and I will help all we can, of course. Under his
rough manner the man can be shrewd and he knows the
politicians in the ward." She paused. "How long have you
been traveling, Niko?"

"About seven weeks," Nick said. "From Smyrna to
Athens and then the ship to America. That voyage took
three weeks. A week in New York with Uncle Valtides
and then the train ride here."

"Poor boy!" Lambri exclaimed. "And I hold you here
chattering. You come and rest awhile before dinner. We'll
have time to talk then since Korakas will make you tell everything a second time anyway." She rose from the couch.
"I'll show you your room."

"I left my bag downstairs."

"Korakas will bring it up."

Nick followed her into a bedroom with a single, curtained window, a bed covered with a woolen spread, an
armchair, and a dresser.

"Nothing fancy like the Metropole downtown," Lambri
said, "but it's clean and you'll have privacy. Best of all,
God forgive me for flattering myself, you'll eat my cook-
ing. I'll get some flesh on your bones."

"Don't you eat down in the café?"

"Are you mad, Niko?" Lambri said in shock. "Eating downstairs would wreck our stomachs in a week."

"How do your customers eat there?" Nick laughed.

"The poor devils who fill our place have no stomachs left," Lambri said. "Rotgut whiskey has dissolved the linings. Soon a new law will go into effect here, banning the making and selling of liquor. Twenty years too late for most of the drunks." She shrugged. "Never mind them now. You rest. Let me hang up your suitcoat."

Nick started to remove his suitcoat, hesitating when he knew he would reveal the bulge of the money belt. He looked at the open, devoted countenance of Lambri and felt a twinge of shame.

"I am carrying a large sum of money," he said, as he removed his coat and vest. He unbuttoned his shirt and unbuckled the belt, pulling it free from around his waist with a sigh of relief.

"You carried that all the way from Smyrna?" Lambri said. "How could you sleep at night?"

"Only from New York," Nick said. "The money is from Uncle Valtides, for me to use to start the business."

"God bless that man!" Lambri said fervently. "How much is there, Niko?"

"Twenty-five thousand American dollars," Nick said, and he enjoyed Lambri's gasp, feeling the importance of the trust placed in him. Lambri quickly closed the door.

"You must be careful, Niko!" she said. "A few blocks from here is one of the most depraved districts in the city. They'd cut a man's throat for ten dollars, let alone the fortune you carry."

"The taxi drove me through that district on our way from the station."

Lambri let loose another cry of outrage.

"You came through that hellpit with that money banded around your body!" She stared up toward heaven and made her cross. "Sunday morning in church I'll light three extra candles in thanks to St. Nicholas."

"They would have had to kill me to take this money!" Nick said vigorously. "This belongs to Godfather, Godmother, and the girls. You won't believe, Cousin Lambri, the incidents in Smyrna these last years. A priest is beaten by Turkish thugs, a church defiled, a shop burned. Godfather is in terror for the girls, most of all. This money will become their salvation!"

"Well, you've gotten it here safely now," Lambri said. "Now you should put it in a bank."

"Do you know a good bank, run by trustworthy people?"

"I have never had money enough to need a bank," Lambri said. "But we will inquire of some of the respectable people at church. Meanwhile"—she motioned to the belt—"I'll get a cashbox and show you a place to store it."

Lambri brought a metal box from another room. She helped Nick remove the money from the belt.

"My fingers are numb," she said in a shaken voice. "Handling only small change for fifty years, this sum congeals my blood. There is something evil in so much money."

"Money is simply a means to trade for the things one wants," Nick said.

Lambri motioned to the dresser. "Push that away from the wall and take off the strip of baseboard," she said. "There is a crevice behind it where I have hidden a few dollars from time to time because Korakas loves to gamble.

He can't control himself when he's got a dollar in his hand."

Nick pushed the dresser away from the wall and knelt down and removed the baseboard. Lambri handed him the box that he stored away. The box had two small keys and he handed one back to Lambri.

"I don't want it!" she protested. "You keep them both. Why should you trust me?"

"Godfather told me he would trust you and Korakas with his life."

Lambri looked at him in gratitude and took the key. Trying to conceal her emotion, she turned away, noisily clearing her throat, and quickly left the room.

That evening, after finishing a delicious meal of roast lamb and okra Lambri cooked for them, Nick and Korakas lounged in the parlor while Lambri finished the dishes. Going to an end table, Korakas reached far back into the drawer for a pair of long, black cigars. He offered one to Nick, who shook his head. Korakas put one cigar away and lit the other, puffing vigorously.

"Lambri was horrified that the taxi drove me through that district today," Nick said. "Is it that bad?"

"There may be districts like the Levee in other cities," Korakas said. "This is just the worst."

"Why is that true about Chicago?"

"This city has got more of everything than anyplace else," Korakas said. "More corruption, more graft, more spoils, more excitement. We got a mayor in Big Bill Thompson who believes in live and let live. When politicians want to get elected here, they send some lackeys to

shoot off giant firecrackers in the flophouses to wake up
the drunks. They lead them to a saloon for a shot and then
to the polling places to hand in ballots marked with names
from gravestones." Korakas snickered. "There are wards in
this city where the dead vote more often than they ever
did in life." He stretched out his legs, puffing up a storm of
smoke. "It's a grand place to live," he said. "The whole
city is on the hustle, everybody racing to get their share.
The only bad thing is the goddam gangs muscling in on everything."

"Gangs?"

"Hoodlums . . . thugs . . ." Korakas said. "The city is
cut up into districts by the gangs. North, south, east, and
west. On the northeast side, between the river and the lake,
there's Dion O'Banion's gang. On the southwest side, the
O'Donnell brothers. West of the river, the Druggan-Lake
gang. Out toward Hammond, Indiana, there are Ragen's
Colts. Right in this area we got one of the most powerful
of the gangs, the Terrible Gennas, who got their headquarters in Little Italy. The undertakers love that family!
Six brothers, one meaner than the next. 'Bloody' Angelo
Genna, 'Mike the Devil' Genna, 'Tony the Aristocrat'
Genna . . ." He paused, smiling at Nick's bewilderment.

"Don't the police put them in jail?"

"The police put them in jail?" Korakas laughed boisterously. "I'd like to see them try to put the Terrible Gennas
or Spike 'Four Deuces' O'Donnell or Joe 'Dynamite'
Brooks in jail. The only way we get rid of those thugs is
when they kill each other off."

"They fight often?"

"All the time!" Korakas cried. "One gang trying to take
over from another. They try to divide things up but

they're such greedy bastards, a truce don't last long. Some stick to certain rackets. Like the Irish favor the booze. I don't know what will happen when the amendment on liquor takes effect in January but people won't stop drinking. Then the Italians control whoring and opium . . ."

"Aren't there any Greeks in this gallery of rogues?"

Korakas paused before answering to puff with renewed energy in the direction of the kitchen, exhaling a cloud of thick smoke.

"Well, the Greeks favor gambling 'cause it's in their blood," he said. "We got a few wealthy Greeks who own some gambling clubs on Halsted, a few blocks south. But they got to give a good slice of their action to the Gennas. Before the last south side war, when the Gennas drove the O'Donnells out of here, they paid their cut to them. For the Greeks, it's like living on a volcano. The Irish got the political power, in the wards and in City Hall. The Italians got the muscle, the Black Hand killers. If they stop fighting each other, they'd eat the Greeks, bone and gristle and all."

Lambri swept in suddenly from the kitchen, waving her hands against the smoke-glutted air.

"What is this?" she cried. "A gas attack in France? Have the sinks downstairs backed up? That poor boy will choke in this cesspool!"

"I was just having a little smoke after your fine dinner, my dear." Korakas feigned surprise.

"Then go outside and smoke!" Lambri said loudly. "I've told you before not to stink up my rooms with your soot!"

"Okay, okay." Korakas rose slowly. "I was hoping to relax and get to bed early, but Nick and I can take a walk."

Leaving Lambri coughing as she moved quickly to open a window, Korakas and Nick walked down the stairs to the café kitchen and then out the alley door.

"When I want to get out of the house," Korakas gloated, "I light up one of my strongest stogies. That works on Lambri every time!"

They walked several blocks south along Halsted Street, leaving the area of Greek shops and stores, until they came to a street dominated by several large and garishly lit clubs. There was the Hermes, the Apollo, and the Poseidon, glaring and gaudy houses embellished by lanterns, streamers, and posters advertising varied games of chance and skill. A crowd of men milled along Halsted Street, moving from one club entrance to another, nimbly dodging cars when they crossed the street while angry drivers honked.

"These are the Greek casinos," Korakas said, and the multicolored sparkle of papier-mâché lamps kindled animation in his eyes. Gripping Nick's arms firmly, he pulled him aside just in time to avoid a collision with a pair of drunks who staggered by with their arms linked. Then he guided him through the high double-doors of the Hermes.

They entered a hall spacious as a auditorium, filled with a clamorous throng of men gathered around an assortment of gaming tables. In the tumult were the cries of dealers and croupiers, the spin and click of wheels, the rattle and crack of dice striking the boards.

Korakas paused inside the doors, breathing deeply, his cheeks flushed.

"Can you hear the music of the games?" he asked Nick. "Can you hear the song of the dice and the melody of the wheels?"

"I only hear a lot of noise," Nick said.

"I know! I know!" Korakas said eagerly. "It's a siren's harmony only for certain ears. Once you've heard it though, you're never the same. I can even hear the players breathing, their throats tight with fear or their voices quick with joy."

"Do you play here?"

"This room is for rubes and tourists," Korakas said scornfully. "There are private rooms upstairs for neighborhood businessmen and club members. I'll show you."

They walked through the maze of tables, the players crowded around the rails, intent on the dice, cards, and wheels. They passed through a curtained arch to a stairway where two young toughs recognized Korakas and waved them on. On the second floor, Korakas gestured at a large, paneled oak door.

"That room is for the big stakes men," Korakas said. "The high action gamblers and the owners of the clubs on this street."

They started up to the third floor and Korakas turned back.

"Maybe you'd like to take a peek in that room?"

"Can we?"

"Sure, they'll let me in," Korakas said. "And there's usually a game at night."

He knocked softly on the door. A slot slid open and Korakas stretched on his toes to speak close to the aperture.

"It's Korakas from the No-worry Club," he said in a low voice. "My cousin has come from overseas and I want to show him the big game."

The door was opened and the guard motioned them to

silence. Korakas and Nick entered a narrow corridor and
the guard closed the door quietly behind them. They
walked along to the arched entranceway of a room and
Korakas stopped.

In the center of the room, circled with shadows, a single
light focused a bright glow across a group of men seated at
a round table with a green felt surface. They seemed silent,
motionless figures to Nick until he noticed certain spare
movements of their heads and hands and heard the murmur
of their voices.

"The dandy there is Prince Pierre," Korakas whispered,
pointing to a man with pomaded hair and a large carnation
glistening in the buttonhole of his satin jacket. "He owns
the Hermes. They call him Prince because he sports a
monarch's wardrobe."

Seated next to Prince Pierre was an obese and bloated
man with fanlike jowls that concealed his neck. A diamond
sparkled in his tie and when his hands slipped into the sheen
of the light, diamond rings glittered on his puffy fingers.

"That is Loukanas," Korakas whispered again. "He
owns the Apollo, across the street."

Beside Loukanas was a barrel-shouldered man with the
thick bull neck of a wrestler, and an ape's forehead and jaw.

"Big Gorgio owns the Poseidon and the Spartan Slaughterhouse too. He carries the stink of the killing pens wherever he goes."

The last of the men in the game was dark, olive-
complected, with the lean, predatory features of a jackal or
a hyena.

"Vito Baldelli . . ." Korakas hissed his name. "He belongs to the Genna gang, runs their prostitution. He's cruel

as a Hun and lousy with money made on the agony of poor girls."

At a smaller table, a short distance from the larger one, several young toughs watched the game with the wariness of wolves.

"Bodyguards," Korakas said. "Merciless bastards who'd sooner shoot or stab a man than eat and drink."

The only remaining occupant of the room was a snow-haired old man in his seventies or eighties, sitting alone to one side, his elbows propped on his knees, his long, lean hands hanging down loosely. Attentive on the game, he sat motionless as stone, his ancient, scarred face proof of his long life. Staring at him, Nick felt some sorrow and pain about him.

"Who is the old man?" he asked Korakas in a low voice.

He did not speak quietly enough and one of the body-guards turned to the corridor. Korakas tugged at Nick's sleeve and they walked softly and quickly back to the door. The guard let them out.

"That old man was Nestor," Korakas said. "He was once the greatest gambler of them all, winning and losing fortunes. He can't see or hear too well any more but when he raises a stake, he plays sometimes."

"Do you ever play in those games?" Nick asked Korakas when they started back up the stairs.

Korakas looked at him in shock.

"Are you mad? In that game, one hand could lose me the club. Maybe that wouldn't be so bad, though, I'd end my misery too."

On the third floor they passed another guard and entered a room that was noisy with the cries of men gathered around a long, deep-surfaced table.

"They're shooting craps." Korakas spoke loudly to be heard above the din. "You ever play?"

Nick shook his head.

"The game is played with two dice numbered one to six," Korakas said. "Seven and eleven are naturals and win. Two, three, or twelve are craps or miss-outs and lose. The rest of the combinations are points and when the shooter rolls them, he tries to roll them again before throwing a seven that loses him the dice."

"That sounds easy," Nick said.

"Easy as dying," Korakas grinned. "The fastest game in the world, fast as a bullet or the squirt of sex."

The stickman running the game called a break and there was a lull in the action. Korakas greeted a few of the players.

"You met Banopoulos earlier today." He motioned to the man with the pince-nez eyeglasses. "I didn't mention he also prints and delivers the paper."

"I remember this young pirate very well," Banopoulos said wryly.

Korakas motioned to another man with a dark face and doleful eyes. "Gikas here is a gravedigger," he said, "but gambling is democratic and we even let him play."

"I'm not ashamed of how I earn my living," Gikas said. "It's healthy and honest work. That's more than others can say." He stared balefully at a tall man with a marked slump to his shoulders.

"Score one for Gikas," Korakas chuckled. "This is Dr. Samyotis, our apothecary. He fixes prescriptions but his specialty is brewing an elixir that cures, so he claims, everything from impotence to piles. When the ax of prohibition falls, he's ready to make a fortune."

Dr. Samyotis shook hands gravely with Nick.

"They joke about a secret formula handed down in my family for generations," he said. "You appear in fine health, but if I can be of any service, please call on me."

"And all these other sports"—Korakas swept his arm to include the remaining players—"I would introduce them but they're not worth meeting."

"Table open," the stickman called. "New shooter coming out."

"Hey, Korakas," one of the men asked. "You gonna play?"

"I'm not playing tonight," Korakas said, his voice shaded with regret as the men moved back to the table. "I'm showing my cousin around."

"Let him play too," another man said. "Give us a chance to win back that dough he took from us this morning."

"I wouldn't like to take your money twice in the same day," Nick smiled. He was answered with hoots and jeers.

"He's related to you, all right." Banopoulos winked at Korakas. "The same strain of consummate humility."

Nick nudged Korakas. "Go ahead and play a little if you want."

"I wouldn't think of it!" Korakas said, but when he looked at the table, his eyes struck sparks.

"I'll watch you play and learn something about the game."

"You sure you don't mind?" Korakas moved eagerly to the table, pushing several men aside to make a place for himself. "We'll tell Lambri we stopped to discuss business." He grinned back at Nick. "Not that she'll believe that salami."

The stickman shoved the dice to Korakas. He fondled them for a moment.

"Come on, you buzzards and skunks!" he cried as he

began to shake the dice in the palm of his hand. "Ride my
comet and I'll pull you from the mud to the stars!"

Late that night, in the darkness of the bedroom above
the No-worry Club, Nick lay in bed, weary and not yet
able to sleep. The voice of Lambri, scolding Korakas about
the gambling she knew had delayed their return, carried
through the thin walls. When she grew still, he heard
laughter and voices from Halsted Street below his window,
the rumble of automobiles on their way, he imagined, to
the roistering district a few blocks away.

For the first time in all his weeks of travel, he felt he had
arrived at his destination. His long journey had come to an
end.

Now, retracing his path from the start, he remembered
his departure from his father's house as a boy when he left
the village in Crete for school in Smyrna. His mother had
stumbled alongside the wagon, holding tightly to his ankle,
ignoring his father's pleas that she let him go. The driver,
finally, spurred his horse forward and his mother's fingers
were wrenched away. He turned to wave to her, watching
her figure growing smaller in the distance until he couldn't
see her any more.

He remembered the night he boarded the ship from the
port in Smyrna for Athens, his godfather embracing him,
the smell of tangy lotion in his beard. He kissed each of the
sweet, tear-stained cheeks of his godsisters. In the final moments before sailing, looking down from the deck, their
figures seemed tiny and frail.

Beyond those departures and the journeys he traveled
over land and on water, he felt some rite of passage
into new manhood. For the first time in his life he held not

only his destiny but trust for the welfare and survival of others.

With his spirit quivering and his thoughts still teeming with plans for all the things he wished to do, he slipped, finally, into exhausted sleep.

CHAPTER 2

In the weeks following his arrival in Chicago, Nick set up his business venture with energy and devotion. He hired a car and driver and contacted import merchants, grocers, and restaurant owners, soliciting future orders for figs. He checked numerous warehouse sites, finally optioning a location near the produce markets on Canal Street where the trucks brought in fresh fruits and vegetables each day. He rented office space above the barber shop from Spiro the barber, had the walls painted, and bought desks, chairs, and file drawers. He employed a woman to answer queries, make his appointments, and write letters. His first letters were to his godfather in Smyrna and to Theron Valtides in New York, reassuring them that the project had started well. Even his evenings were not spent relaxing (despite the scolding of Lambri, who thought he was working too hard) but reading and writing to improve his facility with the English language.

Guided by the experience of Korakas, Nick made courtesy calls upon the powerful ward politicians, requesting their help and advice and assuring them of his loyalty and friendship.

"Make the bastards think you're dying for their counsel," Korakas told him before the visits, "otherwise they can prevent you getting a dog license."

Flattering the bosses as Korakas suggested, Nick was still astonished by how simple and artless they seemed. How, he asked Korakas, could such men have acquired so much power?

"They might seem like fools," Korakas said, "but they know all the dirty tricks and low blows. They can wish you long life and plan your wake in the same breath."

"That's hard to believe."

"I'm serious, Nick," Korakas said earnestly. "I know what I'm saying."

"Oh, I'll be careful," Nick said, "but working with Godfather in the marketplace in Smyrna, dealing daily with crafty Greek and Turkish Smyrniotes, took some skill and judgment, I tell you. Godfather said I was a born trader and these politicians don't seem nearly as smart as those scoundrels back home."

Even as he anxiously read the daily papers for news of the Greek Army encamped in Smyrna and the speculations of foreign correspondents as to whether the army would march deeper into Anatolia, he enjoyed his growing bond to American Life. He admired the people, their vitality and their willingness to confront the challenges of each day. He learned to listen to jazz and stayed through a Mary Pickford film three times, entranced by her blond and winsome beauty. He felt totally American when he could casually inquire of a newsstand dealer if he thought Babe Ruth could break Ty Cobb's record.

He shared the aura of excitement and anticipation the end of the war produced. Strikes went on, workingmen demanding raises and added benefits, politicians warned of Bolshevism, but the last of the soldiers returning from Europe were finding jobs and there was a hopefulness about the future. And while the coming of Prohibition was debated hotly, most people seemed to feel the country would be better off dry.

By the end of October, dusk fell earlier each day, and the first chill winds swept the alleys and streets. Sitting with Banopoulos and Korakas in the No-worry Club late one evening, Nick asked them what winters in the city would be like.

"Imagine a cold more frozen than a pimp's heart," Korakas said grimly. "Snow so deep it would drive an Eskimo mad."

"The glacial winds blast us from the lake." Banopoulos picked up the refrain. "Funeral wagons make hourly rounds, the attendants chipping and chiseling bodies loose from the ice with picks and tongs . . ."

"On really bad days . . ." Korakas began.

". . . icebergs crash through the roofs," Nick grinned, "and even farts crack in the cold air with a sound of thunder."

Banopoulos shook his head in disapproval.

"The boy is in this country little more than a month," he lamented to Korakas, "and he's become as disrespectful as the native-born."

"What can I do?" Korakas laughed. "Looks like he's going to make a wealthy and successful businessman in spite of his smart-ass mouth."

He paused, staring toward the window of the club, where a group of men had begun to cluster.

"Here they come," he said.

Late each evening, before the club closed, a crowd of poorly dressed men would line up at the door. When Korakas finally gave them a signal they would enter eagerly and set up a queue to the kitchen where Korakas waited beside a vat that contained a concoction known as a "Korakas Thunderbolt." This was a blend of the drippings of beer and Bourbon that Korakas laced liberally with several gallons of cheap red wine. As each man approached the vat, Korakas filled a metal cup with the brew for him. Leaving the kitchen, the men also took sandwiches from a large tray.

"You pass out all this drink and food and yet nobody pays," Nick said to him the first time he saw the ritual.

"Winners in games of poker, craps, or rummy come by to drop something in the kitty," Korakas said. "I make up the rest."

"Why do you do it when you're not rich?"

Korakas shrugged. "I remember my worst moments came after losing my last buck at dice or cards, when I got thirsty and hungry and had nothing because a gambler don't keep any reserve. The No-worry Club is for losers, so they'll always have someplace to come for a drink or a snack.

"But these men aren't all gamblers."

"Not all. Some are winos, others are wretches down on their haunches, running from calamity to disaster."

"But if you do this every night," Nick asked, "how do you stay in business?"

"Hanging by my balls," Korakas grinned. "But I was

never meant to be rich anyway. The old lady and I eat regular, we got a warm bed to lay our rumps on at night, and I manage a few bucks to play poker and shoot craps. Who can ask for more than that?"

Then catching a glimpse of one of the patrons stealing back into the kitchen, Korakas impaled him with a shout.

"I see you, Lefteris! That's your third sandwich! This is the No-worry Club, not the Salvation Army or the Pacific Garden Mission! I'm Korakas, not your bloody patron saint! Get your ass out of here!"

Sundays were the one day of the week when Nick did not make rounds of the shops and accounts and the No-worry Club was closed, as well. Both men slept late while Lambri, clutching her small Bible, rose early to go to the Greek Orthodox church on Loomis. On the morning of the fifth Sunday after Nick's arrival, however, she wakened both men with a stern request that they escort her to church.

"I should have suggested going with you before," Nick apologized to her.

"But I was there a few months ago," Korakas grumbled.

"That's poor attendance to cleanse a spirit as befouled as yours," Lambri snapped. "You should be there every Sunday and first in line for Confession. Hurry now, Niko is dressed already, and we'll be late.

Clad in their best clothing, they left the apartment. Nick smiled consolingly at Korakas, who continued to mutter, twisting his fingers to loosen the tight collar of his starched shirt, grimacing as if he were being strangled. Walking the two blocks from the club to the church, Lambri set a brisk pace.

Entering the shadowed narthex of the small, stone

church, joined to the scents of incense and candles, Nick was reminded of the churches in Smyrna. The same somber old men handling change for the sale of candles, the strains of the liturgy, chant, and prayers carrying from within the cloister of the church. Nick felt in a rush of nostalgia if he closed his eyes, he might open them to find the portly, smiling figure of his godfather standing nearby.

They lit candles and kissed the icon and walked into the nave of the church. Nick and Korakas joined the men on one side while Lambri moved to stand among the women. His hands folded, Nick listened to the ancient, hallowed Mass conducted by a small, spritely priest, old and venerable in shining vestments of red and gold. That was Father Ladas, Korakas whispered to him with a wink, a priest so hoary in years, rumor had him serving as chaplain to General George Washington at Valley Forge. A man in front of them turned to mutter a reprimand to Korakas, who glared back at him.

Circling the altar, bending to kiss the holy book or raising the chalice of Communion, the priest's movements bore the grace and ease of a thousand Sundays. From time to time a pair of acolytes joined him, solemn youths with scrubbed cheeks and brushed hair, holding long-stemmed candles in their clenched hands and wearing white robes hanging to their ankles. To the side of the altar, a black-gowned choirmaster added his chorus to the chanting of the priest.

At the conclusion of the service, Father Ladas passed out fragments of holy bread. Korakas tugged at Nick's sleeve, anxious for them to leave. Lambri cut them off on their way from the church and told them they were going downstairs for coffee with the parishioners.

"Come on, Lambri!" Korakas pleaded. "Enough is enough!"

Answering him with a scowl, she took Nick's arm and led him toward the stairs. Men and women were descending into a basement hall set with a table holding coffeepots and pastries.

"Now you'll meet the goddam respectable Greeks," Korakas whispered to Nick.

"What did you say?" Lambri bristled.

"I just said that now he would meet God's respectable Greeks."

In the next few moments, trying to balance a cup of coffee and a plate of pastries and still shake hands, Nick was introduced to a laundry owner, a real estate developer, and a dentist. When the priest appeared, clad in a simple black gown, and circulated among the parishioners, Lambri brought him to meet Nick. Nick bent to kiss the back of the old man's veined, bony hand while the priest murmured a blessing. Then Father Ladas turned on Korakas.

"What was it, Korakas?" he asked scathingly. "A nightmare last night, or pains in your chest? What cataclysm produces your astonishing attendance in church this morning?"

"I came for your blessing, Father," Korakas grinned.

"I have been after him to take Communion, Father," Lambri said, "and come to you for Confession."

"That might be more than an old priest can take," Father Ladas sighed. "I think Confession from Korakas requires at least an archbishop."

Someone called to him and the priest moved away. Lambri motioned Nick and Korakas to wait and then walked rapidly toward a tall, thin man standing in the midst of several elegantly dressed young women.

"I begin to smell a rat!" Korakas said ominously to Nick. "All that business of getting us to church today for our blessed souls! I see her design now! That giraffe in a suit and tie is Aristotle Rantoulis, wealthy owner of the Athens Wholesale Grocery and those powdered, overfed pullets are his three unmarried daughters. That man would drink blood to get them wed."

"If he's got money and can provide them good dowries, he shouldn't have any trouble."

"He doesn't want the run-of-the-mill lout," Korakas said. "He's looking for nobility, a professional man or a prince of commerce to enhance his royal line."

"Well, I'm certainly not interested."

"Don't tell me, tell the matchmaker, Lambri," Korakas said. An instant later, talking zestfully to Rantoulis and his wife, a stocky woman in a large flowered hat, Lambri motioned eagerly for Nick and Korakas to join her.

"There she goes! What did I tell you? Like a vampire following the spoor of blood!" Korakas shuddered. "No escape for us now."

"Nicholas, this is Mr. and Mrs. Rantoulis," Lambri said when they reached the group. "One of the most respected families in our parish. And this young man, my friends, is our cousin's godson, Nicholas Dandolos, from Smyrna."

"Delighted to meet you, my boy!" Rantoulis clasped Nick's hands in both his sweaty palms as his wife stood by beaming. "I have heard about your efforts in behalf of your godfather's family. A splendid thing in these days when so many of our young men are infected by nihilism and godlessness. I think the only salvation for society is . . ."

Catching a dart of censure from his wife's eye, Rantoulis stopped abruptly and turned toward his daughters.

"But I have forgotten to introduce my daughters!"
Looking at them, some paternal anguish and solicitude he
could not control leaped to his face. "This is my beloved
Athena, Aspasia, and Artemis . . . all named, I am sure
you will recognize, for goddesses."

The girls tittered and stared with silent, avid eagerness at
Nick, their eyes sparkling under their velvet and satin hats.
They were vacuously pretty, he noticed, soft-cheeked and
plump as garlanded holiday geese. Their expensive clothing
included ruffled blouses visible under their fur-collared
coats and long skirts whose hems modestly revealed less
than an inch or two of their ankles.

"Your daughters have appropriate names." Nick mustered a nervous smile.

"Thank you!" Rantoulis glowed. "I was telling my wife
Alexandra just last night how ashamed I am because you
have crossed the world to come to our little community
and we have not yet offered you the hospitality of our
table."

Mrs. Rantoulis nodded remorsefully and then bright-
ened.

"Aristotle, why can't they join us for lunch today?"

"We couldn't possibly today!" Lambri spoke before
Nick or Korakas could refuse.

"You are busy?" Mrs. Rantoulis asked.

"No, we are not busy."

"Then why cannot you come?"

"An imposition at the last minute, like this."

"Not at all, Lambri. It would be our pleasure."

"But such short notice, Alexandra!"

"The meal would be less sumptuous than I would like,
but if you do not mind sharing our simple fare . . ."

"Are you sure we would not be intruding?"

"Not another word!" Mrs. Rantoulis smiled benignly. "You will come."

Their brief, adroit exchange closed like a curtain.

"Too much trouble for you people!" Korakas made a feeble effort to separate the folds.

"Perhaps some other time," Nick said.

"I believe the ladies have settled the matter," Rantoulis said with relief. "After all, the kitchen is their sacred domain where they daily perform their miracles." He grasped Nick's arm firmly. "My automobile is just outside the church and if you do not mind some slight crowding, most of us will fit. The others will follow in a taxicab. You will see we live near the lake in one of the finest neighborhoods in the city."

"Papa, can I ride with you?" Athena asked.

"Please, Papa, take us too!" Artemis and Aspasia pleaded.

"Let the girls ride with you and Mr. Dandolos," Mrs. Rantoulis said. "Lambri, Korakas, and I will come in the taxicab."

Korakas threw a final glare of outrage at Lambri, who ignored him. Nick braced himself to endure a painful afternoon. They moved slowly to the door, the daughters walking close to Nick, when a young woman who had been speaking to Father Ladas joined them. Rantoulis paused, looking at her nervously. He turned to the others.

"Lambri, Korakas, I think you have met my niece, Marina Lefkas. Marina, this gentleman is Mr. Nicholas Dandolos, from Smyrna." He gestured to Nick. "This is my dear, departed sister's daughter."

The girl was taller and more slender than the daughters, clad in an unfrilled jacket, plain white blouse, and untrimmed cloth coat. Beneath the brim of her hat, unadorned by flower or bow, her glossy black hair was cut daringly short, exposing small, fluted ears and a portion of her neck. Her complexion tinted with a natural radiance, she was lovely, but it was her eyes that stirred Nick the most; large and almond-shaped, some shade of deep brown, they seemed innocent and yet defiant. He felt a sudden excitement at the prospect that she would join them for lunch.

"Unfortunately, my niece cannot join us today." Rantoulis feigned regret. "We must complete some items of inventory at the store. She helps me there; indeed, it would only be fair to say she is my right hand." He smiled benevolently at her. "I don't know what I would do without Marina."

"Thank you, Uncle," Marina said.

"I am sorry," Nick said. "Couldn't you join us for lunch and take the inventory later?"

"We must not keep Marina from her task," Mrs. Rantoulis said quickly. "Another time we'll all be able to eat together. Now we must hurry if the girls and I are going to prepare anything for lunch. Lambri, Korakas and I can drop Marina at the store."

They walked up the stairs and emerged on the street outside the church. Rantoulis and his daughters moved toward an open touring car and Nick followed them. Mrs. Rantoulis led the others toward a taxicab waiting at the curb. Nick looked one last time at Marina. For an instant she gazed in his direction. Then she entered the cab and was lost to his view.

Seated at the table in the spacious Rantoulis apartment, Korakas cast an all-knowing glance at Nick, suggesting their arrival had been expected. Although they found the dining room table set for only five people, the fine lace tablecloth, delicate crystal, and glistening china attested to a special luncheon. Three more places were swiftly added to the table and after a surprisingly brief interlude in the kitchen (considering she had not been expecting company) Mrs. Rantoulis emerged to announce luncheon and they all sat down.

Rantoulis sat in a regal armchair at the head of the table. His eldest daughter, Athena, was at his right and they sat Nick beside her. After helping their mother bring the bowls of steaming avgolemono soup to the table, the two younger girls converged on the empty chair beside Nick. They reached it at the same time and Nick could sense a swift, silent struggle for possession.

"Girls!" Rantoulis said sternly. "What will our guests think?"

Wilting before her father's censure, Artemis, the youngest, relinquished the chair to her sister. She walked around the table to take a chair beside Lambri, glowering across the crystal at her sister.

Rantoulis clasped his hands and bent his head. Everyone followed suit, Nick looking down at his knees.

"O Lord, bless this food," Rantoulis said sonorously, "and all those about to partake of it, our beloved family and our dear friends, including the fine young man who has traveled so far to join us. Keep us healthy, faithful, and prosperous in these troubled times and assist us in remaining as decent, virtuous, and respectable in the future as we have been in the past."

Rantoulis paused for breath, as if waiting to see what effect the grace was having on his guests. Athena took advantage of the lull to nudge her chair closer to Nick. When he looked at her uneasily, she tried to reassure him with a quick, fluttering smile. Mrs. Rantoulis looked at the bowls of soup that were cooling and stared unhappily at her husband.

"We offer, finally," Rantoulis resumed, "a prayer for our ailing President, and a fervent hope that his recovery will also enlighten him to the faultiness of his recent decisions. We pray that our valiant Greek armies in Asia Minor move soon to regain the holy city of Christendom, and crush the barbarians who occupy it . . . and, in closing, we offer a prayer for our hungry and our poor, the worthy, deserving ones and not the numerous bums and loafers who will not work in spite of opportunities offered to them. We pray we may continue to be as generous to various and sundry charities in the future, as we have been in the past, a generosity, as you so well must know, gratefully acknowledged in writing by His Most Holy Grace, your revered representative in our midst, Bishop Karavellas. . . ."

He paused again for breath. Mrs. Rantoulis uttered a tight, sharp wheeze of breath. Rantoulis looked at her and said, "Amen."

"Begin, please!" Mrs. Rantoulis hurled a final, reproachful look at her husband.

After they had finished the soup, Mrs. Rantoulis carried in a platter of roast leg of lamb that Rantoulis rose to carve. Before the succulent aromas of the lamb and after drinking several glasses of red wine, Nick felt his discomfort diminished. He spoke freely of his long journey, the girls hanging breathlessly on his description of the storms at sea, and of his hopes for the new business. Rantoulis offered him all manner of advice, using his own success as confirmation of his sagacity. Once, after some particularly pretentious assertion, Korakas grunted loudly. When everyone looked at him, Lambri piercing him with her eyes, he smiled weakly.

"Some food caught in my throat," he muttered.

After luncheon, they retired to the parlor. Mrs. Rantoulis brought them demitasses of sweet Greek coffee while Artemis played a sonata on the piano, slurring a number of the notes. Then Aspasia sang an operatic aria, her voice breaking shrilly on the higher notes. Athena had left the room during her sister's song, drawing the drapes across the archway of the hall behind her.

"I'm ready, Papa!" she called from behind the curtains a moment after Aspasia finished her song.

"Now, for our final presentation," Rantoulis said breathlessly. "A real feast for the spirit, I tell you!"

The curtains quivered and then parted. Athena appeared wearing a long, brocaded, and gilded Grecian gown, a garland of flowers in her hair. Her eyes were directed demurely at the floor and in her clasped hands she carried a single, long-stemmed rose.

"She portrays her namesake, the goddess Athena," Rantoulis whispered to Nick.

"Wonderful," Nick whispered back.

"O noble Hellas, immortal mother of the earth, flower of the sparkling and cerulean Aegean sea . . ." Athena recited in a loud and fervent voice.

Rantoulis and his wife sat rapt with adoration and awe before this marvel they had created. Korakas stared at the girl as if he could not believe his eyes. Nick tried to maintain an expression of courteous interest but his thoughts fled to the girl Marina. Even as Athena's voice droned on, he recalled Marina's eyes and the last glance she seemed to have given him before entering the cab. He felt a restlessness suddenly. Longings he had not recalled in weeks rebounded in that moment to distress him.

"Never will I forget thee, O noble Hellas, never will my loyalty waver from thee, never will my spirit be severed from your ageless, eternal, and unquenchable soul!"

Athena finished with a surge of passion that shook her voice and then extended the rose toward heaven.

Rantoulis and his wife, Lambri, and Nick began to applaud. Korakas leaped up, clapping vigorously, and crying, "Bravo! Bravo!" apparently delighted, Nick decided, that the ordeal was over.

Rantoulis glowed as if the applause were for him. Lambri smiled at Mrs. Rantoulis, silently commending her exemplary mother's influence. When the flurry of congratulations and applause ceased, Rantoulis and his wife and Athena looked eagerly at Nick, waiting for something more.

"Marvelous!" Nick said with what enthusiasm he could muster. "Marvelous!"

Rantoulis and his wife exchanged a delighted and triumphant look.

"It will never be said of my daughters," he said gravely, "that they are skillful only in the kitchen. They have abundant talents for the parlor, as well."

Later that afternoon, a streetcar rattled and clanged along Harrison Street, coming to a stop at the juncture of Halsted and Blue Island. Lambri, Korakas, and Nick descended and began walking toward the club a couple of blocks away.

"I said it before and I'll say it again," Korakas spoke roughly. "The father is a pompous ass, the mother has her head in the soup, and the daughters, well . . . the best you can say for them is that they are powdered ninnies!"

"Listen to the man!" Lambri said. "So successful and wealthy in his own life, he can judge others. Nick could do much worse than form an alliance with a family as rich and respectable as that one."

They walked in silence for a few minutes, Lambri casting anxious glances at Nick.

"The truth is," she said to him ruefully, "I had not been close enough to the family to fully evaluate the girls. When I talked to Alexandra in church last Sunday, she expressed sharp interest in meeting you. I thought it would be opportune." She paused. "I had an idea one of the girls might please you."

"That's all right, Lambri," Nick reassured her. "There's no harm in having lunch with the family. It wasn't a bad idea."

"Some idea!" Korakas grunted.

"Never had a bad idea in your life, eh?" Lambri glared at him. "Tell Niko about building the basement storeroom last year, so you could stock up on potatoes and vegetables when they were plentiful and cheaper. The boob who drew the plans for him and the morons who dug it out were almost buried alive when the floor of the kitchen fell in!"

"An architectural misjudgment," Korakas muttered.

Nick smiled. Emboldened, Lambri took his arm.

"I had good intentions, believe me, Niko," she said. "It is time you married, settled down with some nice girl. I knew the dowry would be considerable too, and provide you security."

"Why should he worry about a dowry?" Korakas asked. "He's going to make a fortune in business here. Besides, there is the matter of love."

"Love?" Lambri raised her brows. "Of course, I had forgotten love. It's been quite a while since I've had to give that matter any thought." She gave Nick a small, urgent push. "Say something!"

"Yeh, speak up," Korakas grinned. "Tell us whether you wanted the winged rose or the middle one, the one with bowlegs."

"Bowlegs?" Lambri scoffed. "How could you tell she had bowlegs? Did you peek under her skirt?"

"You know what I mean, woman!" Korakas cried. "A mature man can sense these things. Anyway, they're all attractive girls, I'm sure, and some lucky man can choose any one of them and suffer in style. But not Nick . . ."

They reached the corner of Polk Street, the gambling casinos visible a block away. Korakas paused restlessly.

"Listen, my love," he said soothingly to Lambri. "You go on home with Nick. I'm going to visit a few businessmen, discuss some neighborhood improvements . . ."

"You mean you're going to join the bums at craps," Lambri said coldly.

Korakas looked to heaven. "Jesus, what a woman! Give her an opening and she sinks her harpoon to the hilt!" He started at a brisk pace toward the gambling houses, waving back at them in a fleeting farewell.

Lambri and Nick continued walking. A few children raced by them shrieking to join a small crowd on the opposite corner gathered around an organ grinder and his tiny, cavorting monkey.

"Did you see that neighborhood where Rantoulis lives?" Lambri asked quietly. "How lovely the houses were. In summer those trees would be full of leaves and the gardens would bloom with flowers."

"Would you like to live there?"

"Would I like to go to heaven?"

"If that neighborhood where they live is too expensive," Nick said, "there must still be places better than this street. Why do you stay here?"

"This street and its life belong to Korakas," she said. "Take him away from its shabby pavements and you'd chill his blood. He is a goodhearted man, really, without ambition or hope, content to haunt the crap table, winning or losing a few dollars, drinking mastiha with his cronies, now and then finding some young tart to make him feel the bull he was once." She paused, a pensiveness entering her voice. "Our lives might have been different if we had a family, but I couldn't carry a child, would lose them in the first or second month. Korakas was unhappy about that for a while. The street helped him forget. So I accept he will live and grow old on this street and I will live and grow old beside him. We will probably both die here too."

Nick stopped and turned to grasp her arms tightly.

"Listen, Lambri," he said earnestly. "You will not die on this street and you won't have to live here any longer than you want to. That is a promise."

"That's all right, Niko," she said quickly. "I wasn't complaining."

"Listen to what I'm telling you," he said firmly. "I swear it as a pledge to you."

Lambri nodded, touched by his concern. They walked a short distance further in silence and across the street Nick saw the Athens Wholesale Grocery, which belonged to Rantoulis. He felt a leaping in his blood.

They passed a few more stores and stood before the battered exterior of the No-worry Club.

"I don't think I'll come in yet," Nick said. "I may walk for a while longer."

"I'd walk with you, but my groaning feet refuse," Lambri said. "You have your key?"

Nick nodded and kissed her. She patted his cheek gently, with affection. Turning to the door, fumbling in her purse for her key, she stared up at the shabby lettering on the ramshackle sign.

"The No-worry Club indeed," she said grimly. "The No-sense Club would be more fitting for the old man and me."

She turned the key, opened the door, and entered the café. Nick watched her moving slowly among the tables until she disappeared through the swinging door into the kitchen.

Nick crossed the street to stand outside the Athens Wholesale Grocery. He peered over the display of casks and bottles in the window to the store interior. Although several lights were on, there wasn't any trace of Marina. He saw a counter, shelves laden with merchandise, barrels on the floor. At the rear of the store was a potbellied stove, the black tube of the flue curving toward the ceiling and then into the wall. A large coffee mill stood beside the stove and above it hung a banner with large bold letters: FRIENDSHIPS ARE DESTROYED BY CREDIT.

He tried the door and found it locked. Afraid she might not recognize him, he knocked timidly. Then, scorning his caution, he knocked again more boldly. For a tense moment he heard the beating of his heart and looked around to see if anyone might be passing, thinking he was trying to break in. But twilight had begun to shade the street. The organ grinder and his monkey had moved on, the strains of his music floating faintly from another street. When he was about to give up, he saw her.

She stood near the stove, staring toward the door. He knocked again. She walked forward, the slenderness of her body outlined as her skirt whipped against her legs and thighs. As she neared the door and he saw her loveliness again, he felt a fleeting panic.

She made a brusque motion to tell him the store was closed. He pressed closer to the glass, smiling to reassure her, resembling, he was positive, another grinning monkey. Their glances met and she seemed to recognize him. She clicked back the bolt and opened the door. He stepped inside.

"I'm Nick Dandolos, Miss Marina," he said quickly. "I met you this morning after church. I happened . . ."

"I remember you," she said coolly.

He struggled for the next words, angry at himself for his bumbling.

"You have a fine store here." He motioned to the interior. "I was just passing and looked in and thought I might knock on the chance . . ."

"Uncle will be pleased you admire his store," she said. He sensed a faint teasing smile.

"My reason for knocking," Nick said stiffly, "was that I had brought some sugared loukoum as a gift for Lambri Korakas and it was lost. I wonder if you might sell me some?"

"We are a wholesale outlet," Marina said politely. "But for an important gentleman like you, a potential suitor, I am sure Uncle . . ."

"I am not a suitor," Nick protested.

"Really? Then, Mr. Dandolos, perhaps you are trifling with the affections of my cousins. I'm quite sure they regard you as a suitor."

"They are in error."

"You did join them for lunch, didn't you?"

The absurdity of the exchange made him smile. He admired the way she had put him at once on the defensive.

"Lunch is hardly a proposal of marriage," he said.

She stared at him for a moment and he was awed again at the treasure contained in her eyes.

"I'll get the loukoum," she said. She turned and walked behind the counter. He followed her and she bent and brought up a tin of loukoum.

"If you were a serious suitor," she asked, "which of my cousins would you choose?"

Nick started to smile again and then hesitated.

"I'm not sure."

"Of course, Uncle would prefer it to be Athena, because she's the eldest," Marina said. "But Artemis has a more even-tempered disposition. You would have to decide whether that was worth a smaller dowry."

"Why talk only about me?" Nick asked. "Are there suitors asking for your hand? Are you engaged or planning to be married?"

"I'm not engaged and not planning to marry for quite a while," she said. "My cousins may be eager to marry, but I must plan my life with more purpose than bearing children and doing housework."

"Many women are satisfied with those things."

"Many women are not satisfied!" He was startled at the vehemence of her response. "They are simply dominated by the values of men and cluttered with possessions they are afraid to lose!"

For a tense, curious moment they stared across the counter at one another.

"Well, the luncheon wasn't my idea," he said. "You know, Lambri, my cousin, wanted me to go. I'm not ready to settle down either."

"I heard my uncle talking about you a few days ago," she said more quietly. "You are considered an eligible catch, a young man with potential."

He shifted uneasily.

"I have some important business to conduct here," he said. "For my godfather back in Smyrna, business that will help them come to this country."

"Business is all right," she said. "But for men as well as women, there are other things. To read, travel to distant places, meet many people. The years can pass quickly and then it is too late." She waited gravely as if she expected him to laugh or chide her. He was careful not to smile.

"I understand that feeling," he said.

He had a strange sense she was drawn to him in the same closeness he felt to her. They were silent and then she drew back, reaching for a fragment of paper to wrap the tin. He would have to leave.

"Miss Marina." He spoke quickly. "Will you come to a restaurant nearby. We might have coffee and a sandwich or some dinner."

"Haven't you eaten lunch?"

He nodded sheepishly.

"I'd like to sit and talk with you for a while."

"I couldn't go out with you, Mr. Dandolos," she said. "My aunt and uncle would be horrified. You'd be shocked at the dreadful things people say about me now. My hair is six inches too short and my skirt is two inches too high. Being seen with me won't help you either."

"I don't care about that," he said. He pulled out his purse, fumbling at the clasp, trying to conceal his disappointment. "How much do I owe you for the loukoum?"

"A dollar," she said. As he handed her the money, her fingers touched his palm. The feel of her flesh sent a quiver through his body. He reached despondently for the wrapped tin of loukoum.

"I was just about to make a cup of tea when you knocked, Mr. Dandolos," she said quietly. "We could have a cup together, if you like."

He had to restrain himself from shouting.

"That would be fine." He spoke as quietly as she had spoken.

They sat in wicker chairs in a small office sipping orange pekoe tea. The aromas of pungent cheese and olives came from a storeroom nearby. Marina sat in the beam of a lamp and the light glowed across her cheeks and throat.

He told her about his parents in Crete, who had both died while he was at school in Smyrna. She told him that her mother and father were dead, as well.

"My mother died when I was fourteen, and my father about two years later," she said. "I lived for a few years with my uncle but last year I left his house, found a small place of my own. He and my aunt were angry with me but I couldn't endure living there any more."

"Why?"

"Because of the way he protected and shielded us, his daughters and me," Marina said. "Guarding us until proper husbands could be found for us. We were to stay sweet and carefree and then be married and raise a family. But I knew something of what life was like. My parents and I lived not far from here and I knew the Levee, the bars that never close, the drunks fallen in alleys, the poor women with their painted faces and haunted eyes. My father was part of that life, a drinker and a gambler, and I saw how my mother suffered with him."

She paused, suddenly unsettled.

"Why should I be telling you these things?" she asked. "We've just met today and I'm telling you these personal things."

"I'm grateful you feel you can tell me."

They were silent for a moment.

"When your godfather comes with his family," she said, "will you remain in the business with him?"

"I'm not sure," he said. For the first time in months an uneasiness gripped him, a wavering of his purpose. He yearned to share secrets and confidences with her. "I wanted to be a priest once," he said. "I don't remember why or when I gave up that dream. It seems foolish now and didn't seem foolish then."

She waited for him to go on.

"That seems a long time ago," he said. "And had something to do with my mother's wishes. I suppose now I want to make a place for myself here, become a citizen, earn people's respect. Then, I suppose, I want those things you don't feel are important, marriage and children."

"They are important, Nick, but there are injustices that have to be cured first," she said. "Marriage should be a partnership, not a form of bondage. Women must have some choice in their lives with political and economic equality."

"How will they get this equality?"

"By gaining the right to vote. Do you realize that after

the Civil War was fought in this country to abolish slav-
ery, the freed black men were given the right to vote.
Today, fifty years later, white as well as black women are
denied that right in all but a handful of states. Do you think
that is fair?"

He shook his head slowly. "I don't suppose it is fair, but
simply the way things are. Men have always had the power
in society and in the government."

"That will change!" she said, a fervor entering her
voice. "Since the middle of the last century, women have
been waging a battle for their rights as human beings. I will
fight with them for the right to vote!"

"Is the vote so important?"

"There are other things women should have too," she
said. "Easier divorces and the right to have abortions, if
that's what they choose. But the vote comes first. Women
couldn't do much during the war with their sons and husbands fighting overseas and they put their struggle aside.
Since the armistice, they have begun to fight again. They
have formed the National American Woman Suffrage Association which I have joined."

"What do you do in this union?"

"We write letters, issue bulletins and a weekly paper,
talk to politicians," she said. "If they ignore us, we attend
their meetings, heckle and jeer them, break up their gather-
ings. Some of our leaders have been beaten with fists and
sticks by hooligans and the police throw them in jail. Then
they go on hunger strikes and refuse to eat!"

He had a shaken vision of Marina beaten and impris-
oned.

"Marina, in God's name! I mean, you're right, and these
things aren't fair," he said earnestly. "But what if you got

beaten up and thrown into prison? Wouldn't that be dreadful for you?"

"If that happened to me, then I pray I would have the strength to do as other women have done," she said. "For our cause is just. We fight for the women who have become old at thirty, worn out by years of working from morning to night and by bearing one child after another. We fight for all the women exploited and abused by men who hold the power to make their lives a hell. Yes . . . and I fight for the memory of my mother, who could only suffer and cry, who was so worn and defeated the only way she could escape my father was to die."

He was moved when he saw the tears in her eyes.

"All right, Marina," he said. "I have never considered these things before. You are right." He smiled at her, trying to lighten her mood. "Today you have made one man a convert to your cause."

She stared gravely at him, uncertain whether he was telling the truth.

"I better finish my work now," she said.

She stood up and he rose as well. He moved aside to let her pass. For a moment their faces were only separated by inches and he longed to kiss her. She left the office and he followed her, feeling a warm and buoyant joy.

"Marina," he said. "When can I see you again?"

"Do you want to see me again?"

"Of course!"

"Why?"

"Because I like you," he said. "I know we just met today, but I tell you now that I like you very much."

"Is that the only reason you want to see me?"

"Yes," he said, then quickly shook his head. "I mean no.

I'd also like to talk to you again about some of the things
we spoke of today."

"All right," she said, and there was a trace of a smile at
her lips. "I'd like to see you again too. Talk to my uncle."

"I don't mean to ask for your hand in marriage the first
day I meet you," he laughed. "Besides, I am not en-
couraged by your attitude about that institution."

"I understand," she said, "but since he is my closest rela-
tive and since that is the way society decrees these things
are done, talk to him anyway. I am sure he'll be surprised."

"He'll be shocked and furious! You know he has plans
for me with one of his daughters."

"I know that," she said, and laughter sparked in her
eyes. "Poor Uncle thought he was pulling off a master
stroke by keeping me away from the luncheon today. I'd
like to see my cousins' faces when they discover you want
to see me again."

"You're a wicked girl! What if he says no?"

"I may decide to see you anyway," she said, "because I
am wicked and a brazen revolutionary who is doomed, my
cousins never tire of telling me, to a sordid end."

He followed her to the door. As she opened it for him,
he struck his forehead with his palm.

"I've forgotten the loukoum!"

He hurried back to the counter for the package. She
waited by the door, and walking by her, he reveled again
in her loveliness. She remained standing inside the door and
waved to him through the glass. He waved back with a
surge of jubilation.

He started walking briskly along the darkened evening
street, for a few moments uncertain of purpose or direction. When he reached the corner, he looked back, resist-

ing as impulse to return to the store. He crossed the street clasped in a euphoria unlike any he had ever known.

Entering the No-worry Club, he passed through the café and shadowed kitchen and sprinted upstairs. Inside the apartment he called Lambri's name but the rooms were quiet. Her bedroom was partly open, the room dark, and peering in, he made out her sleeping form on the bed. He was disappointed because he wanted to share his delight. He went to his bedroom and lay down on the bed, watching the light from the street reflected against his window.

Marina . . . Marina . . . even her name held a magic for him. He closed his eyes and called up the vision of her face and her voice, the intimacy of the moments they had shared.

Restless, unable to remain still, impatient to begin some action, he left the apartment, walking down the street toward the gambling casinos to find Korakas.

He walked into the Hermes, weaving his way among the tables circled by crowds of men. He walked through the curtains at the rear of the casinos, used Korakas' name to the guards, and hurried up the stairs. He passed the thick paneled door of the room where the big gamblers played and went up to the third floor. Clearing that guard as well, he entered the room.

Korakas was pressed against the rail of the crap table, making bets furiously, shouting with the other players, when Nick grabbed his arm. He groaned in frustration as Nick drew him to a quieter corner.

"Listen, Korakas," Nick said. "You've got to help me."

"Sure, Nick, sure," Korakas said, staring longingly back
at the action. "But can't it wait till later? I'm way behind
now."

"No, it can't wait, it can't wait!" Nick said. "You know
Rantoulis' niece, Marina, the one who works with him at
the store?"

"The skinny, big-eyed girl we gave a ride to this morning? Sure," he said. "She's some kind of Bolshevik, I think,
fighting for one of those damn suffrage groups. What
about her?"

"I want you to go and ask Rantoulis to allow me to call
on her formally."

Korakas looked at him in shock.

"Are you crazy, Nick? Have you lost your senses? You
only met her for a minute today! You must be mad or
working too hard!"

"I spent several hours talking with her at the store this
afternoon," Nick said. "I know what I'm doing. Korakas,
you've got to help me!"

"Rantoulis would be outraged!" Korakas said. "He
shows you his three lovely daughters and you pick his
damn niece!"

Several men at the table called for Korakas to return to
the game.

"Will you go to see him?"

"Listen, Nick!" Korakas pleaded.

"Don't start lecturing me, in God's name! I know what
I'm doing! I can't explain now but it's like a miracle!"

"He'll throw me out on my ass! He's got three daughters and his pride! I could as easy spit in his eye as ask him
that!"

"I'm not asking to marry her right now," Nick said. "I

just want to call on her and do it properly, the way it should be done."

"Listen, Nick." Korakas lowered his voice. "If it's a woman, I know this beauty in the Apollo. A body like a volcano and . . ." He saw Nick's unyielding face. "All right! All right!" he said. "I'll go see Rantoulis first thing in the morning."

"He's home now," Nick said. "I want you to see him tonight."

"Tonight!" Korakas cried. "Jesus, Nick, I'm playing now and more than a hundred dollars out! Can't it wait until morning?"

"Tonight!" Nick said. "I want it settled before I go to sleep!"

"Hey, Korakas." Dr. Samyotis moved a few feet from the table. "Your turn. You shooting or not?"

"I'll play in your place until you come back," Nick said. "We may change your luck. For God's sake, do this favor for me now!"

With a final anguished look at the table of players, Korakas hurried out of the room, stamping down the stairs, muttering to himself. On the street he flagged down a taxicab and gave the driver the address of Rantoulis. As the cab jolted forward, he sank back in his seat with a curse.

Alexandra Rantoulis opened the door for Korakas, a flaring of excitement in her rotund cheeks when she saw him.

"I am sorry to be intruding, Mrs. Rantoulis," Korakas said. "Might I see Mr. Rantoulis for just a moment?"

"But, of course! Come in! Come in!"

Entering the hallway, he caught a glimpse of one of the

girls peeking out of a room down the corridor. Mrs. Rantoulis led him into the parlor, lit several lamps, and asked
him to wait. He waited, feeling a nausea sweep from his
belly to his throat.

Wearing spectacles that had slipped down the bridge of
his nose, hastily pulling on his suitcoat, Rantoulis entered
the parlor. He clasped Korakas' hands warmly.

"If I'm coming at a bad time," Korakas said, "I'll be glad
to return tomorrow."

"Not a bad time at all!" Rantoulis said vigorously, and
taking his arm, he led Korakas into a small study off the
parlor. He closed the folding doors behind them, motion-
ing cordially for Korakas to sit down. Pulling up another
chair facing him, Rantoulis leaned forward in anticipation.

"I am, as you know, Mr. Rantoulis . . ."

"Call me Aristotle, please. First names for friends and,"
he paused, ". . . family."

"All right, sure, Aristotle," Korakas began again, the
words coming in slow agony from his lips. "I try to do
things right, but I make mistakes, and my wife Lambri . . ."

"Yes, yes, that's all right, my dear friend," Rantoulis said.
"We can speak frankly, man to man, Greek to Greek." He
moved his chair closer, his bony knees jabbing against the
knees of Korakas, who could count the pores on the
grocer's face.

"Well, all right, since you understand I hope I'm doing
this the proper way," Korakas said. "I'll come to the point.
My young cousin, Nicholas Dandolos . . ."

The lobes of Rantoulis' ears quivered and pendant lights
gleamed in his eyes. Korakas faltered.

"My young cousin, Nicholas," he began again. "Why,

he wants, I mean, respectfully asks your permission to call
on . . ."

With the sentence still unfinished, Rantoulis could not
resist the delight that burst in his cheeks. He composed
himself and spoke gravely.

"You may relay to your fine young cousin, Mr. Nicholas Dandolos, that he has my permission to call on Athena."

Korakas swallowed against the stone in his throat and
shook his head weakly.

"Forgive me, Mr. Rantoulis . . . Aristotle . . . not
Athena."

Rantoulis struggled for a moment to absorb the first
whiff of unpleasant news.

"Not Athena?" he said slowly. "But this is most distress-
ing. If he prefers Aspasia, they must wait until Athena is
married, before their own nuptials. Does he know that?"

"I'm sure he knows that," Korakas said quickly. For an
instant he considered dashing wildly from the house.

"Then if he has decided on Aspasia," Rantoulis said, "we
should discuss the provisions of the dowry, what he might
expect from me, and . . ."

He saw something in Korakas' face that alarmed him.

"It is Aspasia . . . ?" Rantoulis asked.

Korakas shook his head.

"But this is most irregular!" Rantoulis trembled in agitation. "Artemis cannot be betrothed until her sisters have
suitors! Why would he request such an unreasonable thing?
Really, most irregular and disturbing!"

"Forgive me, Mr. Rantoulis . . . Aristotle." Korakas
spoke in a low, hoarse voice. "It is not your youngest
daughter."

Rantoulis looked bewildered.

Korakas closed his eyes and fired the final charge.

"He wants permission to call on your niece, Marina," he whispered and opened his eyes.

The shattered face of Rantoulis loomed before him.

"Marina!" Rantoulis cried her name as if it were a disease. "Marina!"

Korakas, suffering with him, nodded mutely.

"Why?" Rantoulis asked hoarsely. "In God's name! Why?"

"In God's name, I don't know!" Korakas cried. "I don't know why a man should not choose from three angels when he has the chance . . . three such lovely girls and he . . . he . . ."

Rantoulis rose to his feet, stepped backward, and stumbled slightly.

"Despicable!" Rantoulis said shakenly. "Contemptible! An insult to my family! An affront to my daughters! In Greece an offense like this would call for the shedding of blood!"

"I know!" Korakas said in despair. "I know!"

"He must be crazy!"

"He's been working night and day," Korakas said. "Maybe something snapped."

"Unthinkable! Impossible! Outrageous!"

"I agree, I agree!" Korakas said and rose. "I'll give him your message." He started for the folding doors.

"Wait!" Rantoulis cried. His lips trembled as if some fierce struggle were taking place within him. "He may, you know, recover his sanity. We might be wise to humor him."

Korakas stared at him in confusion.

"If I reject him now, he may look elsewhere," Rantoulis

said. "Another family, God help us, would have him. But if I give him permission to call on Marina, he will still remain within the sphere of the family. I will make sure that she spends more time with us, that when he sees her, he will see my daughters as well. He has been impressed with the surface appearance of that girl. He will discover, soon enough, that she is a radical and holds heretical views on the family and society. He will be disillusioned. Who knows? He may decide on one of my darlings after all."

Korakas pursed his lips and blew a low whistle of admiration.

"Sound thinking, Aristotle!" he said. "I can see why you've become a success and why I'm still battering my brains out! I got to hand it to you!"

He extended his hands and, grasping Rantoulis' limp fingers, shook them firmly.

"I'll give Nick the news," he said, and once again started for the doors. Looking back, he saw Rantoulis slumped in his chair.

"God help me," Rantoulis whispered. "God help me . . ." He released a long, woeful sigh. "Three daughters." He looked at the ceiling, in the direction of heaven, grimaced and shook his head. "Some rogues are childless and some scoundrels have sons and blessed Rantoulis plows up three daughters . . ."

CHAPTER 3

When Korakas left the room, Nick took his place at the crap table. Still overjoyed at the finding of Marina, he lacked any desire to play. Even as he looked down on the green felt surface of the table, marked and divided into squares and numbers, he felt curiously detached from the frenzy. When the dice moved to him, he motioned the stickman to pass them on.

Slowly, the play claimed his attention. Something in his mood found an affinity in the swiftness of the action. One player hurled the dice that struck the boards and snapped to a stop. The stickman cried the point and the pay-out man cast his rubber puck to rake in the losses and dispense the winnings. Without a wasted motion, as quickly as a shooter gave up the cubes, they moved to the next player. When the dice came to Nick for the third time, he gestured he would play.

"New shooter coming out," the stickman said.

Nick fumbled in his pocket and pulled out a ten and a

five, which he placed on the front line. Even as he rattled
and flung the dice, imitating the energy of the shooters before him, he remained more a spectator than a player.

"Seee-ven," the stickman called. "Shooter wins the roll."

He returned the dice to Nick, who picked them up,
shook them, and hurled them again, watching them strike
the boards, bouncing off to settle on the table.

"Eee-oo-le-ven," the stickman said. "Shooter wins again.
Pay the front line."

The pay-out man added several more bills to the money
before Nick. He hesitated, thinking of withdrawing and
going downstairs to wait for Korakas. Banopoulos pushed
into place beside him and slapped his shoulder briskly.

"Bravo, Nick!" he said. "You're still a winner! Keep
shooting and we poor clods will tag along to recoup our
turtle losses from the house."

Nick picked up the dice again, extending his arm and
opening his hand so the overhead lamp shone brightly on
the cubes. He felt a power being channeled from his body,
through his wrist, and into his fingers. He hurled the dice
again.

"Nine . . . nine, the point is nine."

Nick threw again, the dice cracking loudly against the
boards and flying off.

"Nine again . . . nine right back with a six and three,"
the stickman said.

He was conscious suddenly of the men around the table
watching him. Banopoulos, Dr. Samyotis, Gikas, Spiro the
barber, and the other players, every face intent upon his
play. He threw several more times, audaciously certain before the dice finished their roll that he would win. The

money before him doubled with every pass. Whatever prickings of caution he felt were vanquished by still another seven.

"Nick, you've got almost a thousand dollars!" Banopoulos spoke excitedly at his elbow. "Do you want to draw some off?"

"Give me the dice!" Nick cried.

The men cheered his bravado and their raucous admiration went like wine to his head. He threw again and won, the men around the table winning with him. Two thousand bucks, he heard a man yell.

He held the dice tightly in his hand once more, a wind of triumph animating his spirit. He saw Korakas had returned, was standing bewildered beside him. Nick threw the dice again.

"He's won again!" Spiro shouted in disbelief.

"An angel is shooting for him," Gikas said somberly.

The pay-out man matched Nick's wager with a sheaf of hundred-dollar bills.

Korakas tugged at his arm.

"Jesus Christ, Nick, that's enough!" he cried. "You've made a bundle! Draw some dough off or quit!"

"One more time!" Nick shouted. The men echoed his pledge with a roar. He felt his blood pounding in his temples.

As Nick gathered the burning cubes in his hand, a tense and suspenseful silence gripped the players. In the stillness a man cleared his throat harshly.

Nick hurled the dice against the boards with a crack that burst like a gunshot. They bounced to the felt and snapped to a stop. The men roared again, as he won once more.

Korakas embraced Nick, dragging him from the table.

"That's all, Nick!" he cried. "Don't shoot again or I'll die right here!"

The game broke up, the players crowding around Nick, pounding his shoulders, pressing in to shake his hand. Korakas gathered Nick's winnings, his fingers trembling as he collected the thick sheaf of bills. He began counting the money, silently at first and then aloud as the amount grew. ". . . thirty-nine hundred dollars . . . four thousand . . . Jesus Christ! . . . five thousand . . . six thousand . . . Oh, my God!" He closed his eyes for a moment as if the money were an apparition that would disappear. Then he opened his eyes and went on counting. ". . . seven thousand . . . Holy Mother Mary! . . . seventy-one hundred . . . two hundred . . . three hundred . . . four hundred . . . five hundred . . . six hundred . . . that's it! Seven thousand, six hundred winged green beauties!"

"I have won nearly a thousand myself!" Dr. Samyotis said excitedly. "Do you know how many bottles of magic elixir I have to sell to make that much?"

"Nick don't have to pay me no rent till after Christmas!" Spiro the barber waved a handful of bills aloft. The men laughed boisterously.

"Fantastic! Simply Homeric!" Banopoulos jubilantly pocketed his own winnings. "I must write an editorial about this game!" He hurried from the room.

"New shooter coming out," the stickman said, his expression and voice revealing he was bored at the theatrics. A few players returned to the table but many of them remained pressed about Nick. A few reached out to touch his arms and shoulders, as if to assimilate his prowess and good fortune.

"Let's get the hell out of here," Korakas said. He tugged

at Nick's arm and they started to the door. Korakas stopped. "For cri' sakes!" he cried. "In all the excitement, I forgot some more good news! Rantoulis says it's all right for you to call on his niece!"

In the lingering spell of the play, Nick needed a moment to absorb the news. He let out an exultant shout.

"My lucky night!" he cried. "I can't lose at anything tonight!"

As they walked down the stairs, Nick paused on the second floor before the paneled door.

"Is there a game going on?" he asked Korakas.

"I think so," Korakas said. He looked suddenly, sharply, at Nick. "Even if they are playing, Nick, don't you get any ideas. They're wolves in there!" He tugged urgently and gaily at Nick's arm. "C'mon, let's go celebrate!"

Nick reluctantly let Korakas pull him along.

"Even if they're wolves," he said. "Does that mean I am a sheep or a puppy?"

"You're the best, Nick!" Korakas cried. "You're the best! You proved that tonight!"

For the next hour Nick stood at the bar, he and Korakas the center of a swarm of men who came to shake his hand and offer to buy him a drink. Without any taste for whiskey, he drank a few shots to be gracious, began to feel the heat of the liquor flush his cheeks. As the crowd about him thinned, the men drifting back to their games, his elation passed, a dissatisfaction burdening his spirit. In the large room about him, he heard the tumult and clatter of the games, the excitement of the players' voices. He was impatient suddenly at the timidness which caused him to stop playing.

"How much did I win?" he asked Korakas.

"Seven thousand, six hundred bucks!" Korakas said.

"What if I had rolled again and won? We might have had fifteen thousand dollars."

"You might have lost every dime, too."

"Not tonight." He shook his head. "Tonight I feel invincible. I shouldn't have stopped."

Korakas stared at him somberly.

"Give me the money," Nick said.

"I'll give it to you, Nick," Korakas said nervously. "But let's go home first. I'll tell you how Rantoulis took the news."

Nick silently stretched out his hand and after a moment's hesitation, Korakas slowly gave him the bills. Nick motioned upstairs.

"I want to play with the wolves for a while," he said.

"Nick, listen!" Korakas spoke in a shaken voice. "Those guys play high and hard. They're a breed unlike men you've ever known and they got the dough to freeze you out of the pot. You don't know what playing with them is like."

Nick slapped him lightly on the shoulder. "All right, my friend, now you've warned me," he said soothingly. "Now come upstairs and tell them I want to play." Without waiting for Korakas to say anything else, he started for the stairs. Korakas walked up behind him.

On the second floor, without hesitating, Nick walked to the door and knocked boldly on the wood. The slot in the door opened and the guard's face appeared.

"Tell him I want to play," Nick said to Korakas.

Korakas stared at him mutely, a plea that Nick ignored.

"He's my cousin and he wants to play," Korakas said gloomily. "He's got money."

"Wait," the guard said and closed the slot.

While Nick waited tensely, wondering if they would allow him in the game, Korakas made a final effort to discourage him.

"Listen, Nick, please!" Korakas pleaded. "I'm telling you this isn't your kind of game. Believe me, I know . . ."

Nick peeled several hundred-dollar bills from his winnings and handed them to Korakas.

"Keep the party going," he said. "I'll be down to join you in a little while."

The slot opened again and the guard's face reappeared. A moment later the heavy door swung open and he motioned Nick inside. Korakas made an effort to follow but the guard blocked his path.

"He don't need a nursemaid, Korakas," the guard said.

As Nick entered the corridor, the guard closed and bolted the door behind him.

The first time Korakas had brought Nick into the gambling room, he had been an unobserved visitor. Now, entering to play, the room seemed larger, almost cavernous, the corners hidden in shadows. An eerie mist drifted from the ceiling to swirl under the single bright light focused over the table. A hand was in progress and the guard gestured for Nick to wait.

His eyes growing accustomed to the dimness, Nick made out the figures of the players he remembered, but they seemed altered, somehow magnified. Prince Pierre appeared even more of a dandy. Loukanas sparkled with a spate of diamonds from collar to wrist. The head and shoulders of the slaughterhouse owner, Big Gorgio, seemed more hulking and powerful. And the features of Vito Baldelli, who ran prostitution for the Gennas, were sharpened to an animal's ferocity.

Looking for the figure of the old gambler, Nestor, Nick saw him sitting in almost the same place he had been sitting before, his white-haired head motionless, watching the game. His slender fingers, resting on the cloth of his trousers, seemed longer and so pale they gleamed like pearl.

The hand ended and a bodyguard moved a chair to the table for Nick. He sat down, murmuring his name and a greeting to the players, who barely looked at him in response. He found the rebuff unnerving.

As he reached into his pocket and drew out the roll of bills, he regretted his foolish bravado. Looking toward the darkened corridor leading to the door, wishing that Korakas was with him, he felt nervous and alone.

In the beginning he played cautiously, dropping out of the hand if his first two cards were not jacks or better. Hoarding his stake, he was awed by the size of the pots that rose swiftly from the opening cards into the hundreds and often into the thousands of dollars. He was also dismayed by the cold silence with which the men played, only muttering or grunting as they won or lost.

After playing about an hour, in a game when Nick folded his hand after seeing his hole card, Big Gorgio slammed his big palm upon the table.

"I thought you wanted to play!" he snarled.

"I do." Nick tried to affect a courage and assurance he no longer felt.

"Leave our guest alone, Gorgio." The diamond-studded Loukanas spoke with a falsely civil tone. "Perhaps that is the way they play in Smolensk."

"Smyrna," Nick said, and felt his cheeks flush. Prince

Pierre smirked and beyond the perimeter of light, the bodyguards snickered.

"Forgive me . . . Smyrna, of course," Loukanas said, his layers of jowls quivering with laughter. "Still, sometimes young men's aspirations do not match their abilities."

Nick began to stay in the games on the same cards he had folded earlier. In the next three hands he lost fifteen hundred dollars and that sobered him more.

He dealt the following hand, unable to restrain his fingers from trembling, worried that his distress was visible. Staying when he might wisely have dropped out, he paired queens on his last card and won a pot that held four hundred dollars.

The next game he folded and Vito Baldelli confronted Loukanas in a showdown for several thousand dollars that the obese casino owner won. Baldelli cursed and roughly pushed his chair away from the table.

"My goddam hands have turned sour since this crud came into the game!" He glared at Nick, rose and left the table. He walked angrily to the door, one of the bodyguards leaving with him.

"You are lucky, Nicky," Prince Pierre said amiably. "Vito has a bad temper. He might have broken your jaw."

"Play!" Big Gorgio snarled again. "This goddam game is too much talk!"

Loukanas dealt the next hand, his fingers deftly skimming the cards across the green felt surface to land in place before each player. Nick's first two cards were a pair of tens. He bet them to the end and won about twelve hundred dollars. Perhaps my luck is changing, he thought gratefully.

"Cheers for our friend from Smolensk." Loukanas spoke

in a slow, deliberate provocation. Nick remained silent, his nervousness giving way to anger.

Prince Pierre dealt the next hand. Nick's first cards were a powerful pair of kings and he felt his confidence renewed by a staunch belief the hand belonged to him.

Prince Pierre, an ace showing, opened for two hundred. Loukanas saw his bet and Nick raised five hundred. Big Gorgio folded.

Nick was dealt a ten on his third card, the Prince a queen and Loukanas a five. Only the Prince, holding an ace in the hole, could beat Nick at that point. When the Prince checked to him, with boldness and a sense of victory, Nick bet a thousand dollars. He was overwhelmed with relief when the Prince shrugged and folded his hand. Only Loukanas and Nick remained in the game.

"I see your thousand and raise five hundred more," Loukanas said softly. Nick stared at the four and five the fat man had visible. Betting a low pair or a possible straight seemed a reckless wager. He saw the five hundred and with mounting tension waited for Prince Pierre to deal the fourth card. He received a jack and Loukanas a six, which did not improve his pair but gave him another card toward his straight.

If he had four cards to his straight, Nick thought, the odds against drawing a fifth were enormous. Yet Loukanas radiated a serene confidence, staring at him, humming softly under his breath. Feeling his throat constricted, his saliva drying, Nick mumbled, "Check."

"Check." Loukanas echoed him with a smirk.

Prince Pierre laughed and Big Gorgio hissed with contempt. Nick knew he had been cowed into exposing his timidity. He should have made a strong bet that would

probably have driven the fat man out of the game. Laced
with regret, he waited.

Prince Pierre dealt their final cards. With astonishment
Nick saw a third king join his hand. He looked quickly
across the table and Loukanas had drawn an eight.

The bodyguards started muttering, several of them
scraping their chairs closer. Loukanas looked sternly in
their direction and they hushed. The silence in the room
weighed like a boulder on Nick's back.

"Pair of kings bet," Prince Pierre said.

Nick stared at the hole card before Loukanas. Looking
up, he caught the same infuriating smirk on the man's cor-
pulent face.

"Would you like to check again?" Loukanas asked with
feigned sympathy.

Fumbling at whatever of his money remained, Nick
counted the bills and pushed them into the pot.

"Four thousand, one hundred dollars!" Nick said, his
loud, bold words ringing hollow in his ears. The bodyguards whispered again.

Loukanas stared thoughtfully at his cards. One of his
fleshy, beringed fingers slipped forward nervously, as if
drawing his hand to fold. Then, his jowls trembling
buoyantly, he reached instead for his money.

"I will see your bet"—he pushed money forward swiftly
—"and raise you ten thousand dollars more."

Nick stared at him in shock. The merciless, mocking
face of Loukanas blurred for a moment and then refo-
cused. Big Gorgio laughed harshly.

"I don't have it!" Nick cried.

"Then forfeit the pot," Loukanas said coldly.

Struggling to subdue his panic, Nick couldn't believe

Loukanas held a straight. More likely, scornful of Nick's ability to withstand the pressure or to raise the needed money, he was trying a massive, blatant bluff.

Nick could fold and lose only the money he had won at craps. Yet, if he let the fat man steal the pot, he would suffer that humiliation as long as he lived. Bitten by frenzy and frustration, each second mangling him further, the alternative was to risk ten thousand dollars of his godfather's money.

"All right," Nick said, and he was filled with terror. "I'll see your raise."

"Do you have the money?" Loukanas asked.

"I'll give you a signed slip that I can make good right after the game," Nick said. "I have the money. Korakas is downstairs and he can vouch for that."

"Of course you have the money," Loukanas said with a parody of politeness. "But, since you are a stranger from far-off Smolensk it seems, forgive my bluntness, presumptuous for you to ask to play on a marker."

"Goddam right!" Big Gorgio spit out the words. "Your marker's not worth shit!"

"Then Korakas will give you his marker!" Nick said desperately to Loukanas. "I'll stand good with him for mine!"

"Korakas is a man of irreproachable character," Loukanas said amiably, "but everyone on the street knows the No-worry Club is about as solvent as the Salvation Army. I am afraid, my friend, that will not do either."

Nick stared helplessly from one player to the other. Their cold and unyielding faces snapped like locks in his eyes. Beyond the ring of the table's light, the old gambler, Nestor, seemed to move for the first time.

"Someone go down and get Korakas for me," Nick said.

One of the bodyguards left the room. In a few moments he returned with Korakas, who came quickly to the table, his cheeks shaken with fear. Nick gripped his arm and drew him down.

"In the wall behind the bureau in my bedroom," he whispered, his breath short and hard. "There is a metal cashbox. Bring it here!"

Korakas looked at him in consternation.

"Nick! In God's name!"

"Get the box, Korakas!" Nick pleaded. "Don't argue and waste time! Believe me, they're trying to steal my pot! Just go quickly and get the box!"

Big Gorgio sent one of the bodyguards for a bucket of beer. Prince Pierre rose and stretched, walking to exchange a few words with Nestor. Loukanas pulled out a diamond toothpick and picked idly at his teeth.

Nick remained in his chair, staring obsessively at the hole card before Loukanas, fearful someone might attempt a switch. In those endless, punishing moments he waited, he condemned his negligence in keeping the money in the box and not putting it in the bank. He cursed his arrogance in blindly joining the game, allowing himself to be goaded to this plight. As the madness of what he was doing drew on him, he was tempted to fold his hand and give the pot to Loukanas. Even as the sanity of that decision came closer, Korakas returned. He brought the metal box to the table. Nick took out his key and opened the lid, his hands shaking as he counted out ten thousand dollars. He put the money into the pot. The room grew silent.

"You have courage, young man," Loukanas said. "That is a trait you might try to develop."

As Korakas breathed hoarsely at his shoulder, Nick fumbled over his hole card, revealing his third king. He stared at the card before Loukanas.

"A splendid hand." Loukanas nodded approvingly. "Indeed, I imagine that might even be a distinguished hand in Smolensk. But here . . ." He peered beneath a corner of his card. Then he looked up at Nick and began raising the card with agonizing slowness. He held it hidden a moment longer and then flipped it over.

The blood red seven of diamonds burned Nick's eyes. He clenched his teeth to keep from shrieking and thought he heard Korakas moan.

"Are you through now?" Big Gorgio asked harshly. "You've delayed the goddam game long enough. If you're done, clear out."

Nick motioned at the box.

"I have money," he said, and his voice seemed to be coming from across the room, echoing strangely in his ears. "I'm in the game to the end."

"Nick, for God's sake!" Korakas was trying to hold back tears. "Don't be a fool! They're too good for you and they got too much dough! Give up!"

"That wasn't my money." Nick made an effort to speak quietly. "My only chance is to win it back."

"We'll find the ten thousand bucks somehow," Korakas pleaded. "Don't risk the rest. Nick, listen, please!"

"Leave me alone," Nick said.

Korakas tried to pull him away from the table.

"Goddam you, leave me alone!" Nick shook him off violently. "Get the hell away from me!"

Korakas stepped back stunned. He stared helplessly at Nick and then he turned and fled from the room.

For the next two hours Korakas waited in the hall outside the room. When the door opened, finally, the bodyguards emerged first, frowning and wary. They were followed by Loukanas and Prince Pierre talking casually to one another. Big Gorgio brought up the rear. The slaughterhouse owner paused to grin at Korakas. Pointing back to the room, he ran his big finger stiffly across his throat.

Korakas walked slowly into the shadowed and totally silent room. Nick sat alone at the table, the beam of light glaring across his slumped head. Korakas walked to stand beside him.

"It's my fault, Nick," he whispered. "I first showed you this room, first pointed out these devils. It's my fault."

Nick did not look up or speak.

"Nick, forgive me," Korakas pleaded. "My fault . . . my goddam fault." He shook his head in grief and remorse. "Lambri is right. I'm too stupid to be a human being. I wish I was dead."

A figure stirred in the shadows and the old gambler, Nestor, rose from his chair. Walking through the light toward the door, he paused at the table, staring down at Nick.

"If you're a fool, boy, you've learned nothing tonight," he said in a quiet, stern voice. "If you're not a fool, maybe now you can understand that for a gambler there isn't any yesterday or any tomorrow . . . all that matters is the moment of play."

The next few weeks were the most tortured days and nights of Nick's life. Everywhere he went along the street, he had to accept mockery, pity, and contempt. He had branded himself Dandolos the dupe, the gull, the arrogant greenhorn that had dared to challenge the big gamblers who devoured him. He was the weakling and scoundrel that had thrown away his family's chance for escape and freedom. He heard, as well, Rantoulis was telling everyone how fortunate he and his daughters were because he would not permit them to become involved with an imbecile like Nick. Compounding this misery, Nick knew Marina must either pity or scorn him, as well.

Lambri and Korakas tried to console him, get him to eat, relieve his dejection and grief. He was grateful for their good wishes and support but he wanted to be left alone.

A dozen times he started letters to his godfather attempting to explain. But he could not explain the madness of what he had done. He wrote to Theron Valtides in New York, pleading for money to replace the money he had lost. Putting details of his betrayal of trust into words pained and shamed him even more and the letter remained unmailed.

Spending more and more time in his room, lying on his bed, staring at the ceiling, Nick tried to unravel the events before the calamity. If he had not taken Korakas' place at the crap table, if he had not won the seven thousand dollars, if he had not insisted on playing with the gamblers, if he had not drawn the third king, if he had done this or done that . . . he thrashed round and round like a dog gnawing the same worn bone.

Sometimes, as twilight fell, the cold, November wind rattling the glass in his window, he lit the lamp and turned the shade to illuminate the bed. He brought out a deck of cards he had bought from a notions store and dealt them across the spread. He studied the assorted hearts and clubs, diamonds and spades for hours, seeking to divine the key to their power. In the end his eyes burned and his head ached and he understood nothing but that the money he had been entrusted with was gone.

There was an evening in late November, about three weeks after the night of the game, when someone knocked at his door. He answered and Lambri entered.

"There is someone to see you, Niko."

"I don't want to see anyone."

Without another word Lambri stepped aside and Nick was astonished to see Marina standing in the hallway. She walked slowly into the room, unbuttoning her coat, her cheeks pinched scarlet from the cold. Lambri reached in and quietly closed the door.

He felt a strange joy in seeing her and yet he was afraid at the reason she might have come.

"Why are you here?" Nick asked.

She looked at him gravely and slipped out of her coat. She wore a muslin blouse and a woolen skirt and boots. When she took off her small fur hat he saw her lovely ears were red from the cold, as well.

"I'm not sure just why," she said. "Perhaps because I remember that Sunday in the store. I thought you wanted to see me again."

"Things have changed."

"Have they changed between us?"

"Don't be childish, Marina." He turned away in exasperation. "You've heard people, your uncle, talking about what I've done. You're too young or else you'd understand the shame."

She sat down on the edge of the bed, folding her hands on her knees.

"I understand," she said. "I told you my father was a gambler and I understand."

"All right, you understand," he said wearily. "Now you better go home where you belong."

She rose from the bed and walked past him to the window to stand looking out upon the street. Her slender figure was outlined within the frame.

"You tell me to go back where I belong." She spoke with her back to him. "I am not sure I belong with anyone. Maybe that is part of the reason I am here."

He yearned suddenly to go to her and take her into his arms. She turned from the window to look at him. The moment was strange and warm.

"You better go, Marina," he said. "Your uncle would kill you if he found out you came to see me."

"More likely he would want to kill you," she shrugged wryly. "No, he wouldn't . . . not really. He would be properly enraged only if it were one of his daughters, one of his precious vestal virgins."

He felt like smiling, a stiff, reluctant loosening of his flesh after the last somber weeks.

"I waited for you to come back and see me," she said sternly. "When I heard what had happened and realized your pride was probably keeping you away, I came to you to see if I can help."

"Nobody can help me," he said in resignation. "I was a goddam fool and I will pay for that as long as I live."

"That's a long time to pay for anything," she said. "Are you sure it's worth the rest of your life?"

He walked to join her at the window. For a moment their bodies and faces were only inches apart and he remembered the longing to kiss her he had felt that Sunday

in the store. Ashamed then to use her as a balm for his despair, he turned away and stared out the window.

The street below glittered raw and cold, a few people
hurrying by bundled into their coats. The windows of
tenements across the way revealed the figures of men and
women moving about, families joined at their tables. A few
blocks away the bright glow of the gambling club lights
illumined the sky.

He felt her fingers groping for his hand. When he
looked at her again, he was shaken by the tenderness he
saw beneath the surface of her eyes. Her body slipped
gently, timidly, into his arms. He felt her cool, soft lips and
vented the anguish and frustration in his heart by kissing
her long and hard, until he heard her moan. Quickly,
remorsefully, he let her go.

"I'm sorry, Marina," he said. "I didn't mean to hurt
you."

"Your teeth hurt for just a moment." She smiled to reassure him.

"I can't do a damn thing right any more," he said despondently. "You shouldn't have come. This is wrong."

"Do you think I've come like some romantic Victorian
heroine determined to surrender herself to her despairing
lover?" she said. "That noble sacrifice belongs in trashy
novels." She paused. "Even if I've come to offer myself to
you, you've had women before, haven't you?"

"Is that question part of the new free womanhood you
believe in?"

"That's not an answer."

"All right, yes, I've had women," he said.

"This wouldn't be the first time for me either," she said
gravely. He wondered if she was telling him the truth.

"Don't you believe me?"

"I don't know," he said. "Maybe. Anyway, what difference does it make?"

"Women should have the same freedom as men about such things," she said.

"All right," he said impatiently. "All right, they might as well have the same freedom. They couldn't do stupider things than men do."

"If I have the same freedom as a man," she said, "then I can tell you I want you to kiss me again."

He was grateful for her honesty and drawn to the lure of her eyes. He kissed her again, careful not to hurt her. There was a fragrance about her, a mingling of night and cold and some sweetness that belonged to her. She pushed her body against him and he felt her nipples like small, nimble buds. When they broke free to breathe, she reached up to touch his cheek, her fingers tracing a lingering caress across his skin.

"I'll go home and talk to my uncle, Nick," she said eagerly. "Maybe we can borrow some of the money you need from him. We can work together and save the rest."

"Do you know how much money twenty-three thousand dollars is?" he asked.

"I know it's a lot of money!" she said. "But you can't brood in this room talking of penance for the rest of your life. You've got to return to living and working. You men are supposed to be the stronger sex, but women can teach you something."

"I have been thinking about what to do," Nick said. "For days and nights now, that is all I have been doing. I lost the money gambling in a few terrible hours. That's the only way I'm going to get it back."

She moved away from him, staring at him as if unable or unwilling to understand what he was saying.

"I've been thinking of that old gambler, Nestor," Nick said slowly. "The skill and craftiness and knowledge that must live in his scarred and battered head. If he'd be willing to help me . . . teach me some of the things he has learned . . ."

"That isn't the way!" Marina cried furiously. "You mustn't do that!"

Startled by the violence of her reaction, he reached out to console her. She pushed his hand aside, her body trembling and her eyes blazing.

"If you do something like that, you'll be a greater fool than you've already been!" she said. "That old man is lost! I can remember my mother telling me when I was a child that he had bartered his soul to the devil!"

"Marina, talk sense!"

"Promise me, Nick!" she cried. "Promise me that you won't go to him!"

"Marina, listen to me . . . there isn't any other way. Even that may be hopeless, I know, but . . ."

"Promise!" she pleaded fiercely. "Promise or I swear you'll never see me again!"

He stared at her for a long, tense moment.

"I can't promise you that, Marina," he said quietly. "When I lost that money, I lost my honor, my decency and pride. I'll do anything to get it back."

She reached abruptly for her hat and coat and walked to the door.

"I should have known better," she said in a shaken and bitter voice. "I should have remembered that a man cannot change his nature, that vanity, conceit, and arrogance are more important to him than love."

She pulled open the door and left. He followed her into the hallway, calling her name. He heard her crying as she walked quickly down the stairs.

Later that night, Nick went to the Hermes to talk to Nestor. The old gambler had left and no one knew where he lived. An aged dishwasher suggested Nick try the Minerva, a coffeehouse beyond the funeral parlor on Vernon Park.

Nick was chilled and shivering by the time he reached the shabby coffeehouse, whose faded, torn curtains in the windows and on the doors concealed the interior. He walked into a large bare room that smelled rankly of sweat, tobacco, and cheap wine. The tables held an assembly of ragged men drinking coffee and ouzo, and puffing at their long-stemmed pipes. Most of them clustered at tables in a corner near a potbellied stove. Walking further into the room, Nick saw Nestor sitting alone at a table almost hidden by the stove.

He walked to the table. For a few moments Nestor did not seem to be aware he was standing there. Looking down on the old gambler's white head and lean, marked face, unshadowed for the first time, Nick was startled at how deeply ridged the furrows and scars were that cut through his cheeks.

"Excuse me, Mr. Nestor."

The old man looked up.

"Do you remember me?"

A flicker crossed Nestor's eyes.

"What do you want?" he asked coldly.

Nick leaned forward, nervously spreading his fingers on the table's stained and battered surface.

"I want to talk to you," Nick said.

At a nearby table an old man groaned and coughed hoarsely.

"What do you want?" Nestor asked again.

Nick vainly searched the old gambler's face for some sign of compassion or mercy.

"I want you to teach me to play," Nick said.

"I know what you want," Nestor said with a sneer. "Vengeance to mend your wounded pride. You think I can toss you a few magic pointers so you can return and reconquer the evil men who parted the fool from his money."

"That may be true," Nick said, "but it is also true that I want to try and understand the things that were in me that night."

"All you have to understand is that they are pros," Nestor said. "Crafty, merciless bastards who've been gambling for years and learned their skill at the devil's elbow. Stay away from them or they'll feed like vultures on your guts again."

Nick drew back a chair and sat down.

"They must have weaknesses," Nick said. "You can help me discover them."

"There's nothing I can do for you," Nestor said.

"If there were any other way I would leave you alone." Nick's voice trembled. "That money was to bring my god-father and his family from Smyrna, to start a new life here. I had no right to play with it and no right to lose it. I . . ."

"Jesus Christ, don't you understand?" Nestor said impatiently. "I can't do anything for you. Even if I wanted to help, I'm tired . . . everything in me is running down."

"I would listen carefully and learn quickly," Nick said. "Give me a chance . . . just a chance."

"Some things can't be taught."

"Let me try, please!"

"It's hopeless."

"If I don't redeem the terrible thing I did," Nick said, "my life will be hopeless anyway. I would rather be dead."

Nestor stared at him for a long probing moment, and then reached for the bottle of ouzo. Nick moved quickly to help him. The old man pushed his fingers away.

"I can pour my own booze!" he said roughly.

Feeling his hopes wavering, Nick made a final, desperate appeal.

"They say you were the greatest gambler in the city, maybe in the whole country," Nick said. "Korakas spoke of you as being a kind of king. Well . . . even kings must have an heir . . . someone to continue after they are gone."

Nestor paused with the glass of ouzo near his dry lips.

"So that's what you think? The king is dead, long live the king!" He broke into sardonic laughter. "How do you know?" he asked when he regained his breath. "How do you know, you young boob, if you are destined to become a king? You may study for years and never be more than one of the lumpish, beef-witted players, jubilant when they win, whining when they lose, blaming luck or chance, fate or the stars, and never themselves."

"I don't believe it will be like that for me," Nick said.

"How can you be sure?"

"In the beginning . . . were you sure?"

Nestor was silent for several moments. When he raised his head, he stared grimly beyond Nick and the room, as if he were recalling some spectral vision only he had ever seen.

"Gambling is a journey," he said slowly and softly. "The true gambler looks to find some land, some uncharted place, some nesting he was wrenched from when he was born. Once he begins the search, there is no turning back."

The old man's voice carried in a desolate whisper across the emaciated, hopeless figures of the men at the tables around them.

"He will play for stakes that mean nothing," Nestor said. "For wagers bet by fools, for reasons built on sand. His life changes and he is damned to look at men as people never bother to look at others, learning how they use their eyes, their hands, the muscles in their arms, how they breathe, swallow, twitch, scratch, cough, how fast or how slow they smoke, how they sweat, how often they empty their bladders. All the earth shrinks for him into the cipher of the table."

He looked at the old men around them, a grave and merciless review that did not spare himself.

"He never finds the journey's meaning, never discovers the land he had lost," Nestor said. "All that remain are the games. He has learned everything about cards and men, become as crafty and cunning as an old wolf . . . and then, time takes the last big pot. His sight fails, his hearing dulls, and the jackals close in for the kill . . . as he goes down, he realizes how wasted his life has been, how empty, no warmth, no joy, no love, no hope . . . only loneliness and the jangling memory of ten thousand burned out games."

For the first time, seeing the agony beneath Nestor's great, scarred face, Nick had an instant of terror, a temptation to rise and flee. He remembered his godfather, and the money he had lost in that night of pain and shame.

"I want you to teach me to play," Nick said. "Please teach me to play."

The old gambler lowered his head. His slumped shoulders shook slightly and for a terrible moment Nick thought he was crying. Then he heard the dry, hoarse rasp of laughter.

"I'll teach you," Nestor said. "I'll teach you." He swept his long-fingered, ancient hand like a scepter over the dismal coffeehouse, the dreary tables, the wasted, dying old men. "And you can become the heir to everything I own, my homes, my lands, my friends, my loves . . . everything that belongs to me now will someday belong to you . . ."

CHAPTER 4

In the beginning of December, as the first snow of winter settled flakes across the city's dark streets, Nick and Nestor secluded themselves in the loft where the old gambler lived. The large and drafty room was meagerly heated by a square, coal-burning stove, the room's spare furnishings placed around that warmed center. There were a pair of cots, each bearing several wool blankets, a table, a battered chest of drawers, and a few chairs. A frigid alcove in the corner held a toilet concealed behind a tattered drape.

Dragging the table as close as they could to the coal bucket and the stove, Nick and Nestor began their task, sitting across from one another, a deck of cards between them. A pot of coffee on the surface of the stove boiled and reboiled to a rank and ink-black fluid.

As their sessions began, Nestor was embittered at his weakness in agreeing to try to teach Nick to play poker.

"I was a fool," he said morosely on their first afternoon in the loft. "There are some skills which cannot be taught. If a man lacks aptitude for remembering, or if he does not possess an intuitive knowledge of human nature, then all the drilling on methods and probabilities is useless."

"You gave me a chance," Nick said gratefully. "I promise you won't be sorry."

"I'm sorry already," the old man muttered.

"I'm not a total beginner," Nick said. "I have been playing poker for several years now."

"Forget all you have learned about cards before!" Nestor cried. "We will start at the beginning, like a child first learning to read and write. We will start with memory, an essential for a gambler. If you can remember the cards that have been played, you gain an edge over 80 per cent of the players in any game."

He dealt a series of poker hands, allowing Nick a fleeting glimpse of cards before discarding them.

"You see player number two folding an eight early in the game," Nestor said. "One other player has an eight up and you hold an eight in the hole. Knowing there is only the case eight still alive lets you assess the chances of another player filling his potential six to the ten straight."

From the simpler pattern of remembering the cards in a single game, Nestor dealt out the deck, stopping a number of times to question Nick about cards that had passed and those that remained undealt. Nick proved adept at memorizing the cards. Nestor gave him only a grudging nod of approval.

"No reason for overconfidence," Nestor said gloomily. "I have known men who could memorize the cards in five decks. Even they were not great gamblers."

In the evenings Korakas brought them some supper that Lambri had prepared for them. Nestor ate a sparse portion, chewing and swallowing a few fragments without relish. When he lay down afterward to sleep for a short while, Nick and Korakas sat beside the stove, talking in low voices so they would not disturb the old man's rest.

"I closed the office like you told me to do," Korakas said to Nick on a night in that first week of December. "And gave the girl a little extra money." He paused, looking at Nick uneasily. "You still determined to give this game a go?"

"I have to try, Korakas. This may be hopeless too but I don't see any other way."

"Lambri thinks the old man is senile and that you've lost your senses," Korakas shrugged. He looked around at the cold and cloaked fringes of the room. "You might learn something about poker, Nick, but not before you both expire from pneumonia. An Eskimo could die in this place."

"We stay close to the stove," Nick said. "You keep bringing the coal. I know it will take some miracles."

"Maybe miracles happen for others," Korakas said somberly. "I never had one break right for me. You better not count on them."

"I will give up the miracles, but not hope." Nick looked at the cot where Nestor lay asleep, only his weary, and aged face visible above the crumpled blanket that covered him to the throat. "A cold loft, a tired old man, and hope," he said. "After what I've done even that is more than I deserve."

In the next two weeks, Nestor and Nick played hundreds of games of stud and draw. Through the day, and late into the night, pausing only to add chunks of coal to the stove or to squat shivering on the frigid stool, the old gambler kept drilling Nick.

"First player?" Nestor pointed to a pair of tens.

"He's high and bets."

"Second player with a pair of sevens?"

"Calls," Nick said.

"Third player?"

"Calls on jack-eight."

"No," Nestor said brusquely. "Fold the hand." He gestured at the next cards. "Fourth player?"

"Folds."

"Fifth player?"

"Folds."

"Sixth player?"

"Calls with the king-queen."

"Seventh player?"

"Folds the small pair."

Yet, even as they drilled and practiced the games, Nestor stressed understanding the natures of the players.

"Gambling strips men naked," Nestor said. "A timid husband, dominated at home by a shrew, becomes a wild beast at cards. He can now be master in a world where his bitch is helpless. A man who is kind to his children and his friends becomes a devil, taunting his opponents. A silent man becomes a babbler. A babbler turns tight-tongued and wary. All of them learn quickly that mercy must be smothered. The man you resist destroying because you feel sorry for him may rise two hands later and cut your throat."

Late at night, huddled close to the stove to catch the waves of heat, Nestor's voice grew hoarse.

"Know your weaknesses and the infirmities of the men you play with," he said. "Even as you study them, don't change your expression. Don't whine when you lose a hand, banging down your cards or tearing them up. Don't

gloat when you win. And never drink while you're playing. You'll need your wits to watch your opponents and to
handle the cards. Drinking dulls your edge and makes you
reckless."

"That's enough for now, Nestor." Nick was concerned,
for the old man appeared exhausted. "Let's stop so you can
sleep awhile."

"I'm all right," Nestor said. "Let's go a little longer.
There's so much . . ." He drew a shaken breath. "Remember that bluffing, I've told you this before and will
keep telling it to you, bluffing is the heart of gambling
well. You don't have to win every bluff to keep your opponents off balance. You might plan to get caught a few
times while waiting for the big hand you'll ride to the end.
In five-card draw a good risk is to raise right after a player
opens, whether you have anything promising or not. Follow that by taking only two cards, pretending you have
three of a kind, or better. Depending on the players, stand
pat or bet boldly when you get the chance. But be careful
those weak players who call on everything are not in the
pot. Once a sucker stays in foolishly, he becomes glued to
his money. Try to drive him out early."

The old man's voice slurred away. He rose from his
chair and walked a few steps to the nearby cot. He lay
down, turning on his side, drawing his feet closer to his
body. Almost at once he fell asleep.

Nick gently pulled off Nestor's shoes and covered him
with the blankets to his throat. He dimmed the lamp and
sprawled on his own cot, tugging up the blankets, longing
for rest. But the darkness flashed with enlarged diamonds
and spades, magnified hearts and clubs, tumbling and spi-
raling around him until he fell into an exhausted sleep.

Nestor shook him awake. "Enough time wasted," he
snarled. "Let's get on with it."

Pausing only long enough to let Nick pour a cup of hot
coffee, Nestor dealt the cards. He barked questions at
Nick, who played the hands.

They practiced steadily until noon and stopped then for
a bowl of soup they heated in a pot on the stove. They
started playing again as the wind whistled under the
dormers and rattled the glass in the windows.

Sometimes the old gambler grew impatient and nagged
Nick for faulty play.

"Why call that hand?" he cried.

"It seemed sensible to call," Nick said.

"You think so? That's what you think?"

"Yes."

"You think wrong, you dunce!"

"Why am I wrong?"

"I'll tell you why!" Nestor said. "You suspect you're
beat but you're also an asshead who can't let loose! Don't
worry about the money in the pot! Ask yourself if it's wise
to play on! Don't throw good money after bad! I've been
trying to beat that into your skull for weeks!"

There were moments when Nick could no longer endure the old man's biting temper.

"I've had enough!" he cried once to Korakas, who heard
Nestor berate him. "I must have been unbalanced to ask
this monster's help! Nothing I do pleases him! Nothing I
do satisfies him! He will end up driving me mad!"

"Nick . . . easy, Nick." Korakas tried to soothe him.

"Lose your temper, my young sport, that's dandy . . ."
Nestor mocked Nick's tantrum. "In a big game they
would dismember you for that display. I have warned you

if you lose your temper playing cards, they'll pluck off your balls and stuff one in each of your idiot ears!"

"Who are you?" Nick cried. "Are you God? Do you think you're God that you can call the cards with such certainty and power?"

"I am not God," Nestor said quietly. "I am only a gambler. But if God wished to learn to gamble, he would come to me."

Through New Year's Day and into January, snow and cold wind swirling icy drifts across the dormers and roofs of buildings around them, the old gambler harried Nick and drove him on. He felt sometimes he had been locked in the loft for years. But he came to marvel at Nestor's skill and craft, which had fashioned an artistry he could never hope to equal. He grew fond of the acerbic old man as well, understanding the angry, mocking, or beseeching moods came because Nestor's antagonism toward the tutoring had altered. The old gambler seemed obsessed suddenly by a fear he would die before passing on his knowledge to Nick.

On an evening in the middle of that month, Korakas came into the loft slightly drunk, carrying an opened bottle of champagne.

"They did it today," he lamented to them. "The goddam drys have won and Prohibition has begun. The workingman is being denied his bucket of suds and mothers won't have that evening shot when the kids and their old men get on their nerves."

"Get that stuff out of here," Nestor grumbled. "Wet or dry outside is no concern of ours."

"I just thought you'd like to know." Korakas sat heavily on the edge of Nick's cot.

"I'll have a sip of that champagne," Nick smiled. "One small drink for workingmen and mothers."

"Fine, fine," Korakas mumbled, tilting the bottle to pour some champagne for Nick into a glass. "Then I'll be on my way. Some of the boys are holding a wake."

But after another couple of drinks, Korakas could not move. Flopping over on the cot, he fell asleep for several hours. From the way he muttered and moaned during that time, his visions, Nestor told Nick wryly, were dry and arid nightmares.

At the end of that month, late at night sometimes, when he was worn out by his teaching and burdened by the futility of knowing how much work still remained, Nestor would fling the cards aside with a curse. A silent and morose despair gripped him then.

In an effort to rouse him from his depression, Nick asked him how he had started gambling.

"Haven't I told you that stunning genesis before?"

"No," Nick said.

"Yes, I have," the old man scowled. "And more than once."

"If you have, why I've forgotten." Nick tried to sound sincere. "Tell me again."

"Well, I was born on a crap table on Christmas Eve," Nestor said. "The stickman was my doctor and the payout man was my nurse. With my first breath I did not cry but asked for a bet on the front line."

"Be serious now!"

"Who cares how I began?" Nestor asked scornfully.

"I do."

"You're lying."

"We are friends now," Nick said quietly, "and I would like to know how my teacher and mentor began."

Nestor gave in with a shrug.

"There isn't any romance or glory in the story," he said. "I was thin and sickly when I first came to this country as an immigrant. I could not work on the railroad gangs, and could not stand the long, hard hours dishwashing in restaurant kitchens. I got a place to sleep in a bakery in exchange for tending the ovens, keeping the fires going. The place was warm and they gave me bread and, now and then, an egg. I knew I would starve slowly to death on that fare and I had to find something I could do with my head. I had played some cards with men in the coffeehouses, seemed to have a small ability in that way. I bought a deck of cards and passed the hours each night by the ovens, memorizing them, learning to deal and hold them. They kept me from loneliness and madness and, after a while, I came to know the kings and queens and knaves as if I were a jester in their courts."

He fell silent, as if he were struggling to grasp and recall the past.

"I began playing poker to make a little money on which to live," Nestor said. "I learned I could outplay most other men. I made my decision then, no God urging me on, no oracle foretelling my destiny. By my own free will I decided to live as a gambler. All the things I lacked, physical strength, money, power, success in commerce, none of these meant anything at the table. My skill at gambling let me conquer them all."

He lowered his head into his hands as if the memories had burdened him. When he looked up again, the wavering beam of the lamp glinted across his white hair and scarred cheeks.

"One night following another," he said softly. "One game after the next until I realized that, to a gambler, winning was only a shade better than losing. He would continue to play even if he knew he would never win again. That was true for me. In all those years I gambled, into my prime and my peak, I was arrogant and merciless, confident and secure. All that mattered was the tension and suspense of the play when I felt incomparably alive."

He looked at Nick with a cold, sardonic smile.

"There is an old story about a man named Faustus who bargains with the devil," Nestor said. "Twenty-four years of more life and power in exchange for his soul. I think of that covenant sometimes, and how Faustus felt when the tab came due. Do you understand, young sport, even a fraction of what I'm saying?"

"I think I understand," Nick said. He felt a chill in his bones that did not come from the loft.

"Even if you do understand," Nestor said, "there is one final lesson as well." He pushed himself slowly to his feet and walked toward the wall, standing for a moment peering at the studs and beams. "See here," he said. "There is a spider clinging to the wood. To make my point to you, no better reason than that, I crush it now."

He pressed his hand against the spot where the spider crawled. When he moved back to the stove and spread his fingers, only a tiny blemish marked his palm. "The terrible uncertainty of life," Nestor said, "that it can be expunged by the whim of a man rising from his chair to crush a spider. In God's hands we are no more than spiders."

There was a week in the middle of February when the temperature did not rise above zero. The loft grew raw and frigid, the stove hissing and glowing in a labored effort to cast off heat. Nestor had not been well for several days, spending his time in his cot, which Nick had pushed still nearer to the stove. When he began to run a fever Nick grew concerned. Despite the old man's protests he had Korakas bring up a doctor, who grimaced and shivered as he entered the cold loft. He examined Nestor briefly, prescribed some medication, rest, and broth, and seemed anxious to flee. After he and Korakas had gone, Nick sat on the edge of Nestor's cot.

"That quack couldn't wait to get out of here." The old gambler mustered a grin. "He looked at me as if he had been called to heal Lucifer."

"Your snarling didn't help reassure him," Nick smiled. "Maybe we should have petitioned a priest instead."

"I have no faith in their pious mumblings," Nestor said. "Their sole function is to comfort losers."

"All right, now, I'll heat you some soup," Nick said. "The doctor wants you to have liquids."

"I'll get all the liquid I need from my embalmers."

Nick pressed the outline of the old man's blanketed arm.

"You are a legend," Nick said. "Legends never die."

"I'm not worried about dying just now," Nestor said. "That would be too easy. When my time comes to leave, I'll begin my descent in the volcano's breath."

When Nick rose to return to the table and practice alone with the cards, Nestor motioned him down.

"Screw the cards. We're finished with your training now."

Nick looked at him in shock.

"Fever has made you delirious!"

"You insolent pup!" Nestor grinned. "Doubting the head that taught you?"

"Do you really mean I'm ready to play with the owners again?" Nick cried.

"They might still tear you apart and gobble the pieces," Nestor said. "I mean only it is time for you to leave this prison icebox and join some games with other players. That will sharpen your edge, let you apply in practice what you have been learning, and, most important, help you raise a stake."

"My God." Nick sat down again. "My God, I can't believe it . . ." He reached down then and fumbled beneath the blankets to catch the old man's hand. He clasped it tightly, feeling the bond of friendship and affection pass along the dry and veined flesh into his own body.

Feeling better in the next few days, Nestor made phone calls to connections in other cities. He selected a game to be played the following weekend in Cleveland. After consulting with Korakas, who desperately pulled together all his available funds, they provided Nick a stake of a thousand dollars.

"That isn't enough, even for this game," Nestor said grimly. "Get a batch of tens and a couple of hundred-dollar bills for the outside of your roll. Give the impression you are holding much more dough than you have."

"Make sure your suit is pressed and your shoes are shined," Korakas said.

"Am I going to Cleveland for a fashion show or for poker?" Nick smiled.

"If you look sharp, they'll figure you as a winner," Korakas said. "Before the first card falls, you got an edge."

"Korakas is right," Nestor said.

"See?" Korakas said in triumph. "I know a few things too!"

"You'll be playing with some small-time gamblers," Nestor said to Nick. "I picked this game for you because I know them all. Watch out for one they call 'Ohio Phil.' He is the best of the lot unless there are men present I don't know. Phil holds his cards a certain way when he is bluffing and holds them differently when he has a solid hand. If you watch him carefully, you'll spot what I mean. Another player with some skill is a ward politician named Fairfax. He plays well except when he has drawn a really strong hand, he edges his chair closer to the table."

Nestor motioned he was finished with his counsel. Nick embraced him and hugged Korakas. He picked up his small suitcase to leave for the station.

"God go with you." Korakas wiped a vagrant tear from his eye.

"I have never asked the Lord to help me gamble," Nestor said, his lip curled in a grin. "I confess, however, a number of times I have prayed that He not help anyone else in the game."

For the following three weeks, Nick played games in a number of cities besides Cleveland, his participation arranged by wires and phone calls from Nestor. He broke even in Cleveland, leaving that city with the same amount of money he had brought into the game. In Detroit he played four nights and days with a group of businessmen sports who talked casually, between deals, of their substantial interests in oil, coal, and steel. He won four thousand dollars from them and from there traveled to Philadelphia, where he played for several days and nights in a game that included a police captain and a deputy sheriff. He found them tight, sharp gamblers and he lost half the money he had won in Detroit.

When he gloomily broke the news to Nestor by phone, the old gambler reassured him.

"You're doing fine!" Nestor said. "They haven't broken you yet and that is what counts. Loosen up now. Don't be afraid to risk your last buck on a winging bluff."

Nick's next stop was across the Canadian border in Toronto for a floating stud poker game at the Hamilton Race Track. The game was a raucous marathon that included, at different times, owners, trainers, grooms, jockeys, and gamblers making the race track circuit. One of the men in the game was a track bookmaker named "Long-Odds" Monahan, a thin, loquacious man who took a liking to Nick and invited him to return to join him in booking at the track.

"I don't know anything about horses," Nick told him.

"Neither do the hicks who are betting them to win, place, or show," Monahan said somberly. "We don't figure we will be right, but that they will be wrong. That's the fate of hicks. And since the damn nags are sour-tempered, cranky, bilious, and erratic beasts, they favor the bookmaker and not the player."

"You make it sound easy," Nick laughed.

"Not easy but damn profitable," Monahan said. "Hurry back here and I'll always have a slot for you."

When the poker game at the track finally broke up after ten days of play, Nick had run his original stake into a total of about twelve thousand dollars.

Preparing to leave his hotel that night for another game in Montreal, Nick found a message from Korakas. He phoned the No-worry Club and after a few moments of static, the excited voice of Korakas came bouncing across the miles.

"Listen, Nick!" Korakas cried. "Nestor wants you to come home! There is a big game scheduled for this Saturday night, all the casino owners and a couple of plump pigeons from out of town. There will be big money in the game!"

Nick felt his heart pounding and tried to keep his voice from trembling.

"They think they wiped me out last time," he said. "Why should they let me play now?"

"I've been spreading word your godfather has sent you another twenty-five thousand bucks," Korakas said. "God forgive me for lying so beautifully! The wolves have gotten wind of it and are delighted at the chance to pluck you naked once more. Loukanas himself dropped into the club and asked me to extend you an invitation to play despite all my earnest protests that you would not want to play, that you should not be permitted to play. The crafty, dishonorable bastard reassured me they merely wanted to give you a chance to recoup your losses. What do you think of that bloody shit?"

"Does Nestor think I'm ready?" Nick asked.

"He says this is the time," Korakas said. "God help us all, Nick, whether you feel ready or not, this is the time."

Nick returned to Chicago on the Wednesday before the game and went once again into secluded sessions with Nestor. He recapped the plays in the out-of-town games while the old gambler evaluated the action.

"You should have called 'Foxy' Ryan on his flush," Nestor said after Nick told him of a big hand he had lost in Detroit. "From the way you describe the pattern of his betting, I'd take an oath he was bluffing. You'd have ten thousand dollars more now."

Nick's stake remained their most urgent concern. His bankroll wasn't big enough to reinforce the deception he held twenty-five thousand dollars that Korakas rumored his godfather had sent him. If he were challenged by a large wager early in the game, he would have to back down and run the risk of being exposed. Once Loukanas, Prince Pierre, and the others knew his weakness, they would be able to finish him off.

"I would mortgage the No-worry Club," Korakas said gravely as they discussed the problem. "But I've already hocked everything in the place except Lambri's corset." He winked at Nick. "Tonight when the angel is asleep, I'll slip off with that."

"I'll make do with what I have," Nick said.

"The odds are raised against you," Nestor said. "Given two players of equal skill, the one with the bigger bankroll has an edge."

"Will you be playing Saturday night?" Nick asked him.

"For a few hours." Nestor spit scornfully. "They are staking me, letting me play so the out-of-town suckers can say they played with Nestor. But they won't want me around for too long and, on one pretext or another, I'll drop out." He looked grimly at Nick. "It will be up to you then," he said quietly.

During the winter when he had been secluded with Nestor in the loft, Nick had not seen or spoken to Marina. In those fleeting moments when he rested between games, or in the final span of time before he fell asleep at night, he sometimes thought of her. Those thoughts were not charged with desire since the spell of the cards seemed to subdue the nerve ends of sexual hunger. He yearned for her presence, for her gentleness and warmth.

While he traveled from city to city in the practice games, he had written her on hotel stationery a few times, restrained and awkward letters which did not convey the things he wanted to say. Back in Chicago, waiting the anxious hours for the big game, he longed suddenly to see her.

Perhaps the first, feeble stirrings of spring loosening the earth-lock of winter had something to do with his emotion. Once or twice he caught a glimpse of a faint sun breaking through the gray crust of sky. Daylight came earlier and consumed more of the darkness each evening.

One twilight he walked past the lighted interior of the Athens Wholesale Grocery. He did catch a glimpse of Marina's slender, erect figure in the rear of the store. But he also saw the threatening frame of her uncle, Rantoulis, and that drained him of any resolve to enter. Later that evening, managing with the help of Lambri to locate the address where Marina lived, he found the building and fumbled at the letter boxes, seeking her name. A straggly haired landlady, resembling the Medusa, emerged from a basement apartment to confront him. He lost his courage again and, muttering something about the wrong address, he fled. I am girding for a game with wolves, he berated himself as he walked down the street, and I cannot muster the spunk to approach one slim-bodied girl.

He determined he would wait to contact her until after the game. He would have kept that pledge if he had not seen a poster in a shop window announcing a Women's Freedom Rally at a neighborhood Masonic Hall on Friday evening. Recalling Marina's passion for the rights of women, he decided to attend the rally in hopes she might be there.

When he arrived outside the Masonic Hall on the evening of the rally, the marquee was hung with bunting and banners proclaiming a new era of equality for women. A bold-eyed girl dispensing programs at the door regarded Nick with suspicion, trying to decide, he was sure, whether he might be a male spy. The interior of the hall was sparsely occupied, small clusters of women with a few men like islands in their midst. The rally was in progress and he seated himself quietly in an aisle seat near the rear of the hall.

On the stage, before a podium, a bulldog-faced female harangued the gathering with a catalogue of injustices. A half-dozen women sat in a row of chairs on the stage behind the speaker. With a leaping in his pulse, Nick recognized Marina among them. She sat solemn and attentive, hanging on the speaker's words.

Nick tried to concentrate on the speaker's strident voice demanding votes for women and for an end to the male attitude that consigned women to the role of vassals, fit only for service in the bedroom and in the kitchen. He made a valiant effort to listen, but Marina held his eyes and his thoughts.

As the speaker finished her address, the women in the audience and those seated behind her rose and applauded enthusiastically. She made a plea for generous donations to help their cause. Several young women carried wicker baskets down the aisles. When one extended her basket to Nick, he dropped in several bills.

A short question period followed, one woman rising to ask that the abolishment of indiscriminate operations on women be part of their platform. That motion was applauded vigorously. Then a burly man rose to demand the assembly cease proselytizing his wife since it was causing her to neglect her family responsibilities. He was hooted and jeered and he stalked out indignantly, with a final flourish of his fist.

After that exchange the rally dwindled, the audience beginning slowly to disperse. The women on the platform clustered around the speaker and then descended from the stage, walking down his aisle. He braced himself and rose as Marina came nearer, talking earnestly to a woman beside her. She would have passed without noticing him if he had not called her.

"Marina?"

She stopped suddenly, startled when she saw him. The other woman looked sharply at him and continued down the aisle. He could not tell if Marina was pleased or displeased at seeing him. Separated for several months, he admired her loveliness again, the rakishly cut short black hair framing her enchanting face.

"Have you come to support our cause, Nick?" she asked quietly.

"I came to see you."

She stared at him for a stern, unsettling moment.

"Did you receive my letters?" he asked.

"Yes," she said. "I didn't understand what you were try-ing to say."

"I was trying to explain about the gambling," he said. "What I felt I had to do, what I felt was right."

"There is no such thing as right about gambling," she said sharply. "All of it is wrong. If you can't see that, then I'm sorry for you." She turned to leave.

"Marina, please understand. Stay a minute."

"The others will be waiting for me, Nick," she said. "Anyway, I don't know what else we have to say to one another. You've made your choice."

"All right, Marina," he said. "Go on now, but I want to talk to you soon. I'm not a madman or a fool."

"Aren't you, Nick? I've heard the gossip on the street that your godfather has sent you more money and that you are planning to play again. Isn't that madness?"

"Don't believe all you hear."

"Isn't it true?"

"Listen, Marina, it's too hard to explain the truth to you now . . ."

Suddenly the two of them were alone in the hall, the voices of a few women still remaining in the corridors coming back to them in echoes. Someone hidden from sight lowered the lights on the stage.

"I'll tell you one truth that is clear to me." Marina spoke in a low voice. "My father was a gambler, a pitiful and tragic man who ruined his life and destroyed my mother. He lied and stole, cheated and schemed to get money with which to play."

"Marina, I understand . . ."

"You don't understand," she said. "One night I found

my father on the bathroom floor. He had stolen money
from the company where he worked, they had discovered
it, and he could not stand the shame of jail. So he slashed
his wrists, no gamble in that, a sure and certain way to
die."

She finished slightly out of breath, the shadow of the
grief darkening her face. He reached out and gently
clasped her arm.

"I'm sorry, Marina," he said with remorse. "I didn't understand before but I understand now. I don't want to
cause you any distress. Just believe that I'm gambling now
only because there is something I must do. When that is
finished, I'll be done with gambling too. If you let me, I'll
come to see you then."

She stood looking at him a moment longer and he could
not make out what emotion her eyes concealed. She left
him then, walking down the aisle to join the women in the
corridor. He waited in the deserted hall until the voices of
the women faded and he heard the door opening and closing for the last time.

When Nick returned to the No-worry Club, he found a
tense and distraught Korakas waiting for him. Taking him
by the arm, Korakas motioned to a corner table where two
lean and impassive men waited, their demeanor and clothing unlike the club's regular patrons.

"They are here for you, Nick," Korakas whispered
nervously. "Someone wants to see you. They didn't say
who, but those guys are muscles for the Gennas."

"The Gennas?"

"You know, I told you, the brothers who control the
rackets in this district," Korakas said grimly, watching the
men. "They got their headquarters in Little Italy, not far

from here, and they control narcotics and prostitution and are into bootlegging now too. Loukanas and the other owners all give them a cut of their profits."

"What do they want with me?"

"God only knows," Korakas said in a shaken voice. "I thought of telling them you were out of town but they'd be back. If they wanted to hurt you, they'd wait for you in some alley." He shook his head. "Nothing to be done, I think, but for you to go along and see what deviltry the Gennas have in mind. Okay?"

Nick nodded slowly, still more confused than frightened. Korakas and he walked toward the men.

"This is Nick Dandolos," Korakas said.

"Someone wants to see you, Nick," one of the men said.

"Who and why?" Nick asked.

The man did not answer but gestured toward the door. As Nick and the men turned to leave, Korakas spoke with his voice trembling.

"Look after him," he said. "Look after him because I'll hold you guys responsible."

One of the men bristled and Nick spoke quickly.

"Don't worry, Korakas," he said with feigned assurance. "Tell Lambri to keep some dinner warm for me."

On the street outside the No-worry Club a third man waited behind the wheel of a dark, sleek automobile. Nick climbed into the back seat with one of the men. The other man sat beside the driver. As they pulled away, he saw the stocky figure of Korakas watching them anxiously through the glass.

They drove in silence through a heavily congested area Nick assumed was Little Italy by the names on restaurants and shops. He saw the Napoli Café and the Unione

Siciliano. Shortly afterward the driver drove into an alley and then into a garage. When Nick got out of the car, he smelled an assortment of sauces and cheeses, as if a restaurant kitchen were near. One of the men led him into an elevator and they rode up several floors. Emerging into an anteroom occupied by a half-dozen men who might have been twins to the ones who had brought him, they stopped before a large, paneled door. A buzzer sounded and the door opened. The man gestured for Nick to enter.

He walked into a mahogany-paneled office with ornate and expensive furnishings. A man sitting behind a long desk motioned Nick closer. When he rose to greet Nick, he was short and swarthy with dark and deep-set eyes. Nick took his hand, feeling the thick, strong fingers and stony knuckles.

"I am Angelo Genna, Nick." He spoke in a curiously muted voice, an effort to sound friendly by a man who did not look as if he had many friends. "Do you want a drink or a cigar? I just got a new shipment of Havanas. The best."

"Nothing, thank you," Nick said. Genna motioned Nick to a chair and sat down once more behind his desk.

"What do you hear about me, Nick?" Genna asked.

"I have heard you and your brothers are men of influence," Nick said. "Not much more than that."

"That's fine." Genna nodded approvingly. "You don't have to know any more than that. But I know a good deal about you. Why you came to Chicago, how you lost your godfather's money in the game at the Hermes. I know you're planning to play with the Greek *paisanos* again tomorrow night." He enjoyed Nick's surprise. "I know also that old Nestor has been training you in secret and that you have been building a stake in out-of-town games. The

word goes around that you're ripe for another fleecing
with more money your godfather has sent you. They say
you're a big *idiota* but I'm not so sure."

Nick watched him, feeling his mouth and tongue suddenly dry. Genna opened a humidor and drew out a long,
green-black cigar.

"You won't change your mind?" he asked. Nick shook
his head.

Genna clipped the cigar with a small cutter. He lit the
tip from a silver lighter, inhaled briskly, then blew a swirl
of smoke through his nose. "A good cigar clears the
sinuses," he said seriously.

Leaning back in his chair, he studied Nick for a moment
in silence.

"You know, you Greeks tickle me," Genna said. "You
fuss about being refined, civilized, all that stuff about cul-
ture . . . but scratch your skin and you got blood as hot as
any Sicilian. You'd kill just as fast for vengeance and
honor. One thing you never learned . . . you never
learned to work together, to accept your vows of brotherhood and blood. That's why we rule and why we'll always
rule. We let men like Loukanas and Prince Pierre divide a
few spoils. That keeps them thinking they got some control. I think they know who holds the power."

"What does this have to do with me, Mr. Genna?"

"I been giving you the background," Genna said, "so
you'll understand that if I don't want you to play tomorrow night, you won't gamble in that game or in any other
game in this city."

"But why?" Nick stared at Genna in consternation.
"Why should it make any difference to you whether I
play or not?"

Genna puffed silently on his cigar.

"This game is important to me, Mr. Genna," Nick said earnestly. "I must play tomorrow night."

Genna nodded slowly.

"I want to help you play," he said.

"Help me? I don't understand."

"You're a young man trying to get ahead. I understand that," Genna said. "I told you we got deep family feelings. Why shouldn't I help you?"

"How can you help?" As Nick asked the question a chill touched his heart.

"I don't believe your godfather has sent you more money," Genna said. "I think that is bait for the fish."

"I have money enough to play."

"You may have some money but your chances are less without a good stake," Genna said. "Nestor would have told you that. But you don't need to worry. I'm going to give you a good stake." He reached into a drawer of his desk and pulled out a thick white envelope that he tossed on the desk.

"There is twenty-five thousand dollars in that envelope," Genna said. "You play with that money or you don't play at all. I send word to Loukanas that you're *fuori* . . . out."

He put the long cigar back to his lips, the tip glowing scarlet for a moment and then subsiding. "If you lose the money, you don't owe me nothing," Genna said. "That proves I was wrong. I got no more interest in the matter. We write it off even."

"Just like that." Nick shook his head in amazement. "Just like that you offer me twenty-five thousand dollars for a stake."

Genna's lips curled in a thin smile.

"I'm a gambler too," he said.

"If I lose, you write it off," Nick said. "What if I win?"

"If you win . . ." Genna said slowly.

"I'll pay you the money back," Nick said quickly. "As soon as the game is over and at whatever interest you want. I will be willing to do that." Even as he made the offer, he knew it would not satisfy Genna.

"No interest, only the principal," Genna said. "You pay me back the twenty-five thousand and you owe me a favor."

"What favor?"

"Who knows?" Genna shrugged. "Nothing I can think of now." He watched Nick for a moment and then smiled mockingly. "Don't worry, I won't want you to murder anyone. Besides, I can hire twenty-five professionals for that money. No, I got a Sicilian hunch about you. I want you to owe me a favor . . . like insurance."

"I'm sorry, Mr. Genna," Nick said. "I can't play for blind stakes. I can't do that."

"I thought you were a gambler," Genna said coldly. "I guess I made a mistake. As long as you're not a gambler, make other plans for tomorrow night because you won't be playing. If you got a girl, call her up. And good luck in your future business. If I see some small candy store or alley lunchroom, I'll let you know. Your *paisanos* favor those ratcribs where they make a few dollars a week."

In frustration and fear, Nick saw the trap.

"Mr. Genna, let me explain why this game is so important," Nick said, his voice trembling. "Let me tell you about the lives of the people . . ."

Genna waved him brusquely to silence. He pointed to the envelope. "You want to play?"

After a moment, Nick rose and picked up the envelope.
He walked back to the door. As he touched the knob, the
buzzer sounded and the door opened. The man who had
brought him to the room waited for him in the hall. They
joined the men waiting in the car and drove back to the
club.

When Nick entered the No-worry Club, Korakas came
at a run across the room.

"Are you all right, Nick?" he asked nervously. "Are
you okay?"

"I'm all right."

"I been crazy with worry for the last hour," Korakas
said. "You sure they didn't hurt you?"

"No one hurt me."

"Who wanted to see you?" Korakas asked.

"Angelo Genna."

"'Bloody' Angelo!" Korakas cried. "What did the bastard want?"

"He wanted to talk to me about Greeks and Sicilians,"
Nick said quietly. "The servants and the masters."

"He just wanted to talk?" Korakas looked at him in disbelief.

"I'm tired, Korakas," Nick said. "I'm going up to bed.
I'll see you in the morning."

"Rest will be the best thing for you," Korakas said.
"Maybe take a hot bath first to relax your muscles. Lambri
will boil you some water."

Nick walked up the stairs to the apartment on the second floor. He heard Lambri in the kitchen and he went
into his room and closed the door. Without turning on a
light, he walked to the window and stood staring down at

Halsted Street. He had an eerie feeling that something implacable in his destiny had brought him to the spot where he now stood.

He thought of Smyrna, his godfather, the aborted business, and the money lost in the game. He thought of Nestor, the months locked in the loft, the game to be played the following night. He thought of the envelope of money from Genna in his pocket. Finally, he thought of Marina and was filled with a longing that swept all other concerns and complexities away. For an instant he considered forsaking the game and turning to her for solace. Yet, he could not be sure whether that escape was simply fear of losing again.

He turned on the light. Pushing the dresser away from the wall, he kneeled down and pulled off the strip of baseboard. He stuffed Genna's sealed envelope into the crevice and replaced the strip, afterward returning the dresser to the wall.

He resolved he would win or lose with his own stake. When the game was over, he would return the unopened envelope to Genna.

He undressed then and wearily climbed into bed. For a long time he could not sleep.

CHAPTER 5

The following evening, the players assembled in the second-floor gambling room of the Hermes. Loukanas, Prince Pierre, Big Gorgio, Nestor, and Nick were present. In addition there were two affluent Greek merchants from Boston who had been invited by Loukanas to play with the legendary gambler Nestor.

Moments before the game began, Loukanas pulled Nick aside.

"Delighted to have you with us again, young man," Loukanas said. "I must confess I have felt considerable remorse about your unhappy streak of bad cards the night we last played." His beefy jowls and cheeks played a charade of concern. Big Gorgio, overhearing him, snickered.

"It is gracious of you to permit me to return for another chance," Nick said politely.

"But, my dear boy!" Loukanas said. "Are we not all Greeks? The most civilized of people since antiquity? How could we refuse you a chance to break even and still affirm our humanity?" He spread his plump, beringed fingers in a travesty of humility.

Prince Pierre called the players to the table. Nick settled himself in the stiff-backed chair. The brightly lit table and the circle of players evoked for him the last game. A terror of failing and losing again stirred a nausea in his stomach. He brought out his handkerchief, coughing to calm his distress, apprehensive one of the other players might notice.

"I would never have believed it!" One of the Boston merchants looked reverently across the table at Nestor. "If anyone had told me that one night I would be playing in a game with so famous a gambler as you, Mr. Nestor, I would have called them mad!"

Nestor stared at him silently. The merchant lowered his head uneasily.

"After that splendid compliment," Loukanas smiled benignly, "perhaps Mr. Nestor would honor us by selecting a new deck and beginning the deal."

One of the bodyguards brought a small wooden chest to the table, which Prince Pierre unlocked. There were a dozen sealed decks inside. Nestor gestured at the merchant.

"You choose."

The man rose eagerly from his chair and stretched to select a deck. Nestor cracked the seal and tore up the jokers, dropping the pieces on the floor. While Prince Pierre stated the ground rules of the five-card stud, no wild-card game, Nestor shuffled the deck, his long, slender fingers slipping deftly over and between the cards. The merchants gaped at his swift and facile mastery. Nick understood they saw only the spurious surface skill. Many gamblers handled the cards well. But there was about Nestor a sense that the cards were an extension of his hands, their symbols joined in some mystical union with his flesh.

The game began slowly, the owners playing in the leisurely manner of men starting to eat a grand meal and determined to linger over each course. Nick played tensely, trying to subdue the flutters of his anxiety. The merchants played with erratic jubilation, betting every hand like skittish birds. Pigeons, Nick thought, wretched pigeons in the game to be plucked and devoured, the same kind of quarry he had been the last time they played.

Taking Nestor's advice, Nick had placed larger bills on the outside of his roll. He made certain to display the money within the circle of the light, his movements careful and slow to assure that the other players noticed.

The first few hours of the game focused about the two visitors. Loukanas and Prince Pierre treated them with ex-aggerated courtesy, complimenting their clumsy play, al-lowing them to win a few modest pots while folding what appeared to Nick to be their own winning hands.

Nick dropped out frequently, refusing to join the bla-tant fleecing of the merchants. He watched Nestor taking a share from them, unable to understand how the proud old man allowed himself to participate in the deception.

Nick also used the hours to study the manner in which the other gamblers played. He saw the subtleties he had missed in the earlier game. Loukanas and Prince Pierre were shrewd, canny players, adept at bluffing and calling, varying their styles of play to disconcert their opponents. Big Gorgio played for the sadistic joy of mauling and beat-ing another player, reaffirming one of the lessons Nick had learned from Nestor. Human beings were scaled down to their true nature at the card table.

Shortly before midnight, both visitors conceded defeat. One man had lost eight thousand dollars and the other one six thousand dollars, Loukanas and Prince Pierre splitting most of that sum.

The merchants departed, thanking everyone effusively for the privilege of being cleaned out. Returning to their cronies, they would boast of having played in a colossal, high-stakes game with the great Nestor. The sums involved would grow each time they recounted the story until, after the tale had been told a hundred times, the monies they had lost would accumulate to become a fortune.

After they had gone, the players tested their ability against the old gambler, knowing the stakes he played with did not really count, but wanting to force him into submission.

There were hands during the next few games when Nestor displayed his mastery, routing the other players by his bold and cunning play. At other times he wavered, his skill blunted by his diminished faculties and age. Finally, he grew resigned and careless.

Painfully joined to the old gambler's anguish, Nick was grateful when Nestor dropped wearily from the game, a little ahead of where he had been when they started. After repaying the stake he had been provided to join the game, he would have enough money remaining to buy his ouzo and pay his rent for a few weeks.

Nestor pushed his chair away from the table and rose stiffly, grimacing as he stretched his cramped muscles. He moved to a seat within the mantle of shadows, watching the progress of the game from there. The players turned their attention to Nick.

He had been careful to exhibit the same artless and erratic play he had shown in the earlier game. He bluffed once and they gave him the pot. His jubilation afterward convinced them of his deception. The next time he bluffed he was called and lost the pot. He repeated that reckless

play doggedly and lost several more times. He saw Loukanas and Prince Pierre exchange amused and scornful
glances.

For a while then he played his hands cautiously until he
drew strong cards. He played them as though once again
he were bluffing. Big Gorgio called him and was burned
when Nick turned over the winning cards.

"I could have sworn you didn't have those queens!" The
slaughterhouse owner caught the cards between his powerful fingers and ripped them apart. He threw the pieces
aside and called for a new deck.

Yet, even as he alternated his bluffing, Nick began
revealing a small mannerism when he bluffed, a slight
twitch of his left eyelid that he knew would not be lost on
Loukanas and Prince Pierre. When they called several of
his bluffs after that and won, he knew they had swallowed
the bait.

In spite of playing his cards well, Nick lost several siza-
ble pots in a row. His stake was diminished and he became
afraid he might be boned with a bet he could not meet. But
he took money from his roll with an assurance that
suggested the big bills went all the way down.

Just as quickly as he had been losing, he began to win.
He played one victorious hand after the other and with a
surge of joy he sternly masked, he saw the hunters become
the prey.

They took a short break. Nick walked around the room
to stretch his legs. In the small washroom that smelled of
urine and disinfectant, he emptied his bladder and washed
his face. On his way back to the table he passed Nestor,
but the old man looked past him without a sign.

When they resumed playing, Nick was about forty

thousand dollars ahead and no longer impaled by the fear that his bankroll was inadequate. He stressed his surprise at his good fortune in an effort to suggest to the others that luck rather than skill was at work.

"You're sitting on the sunny side of the hedge tonight." Prince Pierre spoke in an aggravated voice.

Slowly, the games developed into a contest between Nick and Loukanas, the others merely enlarging the size of their pots. Big Gorgio was the first to drop from the game, throwing his cards aside in fury.

"I can't play with goddam cards like I'm drawing!" he cried hoarsely. "To hell with you all!" He settled back in his chair, arms folded, scowling as he watched the progress of the game.

A few moments later, after a hard-fought hand in which Loukanas won a large pot from him, Prince Pierre quit with a shrug as well.

"Enough of my blood on the table tonight," he said and motioned at the cards. "If neither of you object, I will relieve you of the chore of the deal."

Nick and Loukanas agreed and Prince Pierre dealt the cards. Nick won one pot and Loukanas the next one, a pattern that prevailed for half a dozen games. In an effort to break the seesaw they switched for a while to seven-card stud.

Once again a brief halt was called when a waiter brought in sandwiches, coffee, and beer. Nick tried to eat but the food seemed tasteless. He had lost track of time, uncertain whether it was day or night. Only the moments that began and ended a game could be counted.

Prince Pierre dealt a hand of seven-card stud and with a flare of excitement, Nick saw a third ten fall up to match the pair of tens he held in the hole. Loukanas had an ace showing and, from the first card, the betting was strong. Loukanas bet five thousand dollars on the ace and Nick called.

Nick was dealt an eight on the next card, Loukanas receiving a seven. When Loukanas bet another five thousand dollars, Nick was tempted to raise but did not want to reveal his strength too soon. He felt a chill when he considered Loukanas might be holding three aces. He put in his five thousand dollars.

The next card dealt to Nick was the fourth ten and he stared at it in shock. He caught himself quickly, fearful the lapse had been noticed by Loukanas. But the portly owner was absorbed in his own delight at having received another ace. He smirked at Nick and brusquely peeled off a sheaf of bills that he tossed into the pot.

"Aces bet ten thousand dollars," Loukanas said.

Nick stared at the pot, frowning for several moments so he could collect his senses. Once again he fought the temptation to raise the bet, unable to stifle the nagging uncertainty that Loukanas had filled out four aces. He saw the ten-thousand-dollar bet and Loukanas leveled a quick, puzzled glare at his cards.

Prince Pierre dealt their sixth cards. Knowing his own hand could not be improved, Nick was hooked to the owner's card. Loukanas received a nine and Nick was dealt a queen.

"Aces bet another ten thousand dollars!" Loukanas said loudly.

Nick stared at his cards, giving the impression he was gravely evaluating the wager. He nodded slowly and counted out the amount.

"I call the ten thousand," he said.

Loukanas grunted in disbelief.

"You are still too young to realize the danger of reckless play." The words came tensely from the owner's throat.

The room grew still, the watchers sensing a kill. Big Gorgio leaned forward to rest his elbows on the rim of the table. Prince Pierre stared sharply at Nick. In the perimeter of shadows Nestor sat motionless, barely breathing. Nick knew the old gambler must hear the hammer of his heart.

Prince Pierre dealt them each the final card. Appearing to fumble eagerly at the tip of his own card, Nick stole a swift glance across the table. He looked at Loukanas, searching for the faintest trace of quickened breathing, the pulsing of a vein he could not control, a beading of new sweat on the fleshy cheeks.

"Aces bet twenty thousand dollars!" Loukanas stared fiercely at Nick, as if by sheer bravado to convince him to submit and flee.

Nick did not believe Loukanas held the four aces that could beat him. There was enough money in the pot for the owner to have bet every dollar he had left on that matchless hand. More likely he held an aces-up full house, figuring Nick to hold a smaller one.

A jubilation seethed through Nick, the first sweet taste of retribution. He counted the money before him to a total of seventy thousand dollars. He pushed twenty thousand of it into the pot.

"Your twenty thousand," he said. He paused an instant, suspense looping the table like a noose. "And fifty-thousand-dollars raise." Nick let the frailest twitch hook the corner of his left eyelid.

Loukanas stared at him in shock. His fleshy jowls shuddered, his mouth opening and closing as if he were chewing on a stone.

"You are a madman!" Loukanas hissed. "You have been lucky and it has unbalanced you! Time for a reckoning now! When I finish with you, a bum will spit as you pass!"

He spoke as if to reinforce his own resolve, his tongue emerging like a small pink snake to lick his dry, caked lips. He gripped the bills before him, counting the money slowly.

"I call your raise," he said hoarsely. "I'm seventeen thousand short. I'll throw in my marker."

"The last time we played," Nick said quietly, "you told me that markers were a privilege I was denied in the game. I don't think we should use them now."

"Are you saying my marker is no good?" Loukanas cried.

"I am reminding you that you would not allow markers in our game before," Nick said. "We did not mention changing that rule before we started."

"You impudent bastard!" Loukanas shouted. "I . . . I . . ." He made a wrenching, violent effort to calm himself. "All right," he said in shaken fury. "In a few minutes the end will be the same." He motioned to Prince Pierre. "Will you lend me the money?"

"I don't have it," Prince Pierre shrugged. "I'd countersign a marker for you but I don't think that will satisfy the young wolf."

Loukanas looked desperately at Big Gorgio. The slaughterhouse owner smirked at his distress.

"It wouldn't be fair," Big Gorgio said mockingly.

Loukanas sat riddled by anger and humilation. His

pudgy, ring-adorned fingers bent the cards in his hand so tightly it seemed they would be torn apart.

"I'll send my boy across the street," he said finally in a low, choked voice. "He'll bring back the money." He snapped his fingers and the bodyguard hurried to the table.

"Go to the cashier's office and see Leo," Loukanas told him. "Bring me the money."

"How much do you want me to bring?" the bodyguard asked. He spoke in a whisper but everyone heard the question.

Loukanas looked at Nick, his pride pricked once more.

"Bring just seventeen thousand," he said. "I won't need any more."

They waited in silence for the bodyguard to return. Nick suddenly lamented not allowing Loukanas to put in his marker. The waiting made him consider that Loukanas had baited him, his anger a deception to draw Nick's last dollar into the pot. He looked anxiously toward Nestor in the shadows, seeking a reassurance the old gambler could not provide him.

Loukanas sat stiffly in his chair, staring at Nick's cards. Big Gorgio sucked at some particle lodged between his teeth. Prince Pierre lit a cigar, the glowing tip settled quickly into a point of fine ash. One of the bodyguards whispered to another. Big Gorgio glared at them and their voices snapped to silence.

The bodyguard who had been sent across the street returned and handed an envelope to Loukanas. The owner ripped it open and drew out a thick sheaf of bills.

"Seventeen thousand!" he snarled at Nick. "Do you want to count it?"

Nick shook his head. Loukanas tossed the money into the pot.

"I call you, punk!" he cried. He did not wait for Nick to show his hand but fumbled with his fingers and flipped over his hidden cards. "A full house! Aces and jacks full!"

A tornado of vengeance and power swept through Nick's body, unlike any feeling he had ever known in his life before. He turned over his hidden cards. The light blazed on the four tens, their symbols arrayed in neat black and red tiers.

Loukanas stared at them, a bubble of saliva dribbling from a corner of his mouth. A vein swelled darkly in his temple and he tried to speak, but no sound passed his stricken lips.

Big Gorgio whistled stridently and Prince Pierre uttered an exclamation of disbelief. The bodyguards muttered in hoarse whispers to one another. Nestor leaned forward, his shoulders and head entering the arc of light. Nick saw the sparks of fire in his eyes.

"You're through!" Big Gorgio laughed raucously at the fat owner. "The punk baited you in and slit your throat!"

"There will be other nights and other games, Loukanas." Prince Pierre made an effort to console him.

Nick reached with trembling fingers to the center of the table and drew the mass of money toward him.

"Must be more than two hundred thousand bucks in that goddam pot!" Big Gorgio said.

"Hurry and count it!" Loukanas found his voice and cried shrilly at Nick. "Count it and say a prayer because you carry the devil's luck! Run with your winnings, punk, and be thankful the game hasn't lasted any longer!"

They watched Nick as he counted the money into

stacks of twenty-five-thousand-dollars. There were eight stacks when he finished and a smaller pile. Remembering the agony of his humiliation and defeat, the taunts and scorn he had suffered, he felt a wanton rage to destroy Loukanas.

"You want to gamble some more," he said to the owner. "All right. Let's cut the cards once for my two hundred and ten thousand dollars. I'll take your marker for that amount now."

The room was hurled into silence. Prince Pierre, Big Gorgio, and the bodyguards stared at Loukanas. Flushed and stunned, he sat there as if the earth had suddenly split apart before him and he tottered on the edge of a chasm. For a moment he tried to find refuge in the possibility that Nick was joking. When he looked at the faces of the others, he understood the horror was real.

They watched his suffering with a curious fascination, Big Gorgio savoring the spectacle the most. A dazed and bleeding animal, reeling after the slash of the knife, was a familiar sight.

For a frantic moment, stiffened by vanity and rage, Loukanas seemed to accept the challenge. His fingers twitched forward as if reaching to sign a marker. Then a panic he could not subdue plundered him. A terrible moan burst from his lips. His bones and organs appeared suddenly to collapse, and he slumped like a corpse in his chair.

For years afterward across the city, they spoke of the game in the Hermes that night. Men told of the tension of the confrontation, the staggering sum of money involved, the boldness of the young challenger who, after winning everything, dared to risk the total on the cut of a solitary card. A district that had glutted itself on titillations, that did not believe in the heroic, suddenly had a hero. Nick had defied and beaten the entrenched monarchs of power.

If the citizens of the city talked of the game, they also spoke with awe of the celebration that followed, a bacchanalian binge that spread to include every club and casino on the south side. Lasting for two days and two nights, most of the original revelers worn down or passed out, the festivities were sustained by hundreds of people who kept pouring into the area from other parts of the city. They came from the north side Gold Coast, from the west side policy rooms, from the provinces of Hammond and Gary. Society matrons, businessmen, black jazzmen, conventioneers, police officers off duty and their sergeants, all swarmed together joining young harlots, lean pimps, and graying madams. Every bootlegger in the area was pressed into service, every alky cooker with a homemade still recruited to provide the vast quantity of booze the bibulous mobs required.

Nick and Korakas hosted the hugest and most convivial of the celebrations in the No-worry Club. With the exception of Loukanas, who had gone into anguished seclusion, even the gambling owners who had played in the game joined the affair and basked in the acclaim.

For Korakas it was the most magnificent event of his life. He distributed his largesse with enthusiasm and abandon, pouring endless bottles of bootleg whiskey, gin, and wine, every emptied glass posing a challenge he could not resist. Bums and vagrants hurried from the Salvation Army soup kitchens and the Pacific Mission halls to share the bounty. Men who had begged and cadged drinks for years were suddenly afloat in free booze.

Nick danced at the head of a line of fifty men and
women that circled the tables and chairs of the No-worry
Club. When he stopped for breath, he became the center
of a milling, applauding mass of admirers. The magnitude
of the festival befitted the coronation of a young prince
and the citizens came to accord him homage.

Through the hours of the celebration, Nestor remained
at a table in a corner of the No-worry Club, a bottle of
ouzo on the table before him. He drank silently, calmly
watching the dancers and drinkers carousing. Every so
often old acquaintances came to sit with him for a few moments, eagerly soliciting details of the game. A number of
times Nick and Korakas sought to draw him into the circle
of the celebration.

"Come and share the triumph with me, old friend,"
Nick pleaded. "It is your victory as much as mine."

Nestor would not move from the table.

"Enjoy yourself," he told Nick. "This is your night, the
first such triumph, but not the last. There will be many
victories to be celebrated for Nick the Greek."

Korakas, drunk and sobered and rapidly becoming
drunk again, heard the old gambler's words. He made an
effort to climb up on an adjoining chair. He slipped off
several times until a dozen willing hands pushed him back
up and held him from falling. Raising his arms above his
head, he bellowed for silence. Those around him echoed
his cry. As more voices shouted for silence, the room grew
quiet, the furthest corners the last to relinquish their laughter. Only the noise of revelers passing in the street echoed
indoors.

"Give me a glass of wine," Korakas called. When a full
glass was handed up to him, he gripped it unsteadily.

Slowly, spilling liquid over the rim, he managed to raise the glass above his head.

"I drink to my cousin," he said loudly. He paused and, overwhelmed by the intensity of his emotion, the glass quivering, he used his free hand to wipe a vagrant tear from his eye. "My cousin from Smyrna . . ." he went on. "Even before his win, we all loved him, a marvelous man . . . but now . . . He choked up again, unable to proceed. He waved the glass of wine, spilling most of the liquid down his hand and wrist. "For Nicholas Andreas Dandolos!" he cried. "A toast for Nick the Greek!"

A thunderous roar followed his toast and Nick felt the acclaim reverberating through his blood. For me, he thought in gratitude and wonder, they are shouting and applauding for me. He looked down at Nestor.

There was satisfaction in the old gambler's face, a vicarious sharing of the excitement. But there was also, Nick noticed, a sadness in his eyes and lean, scarred cheeks. He raised his glass to Nick after the others had drunk, a toast from an old battle-weary king willingly relinquishing his crown to a successor, without malice, regret, or envy, because he understood the burdens he passed on as well.

"For Nick the Greek." His lips echoed the words softly. A smile flickered for an instant around his mouth. Nick smiled in response, accepting the legacy that included the old gambler's sorrow.

Rantoulis, the owner of the Athens Wholesale Grocery, father of three daughters and uncle of Marina, came to the No-worry Club with a delegation of merchants. They had wakened him with news of Nick's victory, recounting the rumors that grew more turgid and inflated with each telling, that Nick had won a million dollars, that he now owned prime city real estate in addition to several casinos. Lending even more drama to the epic game were the grimmer whispers that the disgraced and defeated Loukanas had hung himself.

When Rantoulis, quivering from one bombastic hearsay after another, finally managed to push his way through the revelers to Nick, he congratulated him with the awe one reserved for a feudal lord.

"Salutations! Felicitations!" Rantoulis cried, clasping and pumping Nick's hand vigorously. "Since the day you honored our house I have been telling multitudes that you were a young man blessed by destiny! My wife and daughters and I were massively impressed with you! They join me in heartfelt wishes for your continuing good fortune and extend a cordial invitation for you to join us at dinner again soon! Please allow us that grand privilege and exalted pleasure once more!"

He finished breathless and flustered. Nick murmured a few polite words about being pleased to accept his hospitality again. As the delighted Rantoulis took his leave, Korakas winked at Nick.

"From bum to saint," Korakas said. "All it takes is a game of cards. I been trying to tell that to Lambri for years."

A man shoved roughly through the celebrants milling about Nick. The cold, stony circle of his face appeared out of place among the joyous throng. Catching Nick firmly by the arm, he leaned closer to place his mouth at Nick's ear.

"Angelo Genna sends congratulations," he said quietly and slipped away into the crowd.

With that warning, a reminder of his debt to the Black
Hand gangster, Nick felt drained of his last reserves of
strength. He longed suddenly to flee and find a place to
rest. He pushed through men and women, shaking off with
a smile the tugging hands that tried to detain him. He escaped, finally, to the street.

Standing outside the No-worry Club, he saw the first
paths of daylight rising above the rooftops of the shops and
tenements. A few drunken groups of men and women,
arms linked, still swept along the street. He knew by this
time all reason for the celebration had been obscured. The
rejoicing had become a circus without anyone caring how
it began.

Weaving slightly, he realized he was drunker and
wearier than he had imagined. He left the lights and glitter,
willingly entering the solitude of darker streets, the cool
air soothing across his flushed cheeks. He was conscious of
a silence that let him examine fragments of his soul. He felt
the wonder of the night, triumphant beyond his wildest ex-
pectations just a few days ago. He thought of the beaten
Loukanas and wondered if the rumors of his suicide were
true. He remembered Nestor's sadness even as he shared
the celebration of Nick's victory. And he recalled again
the ominous whisper of the messenger who reminded him
of the nameless debt.

He recognized suddenly the street he was on as the one
where Marina lived. His longing and his weariness had
brought him to her. He peered at the doors of the brownstone houses, stumbled once, caught himself from falling.
He found her house, looking at her darkened window on
the first floor, a nearby light flickering across the glass and
the drawn shade.

He walked up the steps into the hallway and lit a match to find her name. He rang the bell and waited. When there wasn't any answer, he rang the bell again. Finally a door on the other side of the glass entrance opened. In the light from the room behind her he saw Marina, clad in a robe, her posture apprehensive and uncertain. He hurriedly lit another match, held it close to his cheeks.

"Marina!" He spoke her name urgently. "Let me in, please. It's Nick. I want to talk to you."

She hesitated and he feared she would not let him in. He had not realized until that moment how much he wanted and needed to see her.

She moved then from the threshold of her flat and opened the door. He saw her pale, lovely face, luminous in the shadows.

"Listen, Marina." The words slurred off his tongue. "I wanted to see you because I have something to tell you."

She searched his face, drawing back slightly when she understood he had been drinking. After a moment she stepped aside and motioned him inside. He walked through the hallway into her flat, careful not to stumble so she might think him drunker than he really was.

She closed the door behind them. He caught a glimpse of her bedroom, the covers rumpled on the bed. She led him into a small parlor and turned on a lamp. The room was damp and chilly and she sat down on a couch, gathering her robe about her bare ankles.

"What do you want, Nick?" she asked quietly.

"Listen, Marina," he said. "The game I told you I had to play, well, it's over . . . it's over and I won a lot of money. You wouldn't believe how much. I won back my godfather's money and much more besides. I beat the best gamblers in the city and now, right now, on the streets and in the clubs, a thousand people are celebrating my victory."

He knew he sounded boastful, but he did not care, watching her face for a sign that she understood the significance of his triumph. She did not move or speak.

"Would you rather I had lost?" he asked indignantly. "Would that have pleased you more?"

She looked down at her hands clasped together in the lap of her robe.

He was bitter at her silence. The weariness he had experienced on the street overwhelmed him again. He leaned back against the cushion of the chair.

"Jesus Christ, Marina," he said in wonder. "What kind of girl are you? I've won a fortune and come here to tell you the news. I've become a rich man and it proves I was right and you were wrong . . . it proves it doesn't have to end as you feel all gamblers finish."

"I've seen a gambler's moment of triumph before." Her voice seemed to be coming from far away.

"Not like this moment," he murmured. "You've never known a moment like this one of mine."

After another interval of silence, he saw the shadow of her body looming above him. He reached up, fumbling slowly and heavily for her hand. Feeling her fingers in his grasp, he felt content. Closing his eyes, slipping effortlessly into sleep, he lowered a shade on all of life.

He woke to a burnished light that fanned out across the objects in the room. He lay sprawled in an armchair, his stockinged feet propped on an ottoman, a woolen blanket covering him to his throat, a pillow wedged beneath his head. For an instant he was uncertain about where he was. Then he remembered coming to Marina.

"Marina!" he called loudly. "Marina!"

She came from the kitchen, dressed in a long slender skirt and white blouse.

"You're finally awake, are you?"

"What time is it?"

"About dinnertime."

"My God, I came before breakfast!" He pushed away the blanket and swung his feet off the ottoman. He groaned at the stiffness in his body, the muscles knotted inside his shoulders and across his back.

"I've heated water for your bath," she said. "And earlier today, while you were sleeping, I went out and shopped, two fine steaks and from our special reserve at the store, a bottle of wine. I stopped by your room and Lambri gave me your razor and some clean clothes. I told her not to tell anyone you were here."

"What a marvelous girl you are!" he cried. He stood up and stretched. When he lowered his arms, he noticed the shadows of twilight thickening in the corners of the room. He savored the coming of the night, feeling nested and happy.

After he had shaved and bathed, they sat to eat at her small kitchen table. They drank wine from delicate, fluted glasses, looking at each other, content for moments at a time not to speak. He remembered the way he had fallen asleep after touching her hand.

"All the street is talking about the game," she said. "They are saying you won a million dollars."

"That is nonsense," Nick said. "I won around two hundred thousand dollars."

"But that is still a fortune. What did you do with the money?"

"Korakas and I woke Lambros, the locksmith," he said, "and stored the money in his biggest vault."

"They are talking also of the way you risked all you had won on one challenge to Loukanas. Is that nonsense too?"

"He would not accept the challenge," Nick said. He added uneasily, "Did you hear anything more about his suicide?"

"That kind of creature doesn't kill himself when he loses money," Marina said scornfully. "He renews his efforts to steal more from others."

"You are young to be so wise," Nick laughed.

"What if he had accepted the challenge?"

"I knew in my gut he would not accept."

"What if he had, Nick?"

"We would have cut the cards," Nick said.

"But that was madness, Nick!" Marina cried. "You had won back your godfather's money and a fortune besides! How could you risk that all on one card?"

"I don't know if I can explain," he said slowly, "but when you are playing, each card bears the terrible power of an amulet or a talisman. They fall soundlessly on the table but I swear they echo like the call of the muezzin, the Moslem crier in Smyrna who summoned the faithful to prayer. Your throat feels dry, your body goes from hot to cold. In those frenzied moments a thousand dollars, ten thousand dollars, or a hundred thousand dollars . . . the money somehow loses value. You want to win but that is not the reason you are playing."

He saw by Marina's face that she did not understand.

"That seems a kind of hell to me," she said.

"Yes, yes . . ." he said. "Someone might see it that way. But remember in the Bible classes of our childhood how close heaven was to hell."

Beyond the room where they sat together in that moment, a wind rose and shook the glass in the kitchen window. A child's plaintive cry carried from some nearby room.

"I felt these things, Marina," he hurried to reassure her. "Yet I tell you again what I told you the night you came to my room. There was something I had to do and now I am through. I will not gamble again. What sense would it make? How can I ever match the stunning moment when I beat him? That was not only a victory, but a redemption for me."

"You felt the gambling table was where you belonged," she said uneasily. "Then the rest of the world must seem alien and unreal."

"I feel I belong here now," he said earnestly. "Being here with you is not alien or strange."

She stretched out her hand, moving her fingers shyly against his palm, a gentle caress that made him conscious suddenly of longings he had not felt in months.

"Marina, I love you," he said. "I knew that the first time we had tea together in the shop. I knew it again in the meeting hall where you sat so straight and proud under the banners proclaiming the coming of a new world. I love you and I want you to marry me."

He saw the tremor that swept her breasts. He rose and drew her up into his arms. The clasp of her body seemed to reunite him with something that had been lost a long time. He kissed her lips and found them warm and pliant.

"Do you want to go to bed with me?" she asked.

"Of course I want to go to bed with you," he said. "I mean, that is an important part of marriage. But I love you for many other reasons."

"Do you want to go to bed with me now?"

"Marina!" he said. She had flustered him and he struggled to regain his composure. "What an incredible girl you are! You would make a splendid gambler because you know when to bluff."

"I'm not bluffing," she said. "Women have as much right as men to say things they want to say."

"I understand your philosophy," he said patiently. "I think it is sound in principle. But I am perfectly willing to wait for us to go to bed until after we are married. We can speak to Father Ladas at once and arrange for a date. You will want to order a gown. We can . . ."

"Don't you want to make love to me?" she asked.

"Of course I want to make love to you!" he cried. "I love you and want to marry you! But we don't have to stampede to bed draped with banners and bunting announcing the emancipation of women!"

"I am not campaigning now," she said gravely. "And I am a little scared you might think me bawdy and immoral. But for generations, women have waited until after they are married to sleep with a man. The man has never been bound by that rule. I love you, Nick, and I would like us to make love now. Is it improper for me to make such a decision?"

He shook his head in wonder at her candor. He reached out and took her firmly into his arms, and kissed her again.

Marina's small bedroom contained a delicate scent of lavender. The four-postered bed was covered with a brightly flowered spread. When they first entered the room she left his side and entered the shadows of a corner. He heard her garments rustling as she began to undress and he fumbled at his own clothing.

"I want you to know," she said quietly, "that I have never been with a man like this before."

"Marina! You told me you weren't a virgin!"

"I was showing off," she sighed. "But you're experienced and have had many women, so it's all right."

"I have not had many women!" he exclaimed, feeling the absurdity of the exchange. "If I gave that impression, it was wrong. I am not Casanova and I've never been to bed with a virgin before!"

"That's rather like both of us being virgins," she said, and he thought he heard her giggle softly.

"You are a wicked girl," he said reprovingly. "You are teasing me and making the whole act of love a plank in your feminist platform."

She walked from the shadows into the frail light that shone from the other room. Her blouse was unbuttoned and her throat gleamed like a sliver of moon.

"If that's what you think," she said somberly, "we can return to the kitchen and I will brew some more tea."

"I don't want any more tea!" he cried. "And let us, for the love of God, stop talking! This is a bedroom and not a debating club!"

He was instantly remorseful, afraid he might have hurt her.

"Marina, I want to make love to you," he said softly. "That is my decision too. I am more scared now than I was when I sat down at the table for the game. But I want to make love to you."

She came slowly toward him and he reached out and drew her into his arms. They came together like lovers reunited after years of separation.

He would often recall that first night with Marina. How
he felt as if both of them indeed had been virgins, ex-
periencing the marvel of love for the first time. He had
touched women before but never flesh as smooth and vel-
vet-sheened as her naked body. He caressed her, feeling
each cove and recess enclose a special pleasure. She
touched him as well, her fingers stroking his chest and arms
and shoulders with an innocent ardor. When he finally entered her body, gently, careful not to hurt her, she cried
out less in pain than in awe at what was happening to her.
She bled slightly and he felt moments of panic while they
fumbled for a towel and cloths. Afterward she soothed him
with the delight of a child who had been granted a rare
gift. She fell asleep in the embrace of his arm, her toes
pressed against his ankle, her face hinting some mystery of
contentment only a woman could ever know.

Wakeful as a sentry beside her, he was conscious of the
vault of the night around them, his beginning and, with a
curious sadness, the inevitability of his end. He came to understand then how much foreshadowing of death existed in
the act of love between a man and woman.

He remembered the great game he had played at the
Hermes and could not fathom how another joy could follow such a triumph so quickly. He had a chill of apprehension, an old Greek presentiment that good fortune must
be equated by a measure of ill fate.

A strand of her hair, tickling his cheek, banished his
uneasiness and he stifled an impulse to laugh. He could not
resist kissing her eyelids. She stirred and opened her eyes
and for a stunning moment he saw them luminous with
love. She snuggled sleepily within his arm, closed her eyes
again, and in a moment was asleep once more.

In the morning he woke as she tried to disengage herself quietly from his arms. She moved slowly and gingerly, sliding along the mattress a few inches at a time, trying not to wake him. He pretended he was sleeping and watched her through slitted eyes.

She remained poised on the edge of the bed for an instant, watchful as a fawn, and then rose to walk barefooted and naked toward the bathroom. He admired the ungarbed, graceful litheness of her body, the crystal curve of her back flowing into the swell of her buttocks, her slender, shapely legs. When she disappeared through the door, he closed his eyes, moving his body into the warm portion of bed she had left.

"I have only a little food left," she said to him later. "There is some cheese and a small chunk of salami and a glass or so of wine."

Nick stood in the doorway of the kitchen, a spread draped like a toga about his naked body; Marina wore a nightgown and white mules.

"That's not very splendid fare for lovers like us," he said with a grimace.

"We had steak and wine last night."

"That was before we made love," he said. "Tonight we should have vichyssoise, roast duckling, champagne . . ."

"Shall I go out and shop?"

"Certainly not! You may get lost or decide not to return."

"I would come back to you," she said quietly. "I will never leave you now, for as long as you want me."

"I want you, Marina," he said earnestly. "I will always want you." He parted the spread to free his arms and started toward her. Before he could touch her she laughed and dodged swiftly aside, circling around him to take his place in the doorway.

"Catch me!" she cried.

"Marina, no games now!" he said sternly. "I am older than you and deserve some respect!"

"You must earn my respect!"

"Marina, come here!"

She turned and ran and he started swiftly after her. The spread tangled about his knees and he stumbled and nearly fell. He heard her laughing at his mishap.

"All right, my girl!" he cried jubilantly as he untangled the spread and hurled it away. "You'll pay dearly for your sassiness now!"

Late in the afternoon Marina asked a neighbor to shop for her. The neighbor returned and carried the bag of provisions into Marina's kitchen while Nick hid in the bedroom. He emerged the moment the woman had left.

"I told Mrs. Caravagi I wasn't feeling well," Marina said. "Then I ask her to buy barbecue chicken and artichokes and fresh corn for me. She must think that is odd."

"She will think you have a unique doctor," Nick said, "who believes in treating a minor illness with barbecue chicken, artichokes, and fresh corn."

"Of course," Marina said. "What else does my doctor prescribe?"

"A bottle of champagne, but that takes more magic than Mrs. Caravagi can provide."

"Just a moment," she said. "Magic is my specialty." She reached into a cabinet above the stove and brought out a dusty bottle of champagne. "See?" she said triumphantly.

"Wonderful!" he cried. "Where did you get it?"

"A present for my birthday last year," she said. "I knew I was saving it for a purpose. We can chill it for a while in cold water."

"God, I'm starving!" Nick said. "And dry as a desert! Hurry and let's eat! Then your doctor requests that you return to bed and make love with your companion and then sleep awhile and then get up to drink and eat again. And so forth and so on . . ."

"Until we grow slow and fat and warm like two great love birds snuggled in their nest," Marina said.

During the middle hours of their second night together, it began to rain. The drops pelted the bedroom window, lightly at first and then striking harder. A peal of thunder rolled across the sodden sky.

Nick knew by her breathing that Marina was awake. For a few moments they listened to the thunder and the rain without speaking. A streak of lightning burst at the glass and in the transient flash he saw the tears that glistened on her cheeks.

"My darling! Why are you crying?"

"I'm not crying much. Just a little."

"Why?"

"Because I'm happy. Haven't you heard of a woman crying when she is happy?"

"Yes, of course," he said. "But I thought that was true of old-fashioned women only . . . not the new, liberated banner-carriers of your movement."

"I am a liberated woman in the streets," she said softly. "Here, in bed beside you, I am only a woman whose love seeks the power of an amulet or a talisman . . ."

He reached over and held her tightly in his arms. Outside their room the torrent of rain fell upon the streets,
washing away the refuse of the city, leaving behind a
renewed and untainted landscape they would walk upon
together.

CHAPTER 6

After the nested days and nights he spent with Marina, Nick attempted to return the twenty-five thousand dollars that Angelo Genna had given him. Using Prince Pierre as an intermediary, he tried to arrange contact with the Sicilian leader but Genna refused to see him. Nick persisted, enlisting the aid of a powerful ward politician. Finally, a meeting was arranged. On an afternoon in late March, about a week after the big game, Nick was picked up by men in a car and driven to the Napoli Café. Passing through a crowd of diners, he found Genna eating alone in a latticed alcove guarded by half a dozen gunmen. The swarthy leader had a large platter of pasta and veal and a decanter of red wine before him.

Nick started to speak, and with his fork, Genna motioned him brusquely to silence. He had to stand there for a humiliating and interminable span of time while Genna ate, chewing with a noisy smacking of his lips, drinking wine after each swallow. Only after Genna had finished, pushing his empty platter aside, did he look up at Nick, his face cold and impatient.

"I don't like for anyone to ask to see me," Genna said. "When I want to see someone, I let them know."

"I just wanted to return the money, Mr. Genna," Nick said. He walked forward slowly and placed the envelope on the table. "This is the same sealed envelope you gave me. I swear I never touched the money."

"I believe you," Genna shrugged. "That's a wasted, piddling dodge a Greek would think was smart. But whether you used the money in the game or not means nothing. The debt you owe me still stands."

"I'm ready to return double what you gave me." Nick drew a second envelope containing another twenty-five thousand dollars from his coat pocket. "That's a big profit for the loan of a few days."

Genna raised the decanter and filled his glass with wine.

"Please, Mr. Genna," Nick said earnestly. "Let me square this debt now."

"Listen now to what I tell you," Genna said grimly. "You made a vow knowing that was the only way you could play. That signed a marker with me. When I call on you to pay, you'll pay."

"How can I pay when I don't know what you'll ask?"

"You'll know."

"What if I refuse to pay?" Nick said in a low, hoarse voice. "Will you have me killed?"

"Killing a man who welshes on a bet loses the stake," Genna said. "There are other ways of settling with his friends or a girl he cares about."

Nick thought of Marina with a tremor of fear. He stood there a moment longer, Genna's stony and unyielding face making him understand further pleas or words were useless. He turned and left the alcove, the nameless debt carving a wound in his flesh.

In the wind wheel of spring blowing across the city, Nick tried to resume his life as it had existed before the months he spent with Nestor. He wrote his godfather that he had a stroke of great business fortune and for the family to make plans to journey to Greece and from there, to America.

He rented another warehouse and renewed his contacts with restaurant owners and retail merchants for orders and shipments of figs. He reopened an office larger than the one he had closed and hired several people as a staff. He drove himself through the routine and details of business lunches and meetings, poring over orders and bills of lading, making a relentless effort to occupy his hours. When he stopped rushing for a little while, he felt his spirit wearied by an emptiness and boredom.

Only the time he spent with Marina eased his restlessness. Although her uncle Rantoulis was disappointed because Nick had not chosen one of his daughters, he consoled himself (Korakas explained to Nick) that Nick's wealth and bright future would remain within the family.

Marina was busy with the Woman's Suffrage Association preparing for the municipal elections in April when women would be voting for the first time. He and Marina agreed on a small wedding but Mrs. Rantoulis projected plans for a larger, more grandiose affair. She commissioned the most expensive seamstress in the city to make Marina's wedding gown. She reserved the ballroom of the Metropole Hotel for the throng she planned to invite. After

some initial resistance and a few arguments with her aunt
and uncle, Marina gave in.

"They have been good to me," she said to Nick. "If you
don't mind, let them plan the wedding as they wish. That
will fulfill my last obligation to them. Then, when it is all
over, you and I can go away together."

"I wish we could go away now," Nick said. "I wish we
could be married next week instead of waiting for June."

The fame of the game Nick had won did not diminish
but grew more celebrated with the passage of time. When
he appeared on Halsted Street, a crowd of men and women
followed him. Some wanted merely to look at him, others
had an almost obsessive need to touch him, hoping by that
contract to absorb his good fortune. The bolder ones solic-
ited him for money to aid their sick relatives, to help pay
for their children's schooling, to finance their inventions or
business ventures. He began receiving letters, as well, from
people in other cities asking his help. He was touched by
the travail they recounted and sent money in response to
the most urgent pleas. That produced only a greater surge
of mail.

The relentless attention and pursuit became oppressive
to Nick. He could no longer move about with any freedom. The limit to his patience came on a night when he
was taking Marina to dinner. A group of a half-dozen
shabby, unwashed beggars cornered them near the entrance to the restaurant. They shoved Marina roughly
aside to get to Nick, tugging at his clothing, pawing at him
as they implored his help.

Marina became frightened and Nick shouted angrily at
the men to leave them alone. The beggars retreated, mut-

tering and baleful. As Nick opened the door of the restaurant, one of them called after him.

"When you gonna play again, champ?"

The episode shadowed his pleasure at being with Marina and he was somber during the evening.

As word of the game at the Hermes spread to other cities, Nick received invitations to play high-stakes games in Detroit, Cleveland, Boston, and Cincinnati. He refused these invitations because of his promise to Marina. He reassured himself that he didn't really want to play. But the days and nights passed and his restlessness continued. On several occasions, for trivial reasons, he was sharp and impatient with Marina. She was bewildered, apparently unaware of the reason for his aggravation. He was instantly remorseful and they reconciled fervently. Yet, in spite of those moments of contrition, and his promises to Marina, he came slowly to understand the reason for his vexation and distemper. The stark truth was that he longed for the whipping excitement of a card game once again.

In April the last soiled patches of snow melted. The stunted trees that grew in the back yards of the rooming houses shook off the last winter scales and spotted a few tiny buds. The walls of buildings were plastered with posters announcing the forthcoming Republican presidential convention.

Easter was only a couple of weeks away and Lambri had begun to bake pastries. Along Halsted Street, a score of men raked and swept the large vacant lot between Harrison and Vernon Park where the barbecue pits for the Easter lambs would be set up. The pens in back of Big

Gorgio's slaughterhouse were full of young spring lambs, whose bleatings and squealings sounded over the noise and traffic of the street.

On a night in the second week of April, Vito Baldelli, who ran prostitution for the Gennas, left the Hermes after an evening of gambling. As he was about to enter his car, two men leaped out of the darkness and put guns to his temples. They fired blasts that tore off the Sicilian's head. The following morning the newspapers blazoned photos of the decapitated body, and rumored the killing as a renewed attempt by Spike "Four Deuces" O'Donnell and his brothers, who ruled the territory southwest of Little Italy, to take over the province controlled by the Gennas.

The last war between the Gennas and the O'Donnells had taken place four years earlier. Both families had imported additional gunmen and for almost a year bombings and murders tore the city. A gang lord named John Torrio had arranged a truce that divided their territories. Now, the killing of Vito Baldelli portended another bloody war.

The Greek gambling house owners, knowing their tribute would be part of the victor's loot, called a meeting, to which Nick was invited. He sent Korakas in his place. When Korakas returned that evening, Nick, Banopoulos, the publisher, Dr. Samyotis, Gikas, and Spiro waited for him in the kitchen of the No-worry Club.

"Shouting and panic mostly," Korakas told them in disgust. "They seem scared of their shadows. Prince Pierre, Loukanas, the pig down thirty pounds since Nick skewered him, and Big Gorgio, all frantic they will have to give up a bigger slice of their action. They want to hold on to what they got but they don't want to hold so tight they can't let go if it looks like they'll get a gun blast in the ass."

"Was anything resolved?" Banopoulos asked, nervously adjusting his pince-nez glasses on the bridge of his nose. "I should have been present at that meeting. After all, I am a journalist, with a responsibility to keep my readers informed."

"There are certain things which should not be printed," Dr. Samyotis said.

"What things?" Banopoulos asked sharply. "Freedom of the press in this country is not to be circumscribed."

"None of them understand that it all works out even in the end," Gikas said sagely. "Beggars and owners, gang lords and mayors, all of them filling holes I dig in the ground."

"Did anyone come up with a good idea, Korakas?" Spiro asked.

"Big Gorgio suggested they hire gunmen of their own," Korakas said. "Once and for all challenge the gangs for control of the street. You know he has never accepted cutting the Gennas in for a share of his profits."

"Good for Gorgio!" Banopoulos cried. "That courage is in the valorous Greek tradition. Did we run from the enemy at Thermopylae? At Marathon? At Salamis?"

"We might have run like hell if the Black Hand had been against us instead of the Persians," Dr. Samyotis shrugged.

"I tell you boys there isn't any place in the city more peaceful than a graveyard in the spring," Gikas said. "The squirrels and rabbits come out and people start visiting their loved ones, bringing little sprigs of early flowers."

Banopoulos was already lost in composing his next issue.

"I can see the headlines now," he said, his voice trem-

bling with fervor. "HELLENES DELIVER ULTIMA-
TUM TO HOODLUMS."

"Change that to 'HELLENES COMMIT MASS SUI-
CIDE,'" Dr. Samyotis said.

Banopoulos glared at him.

"You have concocted so much of that scummy patent
medicine," he said, "you have lost your spirit." He rose
from his chair to leave.

"Before you start printing that stuff about ultimatums,"
Korakas warned him, "let me tell you the final decision
was to stay neutral and hope the wild dogs tear one another apart."

"Then I will write a blistering editorial about coward-
ice," Banopoulos said grimly.

"Be careful, old friend," Dr. Samyotis said. "I will miss
your simplistic interpretation of events."

Banopoulos did not bother to answer but stalked from
the kitchen. Dr. Samyotis rose with a sigh.

"I better go up to the paper with him," he said, "and do
what I can to modify his militance."

"I'll walk along with you, Dr. Samyotis, if you don't
mind," Spiro said. "I'd rather not be on the streets any later
than I have to." He motioned to Gikas. "Are you coming
along?"

Gikas nodded and the three of them started from the
kitchen, the gravedigger pausing a moment beside Nick.

"You should try to come out and visit me sometime,
Nick," he said earnestly. "I'll show you around. We've got
some marvelous people buried out there and I can tell you
all about them."

"I'll try to make it soon, Gikas," Nick said.

After the men had gone, Nick and Korakas sat in silence for a few moments. From the main room of the club they heard the muttering of the patrons.

"You were around during the earlier gang war," Nick said. "What was it like?"

"Bloody and full of horrors." Korakas shook his head gloomily. "The O'Donnells tied up one of the Gennas' boys in a packing crate and then set the crate afire so he burned alive. Then the Gennas hung one of the O'Donnells' boys on a meat hook in an icebox for three days. The medics used ice picks to chip him loose."

"Is the money they get from the gambling casinos worth a war like that?"

"This war is for more than the gambling dough," Korakas said. "Bootleg booze is going to be the big money-maker now. The Gennas got a warehouse over on Taylor Street and a license to handle industrial alcohol. They distribute some legally but most is redistilled, colored and flavored to imitate whiskey. It's 190 proof and goes for five bucks a quart. That's the action the O'Donnells are after." He shrugged. "Best thing for us is to stay low and quiet. At times like this I'm grateful I'm only a small fish. Even a boob wouldn't waste a bullet to gain control of a disaster like the No-worry Club."

Nick reached for the bottle of ouzo and poured a portion into his glass. He sipped a little and looked at Korakas.

"Will they be playing at the Hermes tonight?" he asked.

"I don't know, Nick," Korakas said uneasily. "I mean . . . well, there was talk of a game after the meeting. Even if they play, it won't be much of a game. They're worried and they won't play long."

"Are you still worried about me, Korakas?" Nick asked
sharply. "You still concerned they're going to eat me,
bones and all?"

"Are you crazy, Nick?" Korakas cried. "After the way
you showed them that night! How could anyone think
such a thing?"

"The memory of one damn game doesn't last forever,"
Nick said. "Maybe they think I'm afraid to risk any of the
money I won."

"Nobody believes that, Nick!" Korakas spoke earnestly.
"Everyone knows you're a real champion."

"I don't feel like a champion any more," Nick said.

"I understand," Korakas said soothingly. "You feel that
way because you're not playing. God knows when the
urge comes over me, I almost go nuts if I can't play. But
you're different than me, Nick, different than those other
bastards. You're a decent and educated man, you're going
places . . ."

"To hell with that syrup," Nick said impatiently.

Lambri appeared on the stairs from the apartment above.

"Hanging around in the kitchen again?" She glared at
Korakas. "Have you retired? Don't you care those bums
out front are probably stealing you blind?"

"I'm discussing serious matters here," Korakas frowned.
"I got more important things on my mind than soiled pen-
nies from my patrons."

"Forgive me!" Lambri dipped brusquely in a parody of
a curtsy. "Stupid woman that I am, I did not understand I
had married a financial wizard, an adviser to bankers and
kings. You have hidden your intelligence so well, I was de-
ceived into thinking you were just a moron."

"What a woman!" Korakas grimaced. "Her mouth could drown a whale."

"Don't be hard on him, Lambri," Nick smiled. "He has been keeping me company."

"I made some avgolemono soup, Niko," Lambri said gently. "Come up and have a bowl while it's hot."

"Maybe a little later," Nick said. "I think I'll get some air now."

"Put on a scarf so you don't catch a chill," Lambri said.

He pulled his coat and hat from an adjoining chair. When he reached the door, he turned to wave them both good-by and saw them watching him with troubled faces.

He left the street of closed shops and darkened stores, walking toward the gambling casinos whose lights glowed in the gloomy sky. When he passed the corner where Vito Baldelli had been murdered, he thought of Angelo Genna and a shiver swept his body.

Before the Hermes, several men pushed by him to enter the casino. With the door opened, he heard the buoyant clamor from within. He paused a moment and then walked on.

Marina was at a meeting and would not yet have returned to her apartment. He hesitated, uncertain where to go. He had not seen Nestor for several days and wondered if he might find him at the coffeehouse.

When he entered the Minerva, he was assailed again by the rank smells of sweat and staleness. Starting through the tables filled with old men, several of them recognized him, one man reaching up with palsied fingers to touch his arm. He heard a few others whispering his name. Behind the stove he found Nestor at his table. Nick tugged off his coat and sat down.

The old gambler, a bottle of ouzo at his elbow, greeted Nick with a wry, weary grin. Under the crown of thick white hair, his head was more emaciated than Nick remembered, the curved bony ridge of his nose bearing an even sharper resemblance to a hawk's beak.

"Of all the places you might sit and drink in," Nick frowned, "I don't know why you choose this pesthole. It's oppressive and it stinks."

Nestor motioned to a waiter with a soiled apron tied around his waist to bring them another glass.

"I feel at home here," Nestor said. "I've grown old with many of these wrecks, laughed and celebrated, drunk and gambled with them. They are bare and unadorned old citizens, all vanity and swagger gone. I belong with them now."

"But you don't belong with them!" Nick protested. "You are Nestor! Remember what you told me once? If God wanted to learn to gamble, He would come to you."

"A boastful moment." Nestor spit scornfully. "Most of the time I know I am only a sack of brittle bones enclosing weak kidneys, a battered liver, a frazzled heart. The undertaker who gets my carcass will think he has divined Pharaoh's plague."

"You think too much of death."

"Death doesn't trouble me any more," Nestor shrugged. "I understand now there is nothing to be done about that marker we sign when we are born. The enigma is life as it stumbles and staggers toward the end."

Nick felt the probing force of the old man's eyes.

"But death is far from your thoughts," Nestor said. "You are tangled in life." He stared gravely at Nick. "You should be the happiest of men. You are healthy and young. You're in the first, fair flowering of love. You've taken vengeance on your enemies. Your treasury is full. Yet, a strangeness has come into your life. Your days and nights endure the echo of a hollow heart."

"You helped me gain all these things," Nick said. "And you are right they are all a man could want. Then why in God's name do I feel this way?"

"There was once a Dutch painter," Nestor said. "In the final years of his life he painted wheat that concealed demons. He painted stars like wild glowing rings. And he painted cypresses that were torches of green flame. You see, by that time, he had crossed the boundary and everything had become transformed for him."

"Are you saying I'm mad too?"

"Madness will do in place of a better word," Nestor said. "You too have crossed a boundary, erasing the trail from your past. You have played in a game where every breath is like a gust of wind, where each heartbeat strikes like a hammer on an anvil. Do you think you can go back to your figs now?"

"I still have links to the past!" Nick said earnestly. "Family and friendships, and love for Marina that means so much to me. What about love?"

"For a gambler, love is a beguiling fragment that he can never make the total of his life."

"But what the hell is the purpose of victories," Nick cried, "if, in the end, they become only defeats?"

"Better than losing from the start."

"There must be more sense to it than that!"

At a nearby table an old man expelled a hoarse and exhausted sigh.

"Listen!" Nestor cocked his head and pointed a stiff

finger at the old man. "Did you hear that tempest of despair from Meletis? There is the end of victories and defeats, the end of faith and hope, dreams and love. There is
the wreckage of the power and the glory, proof how irrel-
evant a man's life is to his inevitable fate."

"That ouzo you drink makes you speak in riddles!"
Nick said impatiently.

"Do you want clear and simple answers?" Nestor
snapped. "I have none! If you feel life is barren and boring
unless you gamble, then that is what you should do. If
tracking the spoor of that demon frightens you, stay with
figs and love . . . if you can. Whatever you choose, the
final destination is the same. Decaying old men, sinking
into their haunches, waiting for the end."

"I don't believe it has to finish this way!" Nick cried.
"Sighing and mourning in a dingy coffeehouse, waiting for
death to topple you off your chair!"

He called across to Meletis at the adjoining table.

"What do you still want from life, my friend?" he asked
loudly. Some of the old men at nearby tables stirred from
their comatose slump and turned to listen. Meletis stared
numbly at Nick.

"A bottle of ouzo," Meletis finally mumbled.

Nestor laughed mockingly.

Nick called the waiter. "Bring a bottle of ouzo for this
man." He motioned at another of the old men. "And you,
friend, what do you still want from life?"

"I know Petros," a third old man cackled. "He wants
firmer bowels and a pair of clean drawers."

Petros glared at him and turned to answer Nick.

"Sometimes I sit here and close my eyes," he said
gravely. "I see the island where I was born, the white mon-
astery on the mountain, the village church, and the small

village cemetery. I'd like to go home to spend my last days. And after I die, be buried where my mother and father are at rest."

"And you will go!" Nick said. "I promise you that! I'll buy a ticket for you by the first boat!"

A rattle and chatter of excitement stirred the men. A number of them pushed their brittle limbs from their chairs and hurried to the table where Nick and Nestor sat. Several spoke at once until a tall old man with a body still lean as a stripling tree cried out in a harsh, strong voice that subdued the babble.

"I want to go home too, Nick!" he said boldly. "But not to die! Hell no!" He looked contemptuously at Petros. "I want to dance in my village on my nameday." He braced his shoulders, strutting like a rooster. "I may even marry once more! Some young, peasant girl with soft, big teats and a rock-hard butt who will bear me a litter of healthy sons!"

"Bravo!" Nick shouted. He cast a look of triumph at Nestor. "And you will go home! With money in your pocket to buy a gown for your bride!"

His generosity infused the men with enthusiasm and they crowded closer, shouting to be heard, mounting a din of voices and a scramble of hands.

"Wait!" Nick cried and rose from his chair. "Wait!" He waved them vigorously to silence. Their voices succumbed slowly, the men in front turning to hush those in the rear of the circle.

"Listen to me now!" Nick cried. "Each of you wishing to make the trip back home come in the morning to the No-worry Club. Your transportation will be arranged and I promise you that no man here will be left behind!"

The men cheered loudly and hoarsely. Nick looked at

Nestor, who was coughing in a spasm of mirth. When the old gambler finally mustered his breath, he grinned and shook his head.

"I told you that you were mad!" he said. "You'll launch an ark of old goats and bid them sail like Odysseus to regain Ithaca. They'll retch up their zest on the crossing and end in some island tavern, bleaker and poorer than this hole."

"At least they will have assembled the guts to make the journey," Nick said. "That is better than rotting away here."

"You're mad!" Nestor cried. "Totally mad!" He began to laugh again.

"If living boldly is mad, then I choose madness," Nick said. "I choose the painter's vision beyond the boundary. To hell with caution! To hell with figs!"

He scooped up his coat to leave. The somnolent and hopeless lethargy he had found when he entered the coffeehouse had been replaced by activity and clamor. The men had gathered in noisy, vigorous groups, making buoyant plans, their voices ringing keen and breathless. Nick felt their fervor spark his own spirit.

"I'll see you around, old friend," Nick said gently to Nestor. "My teacher and philosopher of the beginning and the end, I'll see you around."

"Where are you going?"

"To the Hermes," Nick said. "A game is in progress and they are holding a chair at the table for me."

In the weeks that followed the night of decision, Nick joined games at the Hermes and at the Apollo. He played for high stakes with Loukanas (who had recovered from his ravaging defeat but who watched Nick with some strange fear and awe), Prince Pierre, Big Gorgio, and others. As Nick's fame spread beyond the environs of the city and the state, eager gamblers came to challenge him. There were railroad and steel executives, politicians and entertainers, and shadowy figures who had smuggling connections in Mexico and Cuba. Men who would have scrupulously avoided each other in the world outside sat together around the table, their suspicions allayed by a conviction that when Nick the Greek gambled, the game had to be straight.

The renown of these high-stakes games played in the upstairs rooms of the casinos also drew a bigger crowd of lesser players to the street, increasing the action in the casinos. The Greek owners were pleased and yet fearful because the gambling clubs became even juicier plums for the Gennas and the O'Donnells.

Warfare between the two mobs continued with bombings and killings across the south side. Rumors had leaders of both families in hiding while their gunmen prowled the streets searching one another out. The peril that hung over the casinos because of that warfare gave them the aura of citadels under siege and added further excitement and tension to the games.

In the beginning, immediately after making his decision, Nick tried to explain and justify his change of mind about gambling to Marina. In spite of his assurances and his efforts at persuasion, for the first time they quarreled.

"I want you to understand!" he pleaded with her. "I'm not interested in the fig business or any other kind of business. I will keep the operation going, find good people to help run it. If I want to spend time gambling, that doesn't make me a criminal. Ask anyone and they will tell you I am an honest gambler."

"What does that mean, Nick?" Marina asked bitterly. "What does it mean to say you are an honest gambler?"

"That means I don't own brothels, saloons, or casinos," Nick said. "That means I play as a sportsman, winning or losing of less importance to me than the challenge of the contest."

"Nick, you're deceiving yourself!"

"I'm not deceiving myself! Marina, why don't you try and understand what I'm saying?"

"Because I have heard those same excuses before! They ring as phony now as they did then, old, stained lies repeated by gamblers many times, lies to mask an ugly truth you cannot face!"

"I know what you went through with your father," Nick said. "But it's foolish to believe it has to be the same way for me. I am not your father."

"Your promises are the same as those he made," Marina said and her voice trembled. "You promised me you would not play again, swore that oath while you held me in your arms!"

He felt a high tide of anger, a frustrated response to the truth of what she was saying. He had broken his promise. He resented her hurling it in his teeth. And he was surprised, looking at her, how bitterness and anger could disfigure a human face, making someone endearing and familiar somehow alien and strange.

"Things have changed for me now." He made an effort to speak quietly. "When I made the promise, I did not know how I would feel." He drew a deep breath. "But try not to be angry with me. Don't punish us by talking of postponing the wedding. I will not make any more promises I cannot keep but perhaps time will help us. I love you, Marina, you must remember that."

"I love you too, Nick," she said softly. "That love could endure many things. But I am not sure it can survive your gambling. You have to understand that."

She looked so forlorn and wretched in that moment, he felt a stab of contrition.

"If I ever have to choose between gambling and losing your love," he said earnestly, "there isn't any question in my mind as to what I would do. Believe me, Marina, you are more important to me than anything else in this world."

He meant those words to console her and, as he spoke them, he did not doubt they were true. But from the way she watched him, as if longing for him to offer more valid proof than facile words, he understood she did not believe him. For an ardent instant he considered redeeming his pledge of love by swearing he would never gamble again, never touch another card or wager another stake.

The thought of such an oath produced so swift and consuming a disorder in him that he felt his body burn as if with fever. He could not speak. She turned wearily and helplessly away, his silence settling around her like a shroud.

CHAPTER 7

In spite of the distress that Nick's gambling produced in his relationship with Marina, they still planned to be married in the summer. He was in such a season of good fortune that anything less optimistic was difficult to imagine. Everything worked splendidly for him. Indeed, so continuing were his triumphs and delights that the ominous anxiety of his debt to Angelo Genna was sometimes forgotten.

He whirled in the elation of days and nights spent at receptions and parties. He was lionized and warmed by the compliments of important people, the admiration of lovely, refined women, the deference of men who respected only power. Items about him appeared in the columns of city newspapers and a writer from a national magazine came to Chicago to do a story on him. All this time he continued to gamble and, with his skill at cards, won a good deal of the time. These victories, sometimes exaggerated in the retelling, added to his luminous legend.

Promoting his new image and faithful to the aura of

influence in which he now moved, Nick had a dozen fine suits tailored for him. He bought several Borsalinos, which he wore at a rakish angle. His shoes were crafted for him by a bootmaker from England who designed and built footwear for the royal family. Adding to his elegance, he wore a diamond ring and a diamond horseshoe pin he had won in a stud poker game from an oil tycoon in Dallas.

He did not forget those around him. He bought an expensive diamond engagement ring for Marina, so huge and finely wrought a stone that when Rantoulis first saw it, he could not restrain his tears.

"You didn't need to give me anything as big and costly as this ring, Nick," Marina told him when they were alone. "A more modest ring would have pleased me just as well."

"Nonsense, my darling!" he cried. "I resisted getting even a bigger diamond! Nothing is too good for the girl who will soon be my wife!"

He tried to convince Lambri to move from the rooms above the No-worry Club to a nicer apartment or a house. When she refused, he refurnished the small apartment, bringing in couches, chairs, and a shiny porcelain stove. He commissioned a seamstress and, over the vehement protests of Lambri, had the woman design several handsome dresses for Lambri who pleaded with Nick to send the seamstress away because she felt herself, "a stringy old hen adorned in plumage like a peacock."

If Lambri had qualms about her new image, Korakas accepted the change with alacrity, eagerly visiting Nick's tailor and bootmaker. When the tailoring and crafting were finished, the owner of the No-worry Club sported a wardrobe that matched Prince Pierre's in splendor. He was not spared, however, some scathing commentary from Lambri.

"Whoever heard of a yellow suit?" she cried when Korakas modeled his newest garment for her and Nick. "That is covering for some camel in a circus!"

"That shows how much you know!" Korakas answered indignantly. "My tailor informed me that yellow suits are the rage now in Paris."

"You are not in Paris, you boob," Lambri said scornfully. "You are on Halsted Street and the only colors in rage here match the gray and grime of garbage."

"Leave him alone, Lambri!" Nick laughed. "I think he looks magnificent."

"Like a magnificent ass," Lambri muttered.

Korakas gave her a final, baleful look.

"Woman, you'll try my patience once too often," he said sternly. "You keep forgetting I am an important man now. I am associated with Nick and how would it look if I dressed like the relic I used to be? Tell me that?"

Without waiting for an answer, he turned and stamped out of the room.

Of all Nick's friends, only Nestor remained adamant about not accepting any help. He refused Nick's offer to move him from his loft to more pleasant surroundings. He rejected any gifts of money or clothing. Finally, he turned aside Nick's plea that he take a vacation or a cruise.

"I have spent so many years secluded in gambling rooms," he told Nick, "if the sun ever caught me squarely, my carcass would disintegrate like a mummy exposed to light and air." He shook his head and grinned. "Don't worry about me, my friend. Leave me alone to enjoy my wretched existence. It is only what I justly deserve."

That May, a group of journalists, entertainers, show-
girls, and athletes gathered around Nick. They were free
and bold spirits sharing a loyalty to gambling.

With the opening of the baseball season, they gathered
in adjoining boxes at the ball park. They would wager
with one another on whether a pitch would be a ball or a
strike, if the batter would swing, if a runner would steal.
Impatient with those monotonous intervals when the
players changed innings or when a new pitcher warmed up
on the mound, they would bet on how often the vendor
selling refreshments would pass, whether the next woman
walking by their boxes would be a blonde or a brunette.
While they bet, they vied with one another to keep the
greatest number of wagers in motion. If a player lost track
of them and wound up with a "Dutch Book," a swarm of
stakes so confusing and overlapping that he could not win
whatever the outcome, he was hooted and derided and
made to buy dinner for all of them.

The same festive group would gather at ringside for the
fights at the Coliseum. They would bet on the number of
punches thrown by each fighter in a round, the number of
knockdowns, how aggressively or timidly a man fought.

One such evening in early May at the Coliseum, they
watched the main event of the evening's card between a
skillful welterweight named Joey Bengal and a bruiser
named Tornado Jackson.

The welterweight was a pleasure to watch, moving
swiftly and lightly, circling the heavier, clumsier fighter,
jabbing and punching him at will. The bout clearly
belonged to the favored Bengal when, in the seventh
round, he slipped and stumbled into a savage roundhouse

swing to his head from Tornado Jackson. A shudder shot through Bengal's body and he grasped for his eye. Nick saw the blood streaming down his glove.

The fight was stopped and Bengal's handlers helped him from the ring. With a towel and robe draped around him, holding a poultice to his eye, they rushed him up the aisle while the audience jeered and booed the swift, unexpected ending.

Nick had bet heavily against Joey Bengal for no reason except that he had been the strong favorite. Now, several of his companions accused him of hexing the young welterweight with his phenomenal good fortune. Nick asked Baridas, the promoter of the fight who was sitting with them, to take him to Bengal's dressing room.

They left the arena and descended the ramp leading to the dressing rooms. In Bengal's quarters they found the fighter lying on his dressing room table being examined by a doctor. The atmosphere in the dressing room was funereal, the handler and trainer watching somberly, the fighter's heavy-set manager slumped on a chair in the corner, chewing a wet, limp cigar.

"How's them tomatoes?" he said to the promoter. "For a year now I been bringing the kid along, one conditioning bout after another. After winning tonight we had a match scheduled with Mickey Kovar, you know, he's ranked number three in the division." He waved his hand grimly toward Bengal. "You see what I got now."

"Perhaps some treatment can mend the eye," Nick said. "Won't he fight again?"

"I been managing fighters for twenty-five years," the manager said glumly, "I know when one is through." He called to the thin, bespectacled doctor. "How about it, Doc? Tell me I'm wrong and I'll go to church on Sunday."

For a few minutes the doctor did not answer, continuing to wash away the blood and peering intently at the eye.

"I can't tell anything until we get him to the hospital," he said. "But the eye is torn bad, the retina damaged. If we're lucky we might save the sight in that eye . . . but he won't fight again."

The young fighter shuddered as if he had been struck again.

"Whad' I tell you?" the manager grunted. "Do I know what I'm talking about? How's them tomatoes? A year lost now, expenses out of my pocket, time when I could have been working with another contender."

"A specialist might decide things differently." Nick spoke cheerfully to Bengal. "We can arrange for a good one to look at your eye."

"A specialist might help him," the doctor shrugged, "but even if he's able to see with that eye again, another blow could permanently blind him."

"What do I do now, Archie?" The fighter spoke for the first time, his voice quivering in an effort to hold back his tears.

"I don' know what you're gonna do, kid," Archie said somberly. "But I gotta find another fighter. You heard the doc."

"What did you do before you became a fighter?" Nick asked Bengal.

"I've always been a fighter," Joey Bengal said. "Ever since I was a kid."

"When you get patched up and after you're rested," Nick said, "come and see me." He put his card on the table beside the fighter's head. "We'll work something out." He motioned to the doctor. "Make sure he gets the best, and send the bills to me."

"If you're thinking of getting him fixed up to fight again," Archie said sharply, "I got an iron-clad and exclusive contract with him."

"I don't have any plans for him to fight again," Nick said. "You heard the doctor. But I'll give you a hundred dollars for his contract."

"I got ten times that much tied up in expenses and time," the manager protested.

Nick shrugged and turned away. Concealed from the manager's view, he winked at Joey and started for the door.

"Wait a minute!" Archie lumbered from his chair. "I'll take the hundred. That's probably all I'll ever see."

"All right." Nick turned back and motioned to the promoter. "Fix up the papers, Stephanos, and I'll send a check over in the morning."

"What are you going to do with my contract, mister?" Joey Bengal asked.

"Give it back to you," Nick said. "Now don't forget to come and see me. We'll work out something for you to do. I promise you that."

The fighter stared up at Nick. He looked so grateful and awed that Nick was moved and had to turn quickly away.

On the ramp leading back to the arena, he heard the crowd roaring at another fight. He was suddenly weary of the mob and the clamor and he passed through one of the gates to the street. He walked away from the arena, inhaling the night's warm, moist promise of summer. A few drops of rain fell and he raised his head, feeling them strike his cheeks and his lips. The rain returned him to a memory of the night with Marina after his great triumph. That tender interlude might have taken place a year before instead of just a few weeks earlier. Sorry for the estrangement that had developed between them, he longed for their marriage, which would bind them closer together than they had ever been before.

But his own problems seemed minor when he considered the young fighter who would never fight again. A single blow had destroyed his dream of becoming a champion. In such swift and fickle moments, all men were at the mercy of fate.

In that instant, for all his victories, he felt himself a frail and solitary figure under the immense night. Driven by a sudden foreboding, he hurried on to enter some room full of voices and light.

Even as Nick knew he was making Marina unhappy, he continued to gamble. That thrust to play grew stronger with each game, overwhelming any desire he felt to alter his life for her. Then, in the middle of May, something happened that made Nick think he might finish gambling in a stunning, colossal climax.

He received an invitation, written in scroll on fine parchment, delivered by personal courier from New York. Arnold Rosenberg, perhaps the most famous high-stakes gambler in the country, was asking Nick to join him in what might be the greatest gambling contest of all time. Only ten of the most celebrated gamblers in the world had been invited and the table stake required to participate was a half-million dollars per man. They would shoot craps until one man had broken all the rest.

"A half-million dollar stake!" Korakas whispered in awe when he saw the invitation. "Magnificent!"

"Blasphemy and sacrilege!" Lambri said as she made her cross. "Burn that scrap of paper, Niko, and light a candle for those doomed, misguided devils!"

For a few days he hesitated telling Marina. When he finally spoke to her of the invitation, he promised that if he won he would quit gambling forever and live out his life as a millionaire.

"Doesn't such a decision make sense, my darling?" he asked. "Why would any man want to gamble again after playing such a game? Kings could not wager for higher stakes."

He waited for her to speak. She watched him silently, her eyes troubled and shadowed.

"I know you have heard me making promises before," he said gently. "But give me this final chance. I don't even know if I can raise the stake in the next couple of weeks. The owners of the clubs on the street will help me because this invitation accords them honor as well. They have pledged a third of my stake. I must find some way to raise the rest."

"What if you lose?" Marina spoke the words so quietly he could barely hear her.

"I know there is that chance," Nick said. "But I feel destiny has decreed otherwise. Everything that has happened to me up to now, coming to Chicago, my first dreadful defeat, the months of working with Nestor, the triumph of the night I beat Loukanas . . . yes, even my pledge to you that I would stop gambling and then beginning again . . . all of these have happened, I feel, so that I can play in this game . . . and win."

He took Marina into his arms. He felt her body stiff and unrelenting.

"I love you, Marina," he said, and his voice trembled with the intensity of his emotion. "I love you and my wedding present to you will be a vow that I will never gamble again. But I need this one more chance."

Yet when Nick figured the total of the sums available to him, his own winnings and the pledges from the club owners, he was still short almost $150,000.

Holding a strategy council in the kitchen of the No-worry Club, Nick sat with Korakas and the young fighter Joey Bengal. The welterweight had spent a week in the hospital, where surgeons sutured his torn eye. Nick had gone to visit him and they made a decision that Joey would join Nick as an associate and companion. When the fighter had been released from the hospital, he had rented a room in a small apartment hotel on Halsted Street.

Now, in the club kitchen, considering ways to raise the additional money Nick needed, Joey pawed the gauze patch that covered his eye.

"If I were still a contender instead of a palooka," Joey said, "we might have been able to make some good money on my fights."

"Be grateful that you can see," Nick reassured him. "Don't worry about fighting. We'll raise the money somehow."

"I know a way that may add another fifty grand or so to the stake," Korakas said eagerly. "I've heard of others who have made a killing on it."

Nick and Joey waited while Korakas paused to heighten the suspense.

"It's a novelty race!" Korakas said. "They run it once a

year, in May, in this town in South Carolina. They race a
goat, an elephant, a man on his bicycle, and a horse."

Nick burst out laughing and Joey tried to restrain a
smile. Korakas looked at them in dismay.

"I'm not fooling, boys," he said, obviously stung by the
laughter.

"The horse would win easily," Nick said.

"But they are rated and handicapped in terms of their
speed!" Korakas said. "Do you understand? The horse
would be the fastest creature, of course, but would have to
race further. The elephant would cover the shortest
amount of ground. The best odds would be on the cyclist
and the goat."

"I believe you're serious," Nick said gravely. "But I tell
you, Korakas, it sounds crazy."

"It may sound crazy but there's a real opportunity
here!" Korakas said. "Come down to South Carolina with
me."

"I'm staying here," Nick said. "I'll see if I can get some
high action games going."

"If Nick says it's okay, I'll go with you," Joey said.
"Maybe they'll let a broken-down fighter enter that race
too." He grinned. "Racing an elephant can't be any worse
than fighting Tornado Jackson."

"Leave Joey here with me," Nick said to Korakas. "But
if you feel so strongly about our chances to make some
money, take a stake down. How about ten thousand dollars?"

"Fine! Fine!" Korakas said. "I'll run it up to a hundred
thousand for you! The race runs next week and I'll make
plans to leave right away."

"What will Lambri say?" Nick asked.

"She'll wish me farewell with her usual viper's tongue," Korakas frowned. "Probably suggest I enter myself in the race as a jackass."

"If you think you might win, go ahead," Nick laughed.

Two days after Korakas had departed by train for South Carolina, Nick received a telegram from "Long-odds" Monahan, the bookmaker at the track in Toronto where Nick had played poker while raising a stake for the game with the owners. The telegram advised Nick to come to Toronto at once.

"This may be the stroke of good fortune we need!" Nick said to Joey. "Monahan had told me when the season began a big Eastern syndicate would run a ringer in one of the races, a stakes champion that would run under a different name. The odds would be big and we could make a bundle. That must be what the telegram is about!" He slapped Joey jubilantly on the shoulder. "Joey, get us some tickets for Toronto!"

"I don't know anything about horses, Nick," Joey said. "You sure you want me with you?"

"Sure, I want you with me," Nick said. "Besides, a horse race is a simple proposition. The horse that comes in first wins the race."

"Is that all there is to it?"

"That's all!" Nick said. "Of course, the handicappers want you to believe it's a science. But I tell you horses are as unstable as humans and even champions have dyspeptic days. Now hurry and get us a drawing room on the first train into Canada."

"Between Korakas attacking in the South and you and

me invading the North," Joey laughed, "we got to get you into that big game!"

The following morning they boarded a train running from Chicago into Canada. By evening they had crossed the border and, when the moon rose, they pulled up their shades and looked out upon a landscape of forests, the trees forming dark thickets against the horizon.

During the night, as they lay awake in the darkness, the train wheels rumbling beneath them, Joey told Nick about growing up in the cramped, shabby flats of Brooklyn.

"We had small concrete yards under the porches where I learned to fight," Joey said. "The only passage in and out would be blocked by the guys. If one tried to run, they'd all pile on and almost beat him to death. So you fought, alley-style, slugging and kicking, until the bleeding loser begged for mercy."

He fell silent, as if retreating into those grim years. The whistle of the train, wailing across the night, brought him back.

"When I sleep sometimes now," Joey said, "I'm back in those concrete yards seeing the faces around me, and the face of the kid I'm fighting. And I feel scared all over, just like I was then, so scared I was ready to kill. Maybe I'll have those dreams as long as I live."

"Those memories will fade when you add new memories and experiences," Nick said. "You have to go to school, Joey, and study to enter some profession. We'll make plans when we get back to Chicago."

"You think I could really do that, Nick?" Joey raised himself on his elbow, his head outlined against the moonlit window. "Go to school so I can learn something besides fighting?"

"Certainly you can!" Nick said. "You're young, bright and strong and can do whatever you want to do. And I'll help you. I swear to that!"

When they got off the train in the Toronto station, carrying their bags up the ramp, Nick saw Monahan hurrying toward them. He was a small, grizzled man with rumpled clothing and a forlorn countenance. When they reached him, Nick dropped his bag and hugged him warmly. When he released him, Monahan wiped a tear from his eye.

"This is my friend, Joey Bengal," Nick said. "He's with me now in whatever I do."

Monahan and Joey shook hands. As they walked from the station to a parking area where Monahan had left his car, Nick spoke to the bookmaker softly.

"Your telegram was about the stakes horse, wasn't it?"

Monahan nodded mutely.

"I told you, Joey!" Nick said jubilantly.

"He was entered to go next Monday," Monahan said in a low, morose voice. "I seen him in an early morning workout a few days ago and he was flying just off the ground."

"Wonderful!" Nick cried. "What odds will he be?"

"The odds would have been long," Monahan said, "but they don't mean nothing now."

Nick stopped and stared at him.

"Last night some moron of a groom brought a mare too close to his stall," Monahan said gloomily. "The colt got excited and kicked the boards. He shattered a tendon in his foreleg. He won't race during this meet . . . maybe never again."

"What lousy luck!" Joey cried.

Monahan looked so crestfallen that Nick hugged him again in reassurance.

"It's not your fault, Monahan," Nick said. "You tried to share this good thing with us. I appreciate that." He shrugged. "The horse could have lost anyway."

He winked at Joey.

"What do you say, Joey? Ready for the train ride back to Chicago?"

"Listen, Nick, why don't you guys stick around here for a few days?" Monahan said. "The meeting is just getting underway and you could do some bookmaking for me. I'll see you get a fair percentage of the take and if a horse looks good and the odds are right, you can make some good money too."

Nick hesitated, looking at Joey, who motioned that the decision was up to him.

"All right," Nick said. "We'll stay around for a few days to work the cramps and kinks out of our legs and backs. But then we have to get back to Chicago."

Monahan drove them to the Featherton Hotel, where he had made reservations. The opening of the Toronto racing season had lured gamblers and sportsmen from all over the United States and the most notorious and affluent of them gathered in the splendor of the Featherton.

As Nick, Joey, and Monahan followed the bellman carrying their bags into the luxurious lobby, they merged into a colorful, garrulous throng. Monahan told them there were owners and breeders, gamblers and bookmakers, trainers and jockeys, perfumed and lovely daughters of joy hanging on the arms of dandies with pearl stickpins in their cravats. All the snatches of conversation Nick heard as they made their way to the desk concerned horses and wagers.

"I clocked that colt three different times . . ."

"That jockey has lost his nerve since he fell at Garden City . . ."

"I got this tip from the owner . . ."

"Put five hundred on the nose for me . . ."

"Marking another man's form, I told him, is worse than screwing his wife . . ."

They reached the desk and Monahan handed an envelope to the room clerk, who put it quickly into his pocket. They registered and sent their baggage up to their rooms. Then Monahan led them to the long mahogany bar in the large room adjoining the lobby that was staffed by a half-dozen bartenders in bolero jackets. One of them made room for the three of them at a corner of the bar. In the next few moments a number of the patrons and almost all the bartenders greeted Monahan.

"Everybody knows you, Monahan," Joey said. "You're a celebrity."

"I know them too," the bookmaker said gloomily. "That's Memphis Harry over there." He pointed out a portly man in a dazzling, checkered suit. "One of the biggest bookmakers in the business. He took me for twenty thousand on a ringer a few years ago." He pointed to another man. "There's Cardozo, a trainer from Saratoga. I paid for him and his doxy to take a trip to Havana, commission in advance for the tip on a big race he promised me. That was two years ago and I don't hear a whisper from him. And see that little guy, the one with the face of a toad and a mouth full of gold teeth? He's a jockey from Detroit, a specialist in 'foo foo dusting' a horse before a race to make it sluggish or adding a few pounds of lead to its shoes to weigh it down."

The jockey spotted Monahan and waved genially at him. Monahan forced a smile and waved back. "I know the bastards all right," he said. "You can't trust them or turn your back on them for a second." He released a labored sigh.

"You don't sound happy in your chosen profession," Nick smiled.

"That's the truth," Monahan said. "Bookmakers sicken me, crowds scare me, I can't stand the smell of stables, and I think it's nuts to wager money on poor dumb creatures."

"If that's the way you feel," Joey said in astonishment, "why don't you give the whole business up?"

"Punishment," Monahan said grimly. "I stay in it for the punishment. I figure if I take enough lumps here on earth, when I cross the final wire, maybe the good Lord won't bother shipping me to hell . . . maybe He'll figure I done my time already and give me a closet under His grandstand, a dark little pothole that's all a bookmaker deserves to see of heaven."

CHAPTER 8

In the morning, Nick was wakened by Joey shaking his shoulder vigorously.

"Rise and shine, Nick!" Joey said cheerfully. "Monahan will be here to pick us up in ten minutes."

Nick opened his burdened eyes.

"My God, it's still dark," he said. "What time is it?"

"About 5 A.M.," Joey said. "You'll feel great once you're up. Our training camp used to start each day about five, so I'm used to these hours."

"Well, I'm not used to these hours." Nick pushed himself toward the edge of the bed, then rose and stumbled to the bathroom.

After he had washed and dressed, they went down to the lobby. Even at that hour a few patrons still leaned on the bar while others, sprawled on the plush armchairs, slept off drunks from the night before.

"I thought you guys were going to sleep all day." Monahan rose from a chair beside a palm.

Nick grunted.

"He's usually much more polite," Joey grinned at Monahan, "but he's not awake yet."

They walked to Monahan's car and drove the two miles to the track. The bookmaker waved to the guard in the gatehouse entrance and they entered the grounds as the dawn light broke across the looming grandstand, glinting off the long roof. Around the oval of the track, a solitary horse and rider galloped through the shadows like an apparition in the ghostly mist.

"That rider is getting an early start," Nick said.

"Life begins at the track earlier than this," Monahan said. "Around 4 or 4:30 A.M. the stable hands and exercise boys feed, walk, warm up, and gallop their mounts. By eight, the trainers and owners are in the track secretary's office, entering their horses for races the following day.

After parking the car, they entered a shed adjoining the stable area. Monahan introduced them to a couple of men who stood at a small stove where a pot of coffee bubbled and steamed on the lid.

"This is 'Clocker.'" Monahan pointed to a tall black man with a trim, erect figure. "He was a cavalry bugler in the Spanish-American War. Now, he don't use a bugle any more but a stop watch. He checks the early morning workouts and can tell us if a horse looks ready."

Monahan pointed to the other man, who was short, with a professorial demeanor.

"This is 'Saddler,'" the bookmaker said. "Name a horse and Saddler can tell you its dam and sire, the races it has run, where it finished in each one. He remembers races run ten years ago like they was run yesterday."

A handsome, impeccably attired man entered the shed. He nodded to them as he poured a cup of coffee from the pot. His presence and appearance were so imposing, Nick took him to be one of the track officials. When they were introduced, he discovered "Major" was a "tout," working for Monahan.

"The Major here, posing as a horse breeder from Kentucky, will pick a conversation with a hayseed over a mint julep," Monahan said, "and then casually drop a tip about a horse in a later race. The hayseed will do the rest. You wouldn't believe how a rumor we start at nine sweeps the track by noon. When it comes back to us, they swear they heard it from the horse."

"You're putting us on!" Joey scoffed.

"Ask the Major if you think I'm lying," Monahan grinned. "Some hayseed watches the horse coming from the paddock and the nag motions with its head or its tail, paws the ground, tosses its mane . . . anything the hayseed can take for a sign. I even remember one loony who, when a horse farted at him, took it as an omen the nag would run like the wind."

Later in the morning, Monahan walked Joey and Nick to the cluster of cinder-block barns and stables. Several horses circled the smaller exercise track at a gallop, workout boys bobbing in their saddles. Before their stalls, grooms slapped water on the sweat-streaked flanks of horses back from their workouts, skimming the water off with flicks of their scrapers and combs. Stableboys carried buckets of oats to the feeding troughs. A blacksmith worked over a forge, hammering the molten metal of a shoe, the sharp ring of iron echoing in the air.

As they neared the stalls, they were wrapped in an odor of muck and sweat, wintergreen and antiseptic.

"When I get this close to horses," Monahan grimaced, "I

begin to itch. If I stay long enough, I'll even break out in hives."

"What a strange reaction to horses for a bookmaker," Nick said.

"Like I told you," Monahan said grimly. "Punishment . . ."

They paused outside a stall where a groom was rubbing down a strong-legged and deep-chested colt. His coat was chestnut with a wispy white blaze running down his forehead to his nose. The groom brushed energetically, sweeping the hard bristles across the colt's muscular shoulders.

"That's Plate Glass," Monahan said. "He's a champion from New Jersey. They brought him in for next week's Canadian Futurity. Ten victories in ten starts last year, he's a cinch to win here."

A wiry-bodied little man in jodhpurs and riding boots came from the stall. He had sharp black eyes and olive skin that stretched tautly over his cheekbones.

"Long-odds-Monahan, my favorite bookmaker!" he cried. "What are you doing in the stable area?"

" 'Fall-off' Baltazar, my favorite jockey," Monahan said. "I'm showing some friends around but you can bet I won't be here long." He introduced the jockey to Nick and Joey. "One of the best riders around," he said grudgingly. "If you can call anyone who rides a dumb animal the best of anything."

Monahan had moved closer to the horse. The animal stirred suddenly, tossing his head uneasily, a snort of warning erupting from his nostrils. Monahan backed away in fear.

Baltazar caught the horse's head in his hands and then stroked him soothingly.

"He caught your scent, Monahan," he said. "He can tell
you don't like him."

"A dumb animal can't tell nothing," Monahan said. He
motioned at Nick and Joey. "I'm starting to itch worse,"
he said. "I'm going back to the shed. Come back when
you're ready."

After Monahan hurried off, the jockey continued to
stroke the horse's forehead gently, his fingers twining the
wispy white blaze.

"See how quiet he is again now that Monahan's gone,"
the jockey said. "They're sensitive to humans who hate
them or are afraid of them."

"He is a magnificent animal," Nick said.

"He is magnificent," Baltazar said. "And he doesn't care
anything about wagers and odds and purses and trophies.
Cover him in the silks of his stable and put him on a track.
Then he runs his great heart out for you, every race the
best he can do, no shirking or loafing." He nodded
earnestly. "You know a really fine horse is the best of man,
woman, rabbit, and fox. Like a good man, he's bold and
proud. Like a lovely woman, he's fair-chested and fair-
haired. He has the sharp eye and well-running sprint of the
rabbit, the flying tail and keen ears of the fox." He paused
and once again ran his palms in a caress down the horse's
mane. "Put all those qualities together," Baltazar said, "and
you got the most majestic creature God ever placed on this
earth."

They joined Monahan in the betting ring at noon, an
acre of land occupied by about thirty bookmakers, each
one with his booth and chalk board on which were printed
the opening odds for the day's races. A bookmaker's crew

included a sheetwriter, who recorded the wagers and odds changes, and a barker, standing on a box, who with a clarion voice tried to entice the bettors to their booth.

Standing with Monahan and Saddler, a sheetwriter named "Foxy" and a barker called "Caruso," Nick and Joey watched the bedlam with amazement. Bookmakers and bettors haggled over odds, their arguments stormy and abusive. When a bet was finally accepted by both parties, a snap of the finger confirmed the wager.

"How can anyone make sense here?" Nick asked. "There are only howls and yells like an alley full of cats."

"You ain't heard nothing yet," Monahan said. "When the races start and the crowds rush back and forth, then you got to move fast and think quick. Odds change fast and a point can lose a pile or make a bundle. If we tab a horse as four to one and take bets at that figure and the horse goes down to even money and wins . . . why we still got to pay off at four to one."

"Why don't you offer even money from the start?" Joey asked.

"Because the bettors shop around the ring for the best odds," Monahan said. "If we ain't competitive, we don't get the money. Sometimes it works the other way when we spot a horse at a shorter price than he should be. We book bets on him at two to one and before the race his odds go up to four to one. We lay off money on him with other bookmakers at that price. If he wins, we collect four to one and pay off two to one."

"I don't think I could ever learn this business," Joey said somberly. "My head is made for punching and not figuring odds."

"If I can learn it, Joey, anybody can," Monahan said.

"Course, you don't learn it all at once, but after some years you get trackwise."

"Like getting ringwise," Joey said.

Several men joined them at the booth. Almost at once they became involved with Monahan in a truculent argument over a wager. They snarled and shouted, their faces flushed with rage. Nick wondered uneasily if they might come to blows and he saw Joey tense, preparing to go to Monahan's aid. Then the argument ended as swiftly as it began, the men shaking hands with Monahan amiably before sauntering off.

"Can't they bet without those high dramatics?" Nick asked.

"That wouldn't be as much fun," Monahan said. "Besides, this keeps our blood boiling and we need steam for the betting field here." He winked at Nick. "Anyway, the first race will be going soon. Saddler will show you and Joey the box of an owner friend of mine. Go see how different the view is from hickdom."

From the turmoil and disorder of the betting ring to the Olympian perspective of a box seat, they watched the horses parading onto the track for the first race. The rainbow silks of the various stables shimmered in the crisp, clear air. Several jockeys cantered their mounts up the track to warm them before joining the file of horses moving toward the chutes. At that point, one by one, they were guided into the stalls. A black horse, fidgeting and balking, was the last into his stall. A tense silence gripped the crowd in the stands as the starter raised his flag.

"They're off!"

The horses burst from the chutes, lunging at once for positions along the rail. They raced bunched, moving as if they were linked and harnessed together in a team of bob- bing heads and straining shoulders. Around the far turn they broke apart, the fleeter mounts pulling ahead, the slower horses falling behind.

Speeding around the turn, losing a horse that veered too wide, they fanned out for the drive down the stretch. A low rumble began in the crowd, mounting to a roar as the horses sprinted the final hundred yards. With a great, leap- ing stride the black horse took the lead, drawing in front by a head and then by a length, the jockey flailing his flanks with the whip. As the horse flashed by on the track below their box, mane and tail flying, powerful legs whip- ping the air, the jockey crouched low and light on his back, Nick felt the spirited drama of the race. The horse sped across the wire and the thousands of people in the stands joined cries of approval and triumph with the grum- bles and groans of defeat.

At the end of the day's races, having made the trip from the box to the betting ring a number of times, Nick and Joey joined Monahan at his booth. The sun had begun its descent, the first shadows of late afternoon darkening the crown of trees in the distance.

The betting ring resembled the shambles of a battlefield, the ground around the booths and boards littered with dis- carded and torn tickets and slips. The barkers were hoarse, the sheetwriters exhausted, while most of the bookmakers looked like men on the edge of coronaries. Monahan slumped in a chair, his face streaked with sweat and his eyes haggard.

"All right, my friend, we've watched the play," Nick said. "When can we start bookmaking?"

Monahan stared up at him in resignation.

"You sure you want to, Nick?" he asked wearily. "I don't want for you to have a breakdown and blame me."

"I'm ready," Nick said. "Let's see if we can make some money out of this brawl."

"Don't say I didn't warn you," Monahan said. "But if that's what you want, I'll hire you a barker and a sheetwriter. You'll book under my name because you ain't licensed here but your play will be your own. Joey can help you cart your winnings to the track safe." He laughed weakly.

"I'm ready," Joey said. He stared around the betting ring with apprehension. "But I can't help feeling it's like teaching a kid to swim by flinging him into a school of sharks."

For the next four days, Nick booked bets from a booth in the betting ring. As he had promised, Monahan provided him a sheetwriter and barker.

Nick found the activity of bookmaking trivial and dull. Since he was a newcomer and the larger wagers went to the established bookmakers, he booked only small amounts. Yet, each day that passed brought him closer to the start of the big game in New York and his stake was still $150,000 short.

He also was nagged by distress about Marina. He had wired her on his arrival in Toronto, affirming his love, asking her to wire back or write him at once. He had wired her a second time but had heard nothing.

"I think we'll go home," he told Joey gloomily on Thursday evening. "There's nothing for us here."

"There's a train for Chicago late tomorrow night," Joey said. "I'll get the tickets."

Nick nodded. "We'll close up shop after the races to-morrow," he said.

On Friday, Nick's last day of bookmaking, the feature race of the day was the Canadian Futurity dominated by the speedster Plate Glass.

"A really great horse," Saddler told Nick. "His sire, Crystal Ready, was a champion too. He's beaten all these other horses in this race before, and should win in a waltz."

The morning odds on Plate Glass in the betting ring were listed as even money but Monahan and the other bookmakers felt that the horse would go off no better than one to ten. That meant a bet of two dollars to win twenty cents.

"Those are terrible odds," Nick said.

"But he's such a cinch, the bookmakers don't want to get killed," Monahan said. "Some of them won't even take bets on him. They'll close their booths before the race."

When the race before the Canadian Futurity ended, the crowd swarmed into the betting ring to get their wagers down on Plate Glass. The odds on the horse tumbled swiftly to the expected one to ten.

Following the lead of the others, Nick's sheetwriter started to erase the even money posted on the board.

"Leave it alone," Nick told him.

The words rang like a bell in his ears. He felt a sudden buoyancy and power, a wave of boldness that whipped the shores of caution.

The sheetwriter looked at him as if he were crazy. The barker, who had been calling odds of one to ten, almost choked closing his mouth. He leaped down off the box.

"Every bookmaker in the ring is quoting one to ten!" he

said to Nick in consternation. "You can't offer even
money! They'll bury you in bets!"

"You do the shouting and let me handle the odds," Nick
said. He motioned at the sheetwriter. "And you get ready
for some business."

Joey wore a puzzled expression.

"Nick, what are you . . ."

Nick waved Joey's query aside and urgently gestured
the barker up on his box. The barker stepped up and in a
low, hoarse voice began offering Plate Glass at even
money.

"Louder, man!" Nick cried. "Let them hear you!"

A few men passing paused, listening to the barker, staring in astonishment at the odds listed on the board.

"Is that right?" a man in a bowler asked Nick. "Them
odds on Plate Glass really even money?"

"Even money is right!" Nick said loudly. "We'll take
any amount you want to bet!"

"I got five hundred bucks right here!" the man yelled.
"Give me five hundred on Plate Glass to win!"

Several other men crowded in to make their bets. Joey
helped the sheetwriter gather the wagers and return the
slips confirming the amounts.

Word spread swiftly around the betting ring and within
minutes there was a frantic scramble to Nick's booth. In
the midst of the pushing, turbulent throng wanting to take
advantage of what they felt was a bookmaker's inexperi-
ence or stupidity, Monahan shoved through the crowd and
pulled Nick aside.

"You must be nuts, Nick!" he gasped. "You'll get destroyed and wipe me out too! That horse is one to ten and
you're giving even money! Nick, call off any more bets

and I'll announce you're sick! We'll tell 'em you're a veteran of Verdun who has been gassed!"

"Listen, Monahan," Nick said soothingly. "Trust me! I've got a hunch . . . it's crazy but I've got to go with it."

A number of other bookmakers whose business had dried up gathered around Monahan and Nick.

"What's going on, Monahan?" one of them cried. "Your buddy gone loony?"

Monahan, his limbs quivering and his face ashen, tried to compose his voice.

"My friend here is a gambler," he said weakly. "He thinks Plate Glass ain't no cinch."

"Is that so?" a portly bookmaker said. "Maybe he'd like to gamble some big money on that."

"He's not taking no big bets!" Monahan cried. He tugged desperately at Nick's arm. "They want to lay off the money they already took on Plate Glass. They'll only pay twenty cents for every two dollars they win off you. Tell 'em to go to hell!"

"Get your bets down, gentlemen." Nick made an effort to speak quietly.

"Can you pay off, friend?" a heavy-jowled, hard-faced man asked ominously.

Monahan looked at him indignantly.

"Where the hell you get off with a question like that!" Monahan cried. "This is Nick the Greek from Chicago! He'll cover any bets he makes! My bankroll is behind him too!" He looked beseechingly at Nick.

"I have about two hundred thousand dollars in my bank in Chicago," Nick said. "They can wire me the money in a few hours. Your bets will be covered."

"I heard of this guy," another bookmaker said. "He's

supposed to be a high action man. Well," he smirked at Nick, "let's give him some action."

In the final ten minutes before the start of the Canadian Futurity, Nick booked almost $175,000 in bets on Plate Glass from the bookmakers. Monahan called the security guards and had the money and markers, payable at the end of the day, transported to the track safe. By that time the horses moving toward the starting chutes, the booth was deserted except for Nick, Joey, and Monahan. The sheetwriter and barker, fearing disaster, had fled.

"Oh, Jesus Christ, I can't believe this is happening," Monahan mumbled. "This must still be the nightmare I seen in my sleep last night."

"You want to go watch the race, Nick?" Joey asked gently.

Nick shook his head slowly. Trying to control his panic, he felt his throat tight, and his stomach burning. He was terrified at what he had done, yet there was also a sense he was not lodged firmly on the earth, but floating . . . in some eerie and stunning levitation.

"Let's go up to the club bar," he said.

They walked from the betting ring, up the stairs to the bar. Monahan stumbled once and Joey helped him regain his balance. At the big window overlooking the track, Nick caught sight of the horses assembling at the chutes and quickly averted his gaze. He ordered a brandy and sat down at a table without a view of the track. Monahan slumped in a chair across from him and handed his binoculars to Joey, who took up a position at the window.

"Have a drink," Nick said to Monahan.

"My belly is in my throat," Monahan said. "A drink would choke me."

The bartender brought Nick his brandy. When he raised the glass to his lips, he saw his fingers trembling.

A roar from the crowd in the stands outside confirmed the horses had burst from the chutes. Joey held the binoculars braced to his eyes.

"Plate Glass broke third!" Joey called.

"Just where he figured to break," Monahan said wretchedly.

With men and women at the other tables in the bar watching him, Nick struggled to appear calm.

"He's still running third." Joey's voice shook.

"Oh, Jesus!"

"Still third at the half," Joey said. "They're beginning to spread out."

"He comes on with a rush." Monahan put his head in his hands.

"Another brandy, please," Nick called to the bartender.

"They're turning into the stretch!"

"He's a devil in the stretch." Monahan rocked back and forth like a mourner.

Joey uttered a tense, choked call.

"He's making his move, ain't he, Joey?" Monahan looked at Nick in despair.

For a long moment Joey did not answer. A deafening and bilious racket rose from the stands. Joey's voice was lost in the rumble.

"Joey, I can't hear you!" Monahan cried.

"He's fading!" Joey yelled. "He's fourth . . . and going down for the count!"

"You're nuts!" Monahan leaped up and lumbered to the window. "You mixed him up!" He snatched the binoculars from Joey's hands. He fumbled to adjust them and then loosed a shocked cry.

"For God's sake, Nick, he's right! The damn horse won't finish in the money!"

A great howl of anger and outrage burst from the crowd watching their favorite lose. The din did not subside but whirled around like a tempest.

I have won, Nick thought, dear God, I have won. As he savored the exaltation of triumph, he felt a consummation and climax more absolute and satisfying than any he had ever achieved in a woman's arms.

Joey raced around the bar, joyous and shouting. Monahan stumbled after him, yelling with delight. When he returned to the table he stared down at Nick with fear and awe.

"How come, Nick?" he asked in a breathless whisper. "How come you was so sure?"

"It was just a horse race," Nick said. "How can anyone be sure what a horse is going to do?"

"Jesus Christ!" Monahan shook his head. "Why didn't I ever think of that?"

Before the winning horse had been led from the winner's circle, the wreath of victory garlanding his neck, the track officials sent for Monahan and Nick. They walked together into the office where the stewards and a dozen indignant bookmakers waited for them.

"Mr. Dandolos," one of the stewards said gravely. "You offered even money on Plate Glass whose price was quoted by every other bookmaker at one to ten?"

"That's right, sir."

"Were you in possession of any information that revealed the horse would not win?"

"No, sir."

"Then how on earth could you place odds like that on

the horse?" another steward asked indignantly. "If you lost, you would have paid off a fortune!"

"I am a gambler and it was a horse race," Nick said. "The horses in a race know nothing about odds, favorites, and long shots. Any one of the horses might not have felt like running. I gambled that Plate Glass, who didn't lose all last year, was due for a bad race. I offered the improved odds to draw the track money to me."

"Something goddam funny going on here!" one of the bookmakers cried.

"Leo, why don't you go speak to the horse?" Monahan said genially. "He'll explain."

After answering several more questions, Nick was asked to leave. As he departed from the steward's office into the hall, he heard Monahan's voice raised shrilly in his defense.

Nick waited in the shed with Joey and Saddler until Monahan returned with news of the steward's verdict.

"They're ruling you off the track," Monahan said. "They said you was guilty of reckless bookmaking and they're ruling you off the track for what they call the good of racing. The truth is you scared the shit out of them!"

"What about you?" Nick asked. "I'm leaving anyway and the ruling doesn't bother me. Are they punishing you?"

"Suspending me for fifteen days," Monahan shrugged. "My stomach will take that long to settle down anyway."

"The cowardly bastards!" Joey said angrily.

"Well, it's all history now," Nick said. "Joey and I are leaving for Chicago late tonight. Let's plan a gala celebration before we go. You and Saddler, Clocker, and the Major will have dinner with us at the finest restaurant in

Toronto. We'll drink French champagne and eat Russian caviar and say farewell to this grand and hospitable city!"

Late that night, the salubrious celebration ended with all of them, including a guitarist they had conscripted from a café, escorting Nick and Joey to the train station. In an unsteady and noisy procession, they played and sang their way past the astonished travelers sitting on the benches in the waiting room and down the ramp to the train. As they bid one another a series of fervent farewells, the security guards from the track arrived with two suitcases containing the money and drafts that Nick had won. Joey, Monahan, and Nick carried the suitcases to their compartment.

"I'll take a look around," Joey said somberly, his voice slow and slurred. "Make sure no suspicious characters are in this car." He waved an unsteady finger of warning at Nick. "Lock the door after me. I'll knock three times when I come back." He opened the door, moving quickly, pulling it closed behind him. Nick and Monahan stared after him. After a moment the door reopened and a sheepish-looking Joey emerged from the bathroom.

"Everything's okay in there," he mumbled, and went out the compartment door.

Nick locked the door and opened one of the suitcases. He counted out twenty-five thousand dollars which he placed in an envelope and handed to Monahan.

"This is for you, Monahan," he said. "For the generous use of your facilities."

"You don't owe me nothing, Nick!" Monahan stared at the envelope in awe.

"I want you to have this money," Nick said. "Don't give me any trouble now."

Monahan shook his head gratefully. "You're a sport, Nick," he said earnestly as he slipped the envelope in his pocket. "A sport. God bless you!"

He and Nick embraced zealously. Monahan stepped toward the door, paused, and turned back to Nick.

"You got a lot of big games and high rolling ahead of you, Nick," Monahan said. "A lot of action bigger than today. But there won't never be nothing to match today for me. They'll talk about this race and your gamble anywhere dumb horses race and anywhere bookmakers bet. They'll tell the story in the stables and in the clubs. They'll say that Long-odds Monahan was with you on the play." He shook his head in wonder, his eyes glistening. "I been around for almost sixty-five years, Nick, and I been nothing. Now, at the end, you made me famous. I won't never forget you."

Wiping the tears from his eyes, he hurried out the door. For a moment Nick stood there, staring after him, and then he locked the door again and sat down.

Somewhere ahead of the car he heard the first ringing of the train's bell, a slow pealing that echoed and vibrated through the compartment. The train lurched forward, a shudder rising from the wheels to his seat. He leaned back and gratefully closed his eyes. The wheels rumbled and rolled faster and he felt himself lulled by the movement, carried in the grasp of a huge, mighty spirit, hurling through the dark night toward his shining and beneficent destiny.

CHAPTER 9

Nick and Joey had wired Korakas before leaving Toronto, and he met them when they arrived in Chicago. As their train pulled to a whistle-steaming and bell-jangling stop in the station, they spotted Korakas. He hurried along on the platform beside the train, peering excitedly up at the windows. Joey knocked loudly against the glass to snare his attention. Korakas responded with a jubilant wave.

As they descended the step from the car's platform, he hugged them both, one in each arm, the tears in his eyes suggesting to other passengers that they had been parted for years.

"Leave those bags alone." Joey waved a redcap away. "We'll carry them ourselves."

Korakas stared at the bags with his cheeks flushed.

"You got the lettuce in there, eh?" he whispered, looking warily around. "Let me carry one of them will you? I want to feel the weight of a suitcase full of dough." He hauled one of the bags for a few feet. "Not so heavy, after all," he said in surprise. "I bet pants and underwear weigh just as much."

They joined the movement of passengers along the ramp into the station. The brassy voice of an announcer droning over a loudspeaker called train arrivals and departures. At the station exit they entered a taxi, Joey and Korakas holding the suitcases on their laps. As the taxi emerged from the terminal into the traffic along the street, Korakas sighed.

"You guys did great." He spoke in a low, dejected voice. "You came back champions. But my trip to South Carolina was a disaster. I lost the whole ten thousand bucks."

"What happened?" Nick asked.

"Well . . ." Korakas began slowly, obviously suffering. "The horse went off at even money. Considering his handicap, which made him race twice the distance of any of the other entries, the crowd still made him the favorite. I knew Nick wouldn't want to bet the creature with such short odds. Right, Nick?"

"Who did you bet on?" Nick asked. "The man on the bicycle? The goat?"

Korakas fumbled his big fingers nervously together, getting a firmer grip on the suitcase.

"The elephant was fifteen to one," Korakas said mournfully. "So I bet on him."

"The elephant!" Nick said in astonishment. "Losing the money isn't important, Korakas, but, in the name of God, how could you bet on the elephant?"

"On his grand workouts," Korakas said earnestly. "I was up at dawn, three mornings in a row, clocking his secret workouts. I tell you, boys, I never realized how fast an elephant could run! The odds on him made him a real sleeper, so I laid our bundle on him to win."

Korakas turned his head away, staring out the window at the buildings and people along their route. He cleared his throat harshly several times. Nick and Joey maintained a discreet silence.

"He finished the race last, shambling across the line after dark," Korakas said bitterly. "The longest hour of my life was watching that shit-headed, lead-assed monster plodding around the goddam track!"

Joe and Nick burst into laughter. Korakas looked at them reproachfully, his expression embarrassed and pained, until, his frown relaxing, he began to laugh too. The three of them roared with mirth.

"An elephant!" Nick marveled when he could get his breath. "An elephant! You bet ten thousand dollars on an elephant!"

"He looked so good!" Korakas gasped, wiping the tears from his eyes. "Hell, I figured his nose alone was worth an extra two feet!"

That started them bellowing again. The unsmiling taxi driver shook his head grimly, as if convinced he had a trio of lunatics as his fares.

They made a stop to deposit the money in the Central City Bank on Van Buren and then to a florist, where Nick bought a huge bouquet of three dozen roses. He had the taxi drive him to Marina's apartment before taking Korakas and Joey to the club. Opening the front door with his key, the instant he stepped inside he absorbed the cherished warmth of the rooms.

"Marina?" He called her name. As he walked through the empty apartment, his disappointment became loneliness. He put the flowers in the kitchen and sat for a while in the parlor. He found the darkness soothing and he closed his eyes.

He dozed and wakened to the sound of a key turning in
the lock. He saw the apartment door open and the slender
figure of Marina silhouetted against the light from the hallway. He rose from his chair and she was startled and cried
out.

"I'm sorry, my darling . . . I should have put on a
light," he said.

When he took her in his arms and kissed her, he felt a
tender impulse to hold and console her for all the things he
had done to cause her grief.

She was pleased with the roses and put them into a vase.
He suggested they go out to dinner but she wanted to stay
in the apartment. She made them bacon and eggs and he
opened a bottle of wine. They ate at the table in the
kitchen and she talked of her activities in the women's
council during his absence.

He waited impatiently for her to ask him what had happened to him in Toronto. Finally, unable to hold back his
great news any longer, he described his triumph at the
track, the resolute way he had won the stake he needed for
the game in New York. He did not expect her to be as
gleeful or enthusiastic as he felt, but he was not prepared
for the vehemence of her disapproval.

"Don't you see, Nick, how the whole business is a kind
of lunacy?" she said bitterly. "Winning more money on a
horse race than people earn in a lifetime. That is insanity!"

"Whether insane or not," he said sharply, "it's better to
win than to lose."

"Is there any difference to a gambler?"

"Don't be foolish, Marina! Certainly there is!"

"When gambling controls and dominates your life," she
said, "how can you really be satisfied or happy with anything else?"

"Marina, why don't you try to understand . . ."

"I do understand, Nick," she said, her voice low and forlorn. "I understand you don't care what is best for us."

"Of course I care! How can you say something so absurd?"

She looked at him in a silent rebuke. He tried to curb his aggravation.

"You won't admit the simple truth that I won a fortune again," he said. "Don't you see that another victory proves what I have been telling you about my destiny and the big game?"

"Destiny has nothing to do with it," she said. "Gambling is a human weakness."

"I don't understand you, Marina!" he cried, stung by her nagging and censure. "You never answered my wires or my letter! You seem bound to punish me, to make us both suffer! My God, even if she didn't share my delight in victory, another woman would at least say, 'Congratulations!' Another woman would at least say, 'Well done!'"

"Then find another woman," she said.

The moment the words were spoken, both of them were shaken by remorse. He pushed back his chair and as he rose she came quickly to his arms. They held each other tightly. When he saw her tears, he kissed the moist lids of her eyes. Afterward, he kissed her lips, lightly at first and then with ardor. Her body sparked his flesh and he felt a strange bewilderment at the twin forces that fought for possession of him, his passion for gambling and his desire for Marina.

Later, after they made love, in the deepest part of the night, Nick woke from a restless sleep to find the bed beside him empty. He called Marina's name and there wasn't any answer. He got out of bed and, shivering in the dampness, he walked through the hall, past the dark bathroom, into the parlor. He saw her sitting in a chair by the window, a faint beam of street light across her shoulders. When he bent and clasped her arms, he felt her tremble through her gown.

"Marina, come back to bed," he said gently. "You'll get chilled."

"Don't go to New York, Nick," she said quietly.

"Marina, my darling . . ."

"I'm afraid, Nick," she said. "Don't go."

"I have to go, Marina." He pleaded for her to understand. "Wherever in the world men gamble, they'll talk of this game, about the players and the stakes. You might be right that I am a little mad . . . but I could never rest if after coming this far, I drew back from the big game now."

She did not speak again and allowed him to lead her back to the bedroom. She slipped between the sheets and he crawled in beside her, taking her cold body into his arms, afraid she might draw away. But she did not move and their bodies warmed one another.

They lay together, sleepless and silent, until the first trace of daylight rimmed the shade at the window. When she rose for her work at the grocery, he pretended he was asleep.

He kept his eyes closed while she dressed. She left the bedroom and a few moments later he smelled the aroma of brewing coffee. He considered getting up and joining her to dispel the constraint the night had put between them. But he did not move.

She returned once to the bedroom and he felt her

watching him for what seemed a long time. Then he heard the front door close.

He lay there, drowsy and longing for sleep, missing Marina's body nestled beside him. He felt penitent about his deception but he was also relieved he had not again pledged a promise he knew he could not keep.

Several days later Nick and Joey left by train for New York. They were met in the cavernous Grand Central Station by an aide to Arnold Rosenberg, a taciturn man who led them to a waiting limousine. They were driven to the imposing Plaza Hotel and taken up to a suite overlooking Central Park. The aide told Nick he would pick him up again in two hours for dinner.

As the suite door closed behind him, Joey flung his cap in the air, aiming at the scrolled moldings around the ceiling of the splendid room.

"What a layout!" Joey cried. "I bet the King of England stays here when he comes to America. Hey, Nick, you suppose we got to pay for this palace?"

"This is peanuts compared to the stake for the game," Nick said. "I think our host, Mr. Rosenberg, will take care of it to get us into the proper mood."

"Well, he's got me in the mood to live like this forever." Joey flopped down on one of the plush couches. "After all the roach-ridden gyms and stinking locker rooms I been in, this place is heaven."

"Enjoy heaven," Nick said. "I'm going to take a bath."

As he lounged in the hot water, Nick felt confident and calm. He hoped the euphoria would survive the beginning of the game. He thought finally of Marina, the tension continuing between them in the last few days even though

after the night when she asked him not to go to New York,
she had not mentioned the trip again. For a moment he was
bothered by a remorse and agitation that he quickly
dismissed. He could not permit any distraction to dull
his concentration on the game.

Some time later a bellboy knocked on the door of their
suite to tell Nick the car had returned. He went down to
the lobby and the aide was there, the limousine waiting
under the fluttering canopy of the hotel marquee. A
drizzling rain was falling and the doorman held an open
umbrella over Nick's head.

He was driven to Delmonico's restaurant on East Forty-
fourth Street. Led by the maître de through the elegant
main dining room to an elevator, he was conscious of the
stares and whispers of the waiters and diners. They must
have known about the game, he thought, and were aware
he was one of the players. He imagined them wondering
how so young a man could have acquired such a stake. He
could not resist a puff of conceit.

When he entered the Scarlet Room, where the dinner
was being held, he found a magnificent banquet table
adorned with gold-flecked crystal and gold-circled china.
Before each setting, a splash of fresh flowers gleamed like a
peacock's plumage.

A group of men were gathered along a mahogany bar at
the far end of the room. Nick walked to join them and one
of the men came to greet him.

Although Nick had never met Arnold Rosenberg, the
host of the game, he had seen newspaper photos of the political kingmaker and notorious gambler they called, "The
Brain." He was less imposing than the myths about him im-

plied. He was slightly built, with pomaded hair, a sallow complexion, and a thin-lipped mouth that seemed incapable of smiling. His eyes, so frosted they seemed colorless, suggested his ruthlessness and force.

"Glad you could join us, Nick," Rosenberg said.

"I am pleased to be here, Arnold."

Those brief amenities completed, Rosenberg introduced Nick to the other men. As he shook their hands and looked into their faces, he felt the presence of men exuding confidence and power and wealth far beyond the stake the game required. A tremor of nervousness rippled in him for the first time.

There was "Earthquake" Thompson, named after winning a big game when with a brawling jubilation he shattered the table with his fist. "Tiger" Pat O'Neill was one of the most influential politicians in Tammany Hall. "Tiffany" Wolfgang, sporting huge diamonds, owned mines in South Africa. Sheik Farid Ben Hamed, in burnoose and flowing robes, had come from his sheikdom in the Middle East. Efemio Salazar owned sugar plantations in Cuba. There was Joshua Cogden, the steel magnet, and Charles Stoneham, whose railroad had built the first line across the western plains. The last two men to greet Nick were the horse breeder Lance Kingman, from Kentucky, and the yachtsman "Neptune" Daniels, from Maine. Including Nick and Rosenberg, there were eleven men. As they moved to the table for dinner, Nick thought with awe of the five and a half million dollars their stakes would total.

He ate sparingly and drank little champagne. Most of the others showed the same restraint, while the hulking men like Earthquake Thompson and Tiffany Wolfgang

ate and drank with gusto. After an array of rich desserts
and Napoleon brandy, fine Havana cigars were distributed.
As men struck matches and lit the tips, the table clouded
with swirlings of smoke.

Rosenberg dismissed the waiters with a wave of his
hand. They scurried to leave and when the door had closed
behind them, Rosenberg rose to speak.

"I want to welcome you all here." He spoke in a loud,
nasal voice. "I hope you enjoyed the best food and wine
that money could buy."

Earthquake belched noisily and the men laughed. Rosenberg glared at him.

"The whole town has been buzzing about this game for
days," Rosenberg went on. "Hurley mentioned it twice in
his column in a week and even the President of these
United States doesn't get mentioned in Hurley more than
that. Busboys, waiters, cabbies, and sports all over the city
are saying it's the greatest gathering of high rollers in the
city's history."

There was a scatter of applause but most of the men
puffed on their cigars and sipped their brandies.

"When do we begin, Arnold?" Tiger O'Neill said.

"Tomorrow afternoon," Rosenberg said. "Each one of
you will be picked up at your hotel."

"Where will we play?" Tiffany Wolfgang asked.

"Nobody knows that but me," Rosenberg said somberly.
"You'll find out tomorrow. But I want to assure you that
every precaution for safety has been taken. A lot of police
captains are going to take vacations this year on the dough
we've paid out to protect this game."

"The boys in your game at Saratoga last year thought
they were protected," Earthquake sneered. "They say the

gang that knocked you over got more than a half million from the pot."

"I know all about Saratoga!" Rosenberg flushed angrily. "I'm going to catch the finks who pulled that heist and give them a concrete berth in the river!" He made an effort to calm himself. "Don't worry about this game. God help any bastards who try to knock us over."

"Do we set the money up as usual?" Tiffany asked.

"Right," Rosenberg said. "Your money and drafts will be exchanged before the game for packets of ten thousand dollars. The Merchants Bank has bonded every packet."

"The play is strictly cash, isn't it, Arnold?" Lance Kingman asked.

"Absolutely."

"That includes you, Arnold, doesn't it?" Earthquake asked sharply.

Rosenberg stared at Earthquake Thompson and Nick saw the hatred in Rosenberg's face. He remembered the man had a reputation for playing with markers that others found difficult to collect and were afraid to complain about.

"That includes me," Rosenberg said. He brooded a moment longer. "That's enough for now," he said. "This evening you're my guests. I got special box seats for the *Ziegfeld Follies* at the Herald Square. And we're all invited backstage after the show for a party with the girls."

Earthquake slammed his big fist on the table in jubilation and a few other men responded with approval. Most of them remained silent. They had not come, Nick knew, for the ordinary pleasures of food, drink, and women, although they might accept all three as diversions. They had come to play the queen of games, the unmatched excitement of fast action and high stakes.

They were driven by limousines from Delmonico's to the Herald Square. They entered the theater through a stage door and were escorted to the best box seats in the house.

Nick sat in one of the boxes and watched the colorful spectacle of the *Follies*. Looking at the faces of the men around him watching the feathered and sequined dancers, the statuesque models with diamonds sparkling on their nipples, Nick realized how skillfully Rosenberg had used the gratuitous offer of hospitality to his own advantage. Sated with food and drink and titillated at the prospect of a night of celebration and sex, the players would not be at their sharpest for the game the next day. Nick could understand the beguiling allure of the lovely girls. There was a black-haired young dancer in the chorus who reminded him of Marina. She had a slender, flawless back that sloped into shapely buttocks and long legs. He thought fleetingly of her warm flesh easing the chills in his body, loosening the knots of tension he felt in his body as the hour for the game grew closer.

At the end of the show, Arnold led them down the stairs for the party backstage. Nick slipped out the stage door and walked up the alley to the front of the theater to hail a taxi to take him back to the hotel. The last small groups of theater patrons were dispersing, and under the darkened marquee, he saw a girl apparently waiting for someone to pick her up. She wore only a thin, cloth coat and the damp, raw night made her huddle near the doors for warmth. As he passed her he recognized the dancer from the chorus who had reminded him of Marina. He admired her for not remaining to entertain the visitors. On an impulse he paused and returned to where she waited. He pulled a sheaf of bills from his pocket and peeled off a thousand-dollar bill, which he handed to the girl.

"Take this, honey," he said gently. "Buy yourself a fur coat. You'll catch pneumonia dressed like that."

The girl looked at him and then stared at the bill in his hand. When she noticed the denomination, she looked up at him with her eyes blazing.

"You sonofabitch!" she cried. "I know you Broadway wise guys peddling your stage money to make the girls! Go to hell!"

Nick looked at her in astonishment, started to protest and explain, and then remained silent. He put the bill back into his pocket, thinking wryly that even pretty young cynics should not be rewarded for their lack of faith.

He saw a taxi coming and he moved to the curb and hailed it. He entered and closed the door. He looked back at the girl still huddled under the marquee. When she saw him watching her, she poked her finger stiffly into the air, flashing him a final, obscene gesture of farewell.

At noon the following day, the limousine picked Nick and Joey up. After driving for about ten minutes, the car turned into a garage.

"Is this where the game will take place?" Nick asked.

The aide sitting beside the driver shook his head.

The car pulled forward where several men waited. One opened the limousine door for them.

"You'll change cars here, Mr. Dandolos," the man said,

and motioned to a less conspicuous automobile a short distance away.

They walked to the other car, joined by a driver and a
man riding beside him. They emerged from the garage on a
different street from the one on which they had entered.
Moving through a quiet, residential area, the driver swung
the car into a driveway beside a three-story building
enclosed by a stone fence. Nick caught a glimpse of a sign
that read, Greengarden Funeral Home.

The car pulled around the rear of the house to a
canopied door. Several men in dark suits waited there and
one of them, decorous as an undertaker, opened the car
door.

"Good afternoon, Mr. Dandolos," he said. "Please come
this way."

Nick and Joey followed him through a corridor into an
anteroom.

"Forgive me, Mr. Dandolos," the man apologized, "but
we got to frisk you here for any weapons. In case, you understand, a man loses his temper during the game."

"Go ahead," Nick said. The man searched him
thoroughly and did the same to Joey.

"Did you find any weapons on the other distinguished
gentlemen?" Nick asked.

"A few small caliber revolvers and one stiletto, which
we checked until the end of the game," the man said. "All
carried, we were assured, for self-defense."

"Of course," Nick said, and winked at Joey.

A moment later, attired in a solemn black suit and black
tie, Rosenberg joined them.

"We lost you last night, Nick," he said as they shook
hands. "You missed a great party."

"I had a headache and went back to the hotel."

Rosenberg motioned Nick to follow him. They passed between the drapes into a large parlor. Nick was startled to see a wake in progress. There was a platform bearing a bronze casket, the lid open, wreaths of flowers standing along the wall on either side. A score of mourners sat among the rows of chairs.

"Is this real?" Nick asked in a low voice.

"As real as we could make it," Rosenberg said with a smirk. "The daisies cost us a thousand bucks." He caught Nick staring at the mourners. "Out of work bit actors and actresses," he said. "We hired them for as many days as the game lasts, telling them there might be bigger parts later on. Why we even got a young Talmudist who needs the dough to continue his studies."

Pausing at the casket, Rosenberg pointed gaily at the corpse.

"Harry the Hip," Rosenberg said. "He ran some horse bets on the East Side and took in numbers on the weekend. We bought him from the hospital that was going to carve him up for a class of croakers. Did old Harry a favor. The undertaker, a personal friend of mine, did a hell of a job on him. The ugly little bastard never looked better."

Rosenberg laughed raucously, a discordant sound in the somber, shaded room. He pointed to the draped base on which the casket rested.

"If anything goes wrong," he said, "the dough goes into a vault under the casket and we all join the mourners. Anyone coming in will find nothing but a wake." He finished, eager as a child for some commendation.

"Very clever and resourceful, Arnold," Nick said. He noticed Joey staring uneasily at the casket and corpse.

They walked around the casket and passed through a
short corridor to a room occupied by a dozen bodyguards
and companions of the other players.

"Your boy stays with them." Rosenberg motioned
brusquely at Joey. "Only players go on from here."

Nick nodded and Joey clasped his hand in an earnest
farewell. "I'll be close if you need me, Nick." His voice
warned Rosenberg against any intrigue.

Rosenberg led Nick through another hallway. The
building seemed a maze of corridors and rooms, so circui-
tous a labyrinth that Nick lost his sense of direction.
Through another heavily paneled door, they entered a spacious room dominated by a great crap table in the center.
Along the walls, smoking and talking or having a drink at a
bar, were the gamblers Nick had met the night before. Almost at once he absorbed the smells of tension, the almost
audible vibrations of anxiety and fear that sparked his own
emotion.

"Donovan over there is from the bank." Rosenberg
pointed to a man at a table. "He'll give you the packets of
money in exchange for your dough. Then have a drink, if
you like. I'll be back in a few moments."

After Nick had changed his cashier's check for the ten-
thousand-dollar packets which he stored in an attaché case,
he mingled with the other players. As they barely acknowledged his presence, offering only curt nods before
returning to their conversations, he understood they considered him a young upstart. His only credentials rested in
his half-million-dollar stake.

As he stood alone, Earthquake Thompson came to speak
to him, reaching out one of his hamlike hands to clap Nick
genially on the shoulder.

"Glad to see you, Greek," he said. "I thought last night maybe you got cold feet and decided to high-tail it back to Chicago."

"My feet are always quite warm," Nick smiled. "I won't leave for Chicago until I finish our business here."

Earthquake laughed and winked at him broadly before turning away, Nick walked to stand beside the crap table. He stared down at the green felt of the layout marked by squares and boxes, numbers and odds. After a few minutes he sensed that the surface of the table was alive, numerals and lines wavering and glowing eerily before his eyes. Shaken by the apparition, he turned quickly away.

When Rosenberg returned to the room, escorting Sheik Farid Ben Hamed, the roster was complete. They moved to their assigned places around the table, each man stacking his packets of cash on the ledge before him.

"We got two men at the table who will run the game," Rosenberg said. "One of them is Larry Sims here, from the Spa at Saratoga, the finest goddam stickman in the business." He paused, as if challenging anyone to question his judgment. "The other man is Mick Garland, one of the best pay-out men in the world. Any of you played at the Manchester Club in London know what I'm talking about. He came from England just for this game. Larry and Mick will tab the throws and pay-outs and their word goes."

The men nodded silently, closing on the table in a tighter circle.

"You should all know the rules we play by for Open Craps," Rosenberg went on, "but for one or two newcomers, I'll repeat them. Bets have to be down before the roll begins and no 'gating.' Both dice got to strike the

boards or wagers are a standoff. We'll break fifteen minutes
every four hours, and a man gets only five minutes to go to
the can. After that he's docked a thousand bucks a minute.
And if a player gets sick, goes blind or deaf from shock or
fear, if for any goddam reason he can't hold his place and
play, he's ruled out of the game and his dough is split
among the rest. Finally," Rosenberg paused and looked at
them all so balefully, Nick felt a shiver up his back, "any
man caught using 'busters,' switching or palming them in
or out, forfeits his play and has his dough split among the
rest. Then the bastard will have to be carried out because
I'll also break his legs."

The men looked at one another. Neptune Daniels and
Tiger O'Neill lit cigars and a few spirals of smoke drifted
toward the ceiling, circling the bright overhead light like a
noose. Lance Kingman coughed nervously and Charles
Stoneham, trying to laugh casually, managed only a tense
squeak. Earthquake Thompson whispered a few hoarse and
hasty words to Efemio Salazar, who stood beside him. On
the other side of Earthquake, Sheik Farid Ben Hamed
raised his arm, the cloth of his robe falling away from his
wrist. He touched his long brown fingers to his forehead
and then swept them down to rest for an instant over his
heart.

"New shooter," the stickman called. "New shooter coming out."

Tiffany, who had won the toss, reached into the bowl
containing a score of dice and brought out two. He
checked then swiftly by spinning the corners of each cube
between his thumb and forefinger. Holding them as rev-

erently as sanctified relics, he bet forty thousand dollars. His bet was faded quickly and the players made side wagers. At a nod from the stickman Tiffany cupped the dice in his palm. He began to shake them, slowly at first and then rapidly, his hand cutting a swift, short arc. He hurled the dice against the boards. Bouncing off, they whirled to a stop on the green felt surface.

"Nine," the stickman called. "Shooter's point is nine."

The pay-out man adjusted the wagers and new bets were made. Tiffany threw the dice again.

"Nine right back with five and four," the stickman called. "Nine a winner."

Tiffany chortled in triumph and retrieved the dice once more. On his next throw he hurled an eight. Nick made his first wager, betting ten thousand dollars that the shooter wouldn't make his point. Tiffany busted and Nick won his bet. The dice passed on.

"New shooter coming out," the stickman called.

Efemio Salazar picked up the dice and bet thirty thousand dollars. His bet was faded, the players wagering more swiftly. Nick bet twenty thousand dollars the shooter would not throw a pass. The stickman nodded and Efemio let the dice fly.

"Eee-oh-le-ven," the stickman called. "Pay the front line winner."

Nick's twenty thousand dollars was swept away. He waited out the next play and Efemio threw a six. Nick bet another twenty thousand dollars against the shooter. Two throws later, Efemio made his six. Dismayed at the rapid disappearance of forty thousand dollars from his stake, Nick delayed betting as Efemio hurled the dice again.

When he busted on craps, Nick learned the grim lesson
that the mercurial velocity of the game did not permit hesitation or indecision.

In the first hour the men played in a silence broken only
by an infrequent whisper. The sounds from the table were
the packets of money rustling across the felt, the dice rattling in the shooter's palm, cracking noisily against the
boards, and, finally, the stickman's sharp, clear call. As they
passed into the second hour of play, the tempo of the game
escalated, the whispers becoming grumblings and pleas. Finally, their voices rose into a bitter and jubilant clamor.
Nick heard his cries joined to the others as if it were coming from someone else. In the same way, his fingers flut-
tered away and then returned to his body as if they were
animated by a life and purpose of their own.

"Eight," the stickman called. "Shooter's point is eight."

Nick bet against the shooter, sometimes hedging with
side wagers. He lost on a few throws, won some others, his
stake remaining about even. Preoccupied with his own
miniature arena of action, when he looked out and saw the
packets of money like ridges of mountains across the surface of the table, he was shocked. He calculated swiftly
that a million dollars was changing hands with each roll.
The sum mesmerized him and he had to make an effort to
concentrate on the trajectories of the dice.

"Seven," the stickman called. "Pay the front line."

As Nick's turn came to shoot, he held the dice for an instant, conscious of the others watching him. He sought
some mystical affinity between the cubes and his spirit but
their coldness and indifference repelled him. He passed
them on, choosing to bet against another shooter.

"Six," the stickman called as Tiger O'Neill threw the dice for a hundred thousand dollars. "Shooter's point is six."

Tiger busted two throws later. He mumbled incoherently, his cheeks gray as gravestone. The dice moved on.

Nick had gambled enough to know the way time accelerated in a game when eyes and ears were hooked to the play. But he had never before experienced action where despair pillaged elation so swiftly. In a single second's toss a gleeful winner could become a shattered loser.

"Craps," the stickman called. "Shooter busts on craps."

After they played four hours, the stickman called a fifteen-minute break. A few men rushed to the toilets while others had a sandwich and a drink. Nick washed his face with cold water, trying to cool the heat throbbing behind his eyes. Before the lull ended, the players gathered back at the table as if they found the inaction unbearable.

When they resumed playing, as if to make up for lost time, the pace of the action quickened, uncertainty and timidity plundered as the players bet and threw. The instant the dice ceased to roll after a toss, the pay-out man swept the table like a wave. The players shouted and cried their curses and prayers. Only the stickman's call continued a monodic, unruffled chant.

The dice passed to Earthquake Thompson, his face flushed and drenched with sweat. He clutched them in his huge fist, his knuckles whitening as he squeezed them hard. He swept them beneath his lips, blowing a beseeching breath upon them.

"Here's a goddam toss of the devil's dominoes for guts

and glory," he said. He fumbled and pushed packets of his money onto the front line until he wagered all of the one hundred and fifty thousand dollars he had left. The players divided his bet to fade him, Nick staking twenty thousand dollars Earthquake would not make a pass. Afterward, everyone fell silent, understanding that if he busted, Earthquake would be the first man driven from the game.

Earthquake rattled the dice in his hand for a turbulent instant and then catapulted them toward the boards. Cracking like gunshots, they spun off to a stop.

"See-eh-ven, a winner," the stickman called. "Pay the front line."

Earthquake let his bet ride and the men faded him again. Nick bet thirty thousand dollars that Earthquake would not pass.

"Here go the Memphis bones again!" Earthquake cried. "I'm hot now and watch them smoke!" He fired the dice once more.

"Eee-oh-le-ven, a winner," the stickman called. "Pay the front line."

Earthquake yelled in delight, his cheeks puffed and crimson as plums.

"Come on you twits and turkeys!" he shouted. "I'm crap shooting all the way, grit and iron in my balls, screwing everything in sight!"

More cautiously now, yet unable to resist the lure of the big man's destruction, the players laid down their wagers against his mounting stake. Nick bet forty thousand dollars against him. The two heaviest winners in the game to that time, Rosenberg and Tiffany covered the greater portion of the six-hundred-thousand-dollar bet.

Earthquake launched the dice again.

"See-eh-ven, a winner," the stickman called. The lament

of the players rolled off Earthquake as he fondled the packets of money piled like a mountain on the table before him.

"A million, two hundred thousand dollars on the line," the pay-out man said.

Earthquake let his breath out slowly. A sudden faltering, perhaps a foreboding shadowed his eyes, and he fumbled to draw some of his winnings from the line.

"You were going all the way!" Rosenberg said harshly. "Guts and smoke in your balls, you said! Are you making peepee on the fire now?"

"Goddam you, Rosenberg!" Earthquake cried angrily. "I'll show you what guts are like!" He shoved back the money he had withdrawn from the line. "Let the million, two hundred thousand dollars ride! Every last dollar!" He flashed his thumb in an obscene gesture at Rosenberg. "Now let's see if you got the fucking balls to meet me head on!"

Rosenberg calmly counted out the seven hundred thousand he had left in his stake and winnings. When he had pushed in his final packet, his scornful eyes challenged the remaining players.

The players, led by Tiffany, faded the balance of the big man's bet. As Nick joined them, he was troubled that Rosenberg had taunted Earthquake into the play.

Sheik Farid Ben Hamed looked gravely at Earthquake.

"Allah admires a brave man, my friend," he said quietly. "But in the words of the prophet, even courage cannot save a man destined by his fate to be destroyed."

With the table of men waiting motionless and silent, Earthquake raised his head, closing his eyes in entreatment and prayer. He opened his eyes and hoisted the dice, exposing them in the palm of his hand. In the glare of the lamp, they gleamed like sorcerous charms. He closed his fist around them, shaking them slowly and then with fury until echoes rattled and cracked from the corners. When he fired them violently at the table, they exploded off the boards and flew apart. Elbowing and shoving men aside, Earthquake lunged forward to read the cubes.

"See-eh-ven." The stickman's voice quavered for the first time. "See-eh-ven, a winner."

Earthquake Thompson reared back.

"Oh, Jesus!" he cried. "Oh, sweet Jesus!"

Rosenberg stood silent, his face shocked and bloodless.

"I broke you, Arnold!" Earthquake's voice trembled in elation. "All the years you beat me and, finally, goddam you . . . goddam you, Arnold, I broke you now!"

Watching him gloating and savoring his triumph, Nick saw the big man shudder and stare with bewilderment at the men around the table. His hand fumbled to his chest, his fingers groping at the region over his heart. A bubble of saliva, thick as honey, trickled down his chin. He whimpered in terror as another, stronger shudder whipped his body. He collapsed to his knees and made a final, frantic effort to clutch the edge of the table. Then his fingers slipped off and he tumbled like a stricken bull to the floor.

Nick and a number of others moved quickly to his aid but Rosenberg waved them away. Reaching under the table, he pressed a buzzer, and a moment later, several men hurried into the room. Rosenberg motioned at Earthquake on the floor.

"Carry him into the parlor," he spoke calmly, in command again. "Call Doc Sarila."

Bending down and straining to lift Earthquake's huge form, one man gripped him around the neck and two men grasped his ankles. They heaved to raise him and staggered toward the door. His arms dragged along the floor and his head swayed limply. With a grim, chilled certainty, Nick knew he was dead.

"The doc will look after him," Rosenberg said quietly. "By the rules of the game, we split his dough." He gestured to the pay-out man, who divided the huge mound of winnings.

No one at the table protested as the pay-out man gave him a share. When he had finished, Sheik Farid Ben Hamed and Efemio Salazar, who had been standing on either side of Earthquake Thompson, moved together to close the breach.

"New shooter," the stickman called. "New shooter coming out."

Nick waved at the stickman and left the table, crossing the room to a toilet. He hurried inside, locked the door, and crouched over the bowl, nausea twisting in his belly.

Above the stool was a window, the panes latticed with bars. He gripped the handles and heaved, determined to break the glass if it would not open. Then the wood wrenched free from the frame and he felt the night warm with the streamings of new summer.

Peering up at the sky, straining to define the stars, he trembled on the verge of some revelation just beyond his grasp. Between the cubicle, narrow and dark as a grave, and the vast night, he struggled to understand the link. The meaning receded leaving only a sad and unsolved riddle.

He unlocked the door and walked back into the room to rejoin the game.

CHAPTER 10

Ten days after they had departed for the big game in New York, Nick and Joey returned to Chicago. When they emerged from the train at Union Station, and walked up the ramp to the noise and traffic of the city, a gleaming Rolls-Royce with a chauffeur in livery waited for them. They climbed into the rear seat and he drove them to Halsted Street.

With the elegant automobile parked outside the No-worry Club, word spread rapidly up and down the street that Nick had returned in a gaudy and splendid triumph. A crowd of well-wishers swarmed about the Rolls while others pressed into the club. As the throng became a mob, pulling and shoving at one another to get to Nick, he and Joey fled to the kitchen. Korakas defended the door and stoutly turned back any of the celebrants who tried to follow them.

The news of Nick's victorious return was carried to Prince Pierre, Loukanas, and Big Gorgio, and they hurried from their casinos to the No-worry Club. Big Gorgio pushed roughly through the crowd that clustered around the Rolls-Royce. He smacked the glossy silver hood of the automobile and whistled loudly.

"Goddam, what a chariot!" he cried. "Must have cost Nick a bundle!"

He rejoined Prince Pierre and Loukanas, the three of them entering the club, their bodyguards cutting a swath through the jam of celebrants. Big Gorgio hammered with his fist on the barred kitchen door. Korakas opened it warily and motioned the owners inside while the bodyguards took up positions to guard the entrance.

The casino owners found Nick sitting in a small circle of men that included, in addition to Joey and Korakas, Banopoulos, Dr. Samyotis, Gikas, and Spiro.

"The automobile is magnificent, Nick!" Prince Pierre said with fervor. "Worthy of a mafioso or a king!"

"I cannot wait to hear the details of the game," Loukanas said, his jowls quivering with excitement. "The stakes must have been enormous!"

"I don't give a shit about the details!" Big Gorgio said. "All I want to know, Nick, is how much you won?"

There was a commotion at the alley door as several persistent celebrants tried to enter. Korakas hurried to keep them out, bracing his stocky shoulders against the frame of wood.

"Later, boys," he said soothingly. "You'll see Nick later. He's resting now."

He leaned against the closed door and folded his arms.

"Come on, Nick!" Big Gorgio said hoarsely. "Don't keep us in suspense! How much eastern dough did you clip from those bastards?"

"The truth is they clipped me," Nick said quietly. "I didn't win. I lost."

Big Gorgio kept grinning as if he had not heard or understood Nick's words. Prince Pierre stared at Nick in disbelief.

"Lost!" Loukanas said shrilly. "Lost!"

"Nick lost?" Big Gorgio snarled at Loukanas. "You must be nuts!"

"He said he lost!" Loukanas cried.

"He's kidding! Nick's kidding!" Big Gorgio shouted. "Cut the shit, Nick, and tell us the truth."

Prince Pierre stared at the unsmiling visages of the men seated around Nick. He looked at Korakas, a grim sentinel guarding the door.

"He's telling the truth," Prince Pierre said gravely. "He lost."

"Oh, my God." Loukanas swayed as if he were going to collapse and then clutched for a chair. He slumped to the seat and stared in horror at Nick.

"What about the goddam car parked outside?" Big Gorgio shouted again. "That's no fucking loser's buggy!"

"A consolation gift from Arnold Rosenberg, who cleaned us all out," Nick shrugged wryly. "The man's sense of irony was tickled by seeing that each of the losers got one."

For a few stunned moments, the owners were silent, the only sounds in the kitchen coming from the clash and clamor inside the club. Joey rose and went to stand beside Nick's chair, his face sympathetic and forlorn.

"The fates apportion losses as well as victories, gentlemen," Banopoulos said sternly. "You are all gamblers and should not be surprised at that fact."

"That's what I've always said." Gikas nodded somberly. "The cemetery is final proof."

Korakas abandoned his post at the door and came to the circle of men.

"This isn't a goddam wake!" Korakas said indignantly. "This trip they only took Nick's dough, not his skill or his spirit! You can be sure Nick the Greek will play again!"

"Of course that is true!" Banopoulos cried. "One defeat does not lose a war! Nick has shown he could win dynamic victories and now he proves that he can absorb, with grace and Promethean courage, even a shattering defeat!" He leaped from his chair. "There is a marvelous moral here! I must compose an editorial at once!"

He left hurriedly through the alley door.

"Well, I better get back to the barbershop," Spiro said, and winked at Nick. "Come on over for a haircut and shave. You know your credit is always good with me."

"What will you do with the car, Nick?" Prince Pierre asked.

"Sell it as fast as I can find a solvent buyer," Nick said. "The proceeds should provide a solid stake for my next game." He gestured reassuringly at the owners. "Don't worry about your money. You'll get it all back."

Big Gorgio laughed raucously.

"Goddam right!" he said. "I'm not worried! We had you on your ass once and you came back to take us!" He smirked at Loukanas. "Those shits in the East can't be any tougher sports than us!"

Prince Pierre nodded in agreement and Dr. Samyotis muttered approval. While Korakas beamed, Loukanas stared at Nick with a nervous resurgence of awe.

A few moments later Nick left the kitchen by the alley door to escape the crowd in the club and crossed the street to the Athens Wholesale Grocery. He entered the store eager to see Marina and a clerk told him she wasn't there.

Hearing his voice, Rantoulis emerged from the small office in the rear. He stared at Nick in puzzlement and distress.

"First, I heard you won a fortune," he said. "Then word came you lost it all. In God's name, which story is true?"

"I lost," Nick said impatiently. "Where is Marina?"

"You lost it all," Rantoulis whispered. He stood dazed as if he were unable to comprehend the immensity of such a defeat.

"Mr. Rantoulis, where is Marina? Is she ill? Is she at home?"

"She isn't home and she isn't ill," Rantoulis said. Something about his somber countenance cut Nick like the blade of a knife.

"Where is she then?" he cried.

"She's gone," Rantoulis said in a low voice. "She left the city three days after you left for New York. She took her clothing and gave up her apartment. I don't know where she's gone or if she's coming back."

Nick felt a cold unlike anything he had ever known chill his bones and blood.

"Don't lie to me now," Nick pleaded. "I love her and I must know where she has gone."

"I don't know where she is," Rantoulis said mournfully. "She told nobody so you would not be able to follow her. I swear to God, I don't know where she is."

In the next few weeks, as summer spun its hot, moist web across the city, Nick and Joey, helped by Korakas and a few other friends, struggled to uncover Marina's trail. They carried her photographs to train and bus depots, trying to find a ticket agent or conductor who remembered seeing her. They checked with friends of

Rantoulis and his wife's and with their relatives in other cities. Every path led to a dead end.

Nick brooded and waited for Marina to relent and send him some word. From his first feelings of loss and remorse, he grew bitter, alternating between pity for himself and anger at Marina for abandoning him. Even as he tried to convince himself he was better off alone, their union doomed by her lack of sympathy for his aspirations and needs, he found himself peering wistfully into the faces of other young women on the street, seeking resemblances to Marina.

He spent many hours gambling, grateful for the swift passage of hours that produced. He doubled and tripled the stake he had obtained when he had sold the car. But the pleasure and excitement of the games were gone.

The worst times for him were the dark and solitary hours of the night. In those sad and sleepless times he remembered the fragile loveliness of Marina's face and the haunting echoes of her soft voice. After a while even his breathing seemed burdened with despair.

One such night, several hours past midnight, when he read in the small bedroom of the Korakases' apartment, where he had returned to avoid the loneliness of hotel rooms, there was a low knock on his door. He called an answer and Lambri entered, wearing a cotton robe over her nightgown. She came to sit on the edge of his bed, pressing his knee through the blanket, an endearing caress that reminded him of his mother's touch when he was a child.

"I thought perhaps some tea," she said. "Or a little warm soup to make you sleepy."

He shook his head. She was silent for a moment.

"Niko . . . Niko," she said quietly. "I watch you suffering and I am sorry for you. Yet I wonder when you will finish with this madness?"

"How can you call it madness, Lambri?" he asked in aggravation. "I miss Marina and I am trying to find her and why should that be madness?"

"She is gone, Niko," Lambri said. "She left to get away from you."

"But I love her!" Nick said earnestly. "I must find her and explain again how much I love her! If she wishes to leave me again, all right, she can leave. But I must talk to her first!"

Lambri shook her head somberly.

"I have lived sixty-four years, Niko." She spoke in a calm, patient voice. "I still find myself astonished at the way you men work things out in your heads. You knew she loved you. You had many chances to prove you loved her. You wanted her, I know, but you also wanted that cheap and fickle life that is the greatest madness of all . . ."

He tried to interrupt her but she waved him silent.

"Let me finish what I came to say," she said. "I love you, Niko, as if you were my son, but I tell you that you are wrong. You feel loss but you also feel guilt and remorse because you drove her away."

He struggled to accept the truth of her words.

"I have done stupid things, I know, Lambri," he said contritely. "I understood how strongly she felt about them. Yet, I never thought she'd leave me, I kept believing we would work things out. The important thing is that I love her."

"So you love her," Lambri shrugged. "When men wish to excuse the pain they cause women, they say they love them. You love her but you have also hurt her. That's

God's truth and now you must leave her alone to decide if she loves you enough to come back."

"What am I supposed to do while she makes up her mind?" Nick asked bitterly. "Sit here and wait? Night after night, just suffer and wait?"

"Take a trip someplace," Lambri said. "Get away from these wretched streets, this devil's playground. When she lets us know where she is or when she returns, we will let you know." She paused, shaking her head, and he saw the glint of tears in her eyes. "Listen to me now, Niko," she beseeched him. "Marina loves you, but try and understand her pain too. Give her a chance . . ."

Unable to refute the stern sense of Lambri's words, Nick reluctantly gave up his quest for Marina. He made plans to sail for Europe.

He was grateful, in a way, to leave. A frenzy seemed to have captured the city and the country, as if the Spartan years of the war were finally wearing off and people once again beginning to enjoy life. Everything seemed to be moving to a faster, wilder beat. The violence of the continuing gang war between the Gennas and the O'Donnells was pushed off the front pages of newspapers by stories about political bribes and deals, swindles in gold markets, real estate, Indian lands.

With each week that passed, as well, the futility of enforcing Prohibition was exposed. Several speakeasys opened along Halsted Street, a constant stream of patrons moving in and out of the iron-grilled doors. While in numerous neighborhood basements and garages, duplicating the activity taking place across the country, illicit stills flourished. For as modest an investment as five-

hundred dollars, a commercial still could be set up that
would produce fifty or a hundred remunerative gallons of
bootleg liquor a day.

Dr. Samyotis, permitted to sell alcohol on doctor's prescriptions, was becoming a wealthy man. Spiro, the barber,
converted the back of his barbershop into a still, spending
more time selling and delivering booze than he did cutting
hair. Even Korakas would have eagerly joined the alky
cookers but for the ominous threats of Lambri to "blow up
any still he set up."

"She'd do it too," Korakas told Nick grimly. "If the
Revenue boys had a half dozen like her, the bootleggers
would be crying for mercy in a week."

So, in the middle of July, Nick said good-by to his
friends, rejecting Joey's pleas that he go with him.

"I need you here to keep watching for her, Joey," Nick
told him. "You and Korakas are like my eyes and my ears.
When you hear something, I will depend on you to let me
know."

A week later he boarded the liner *Semiramis*, sailing
from New York at dawn. Standing at the rail on the deck
as the ship pulled slowly from the pier, a widening expanse
of water separating them from the port, he watched the
land receding. When everything was obscured, he felt
himself drifting in a gray, ghostly mist that carried him
further and further from his beloved.

He traveled to Greece, was reunited warmly with his
godfather's family, remaining with them long enough to
make arrangements for them to depart for America in the
fall. He journeyed again from Greece, through the Adri-
atic Sea to Venice. From that ancient city of canals putrid

with offal and garbage, he rode a train north through the white-capped and frosted mountain towns of Switzerland and on through the Alps into France. He paused for a while in Paris because he was weary of traveling.

He found the city a shimmering landscape for lovers. Young men and women walked arm in arm along the boulevards or embraced on the grassy banks of the Seine. Seeing them absorbed in one another filled him with longing for Marina. He planned to move on to London as soon as he received an answer to his cable from Korakas and Joey. Their earlier letters, waiting for him at central points on his journey, contained no word about Marina. A despair came over him when he thought he might never see her again.

To pass the time, he began to frequent the casinos of Paris, the Capucine and Haussman clubs, playing roulette quietly, taking his winnings and losses impassively.

One evening when he was dining alone in the gilded hall of the Haussman Club, the casino director came to his table.

"Forgive my interrupting your dinner, Monsieur Dandolos," he said. "A historical event is going on at this moment in the North Room. A compatriot of yours, the famous Greek millionaire gambler Monsieur Zarakas, is dealing the bank in baccarat against the Aga Khan. Zarakas has already lost ten million francs. Tonight may be the first time his bank has ever been broken."

Nick had heard of Zarakas during his stay in Paris but had not seen or met the legendary gambler. Now, curious, he rose and followed the director.

In the North Room all the gaming tables had been abandoned, the players, dealers, and croupiers clustered in a si-

lent throng about one central table. The director led Nick
through the crowd, murmuring a polite but determined
request for passage. They paused at a vantage point that
permitted Nick to watch the two players who confronted
one another across the green baize table.

Zarakas was a small, slim, and dapper man with coiffured
hair, thick sideburns, and a neatly trimmed, pointed beard.
In the pale oval of his face, his dark eyes gleamed like nug-
gets of quartz.

The Aga Khan was a mountainous man, a mass of flesh
overflowing the arms of his chair. His face was the shade
of ripe green olives, his white hair and white shaggy eyebrows sweeping together in a patch that almost obscured
his forehead. Behind his tinted glasses, his large, bulbous
eyes seemed about to burst through the lenses.

Zarakas, the baccarat shoe before him, prepared to deal.

"The sky is the limit, Your Highness," Zarakas said
quietly. A ripple of suspense swept the crowd. Despite his
huge losses, Zarakas was not restricting the amount of any
wager the Aga Khan wished to make.

The monarch stared at Zarakas approvingly. When he
spoke, his low, hoarse voice rumbled from his chest as if it
were emerging from some deep cavern.

"I wager ten million francs," he said.

A gasp shook the watchers, awe at the fantastic sum involved, and a flutter of sympathy for Zarakas. But the trim
little Greek remained as calm as if the enormous bet had
been only a thousand francs.

A slight movement of his eyebrows accepted the wager.
He dealt from the shoe, sliding out two cards for the Aga
Khan and two for himself. The Aga Khan moved one
fleshy-fingered hand slowly toward the cards. He raised

the corners a fraction to examine them. With a quick snap
of his fingers, he flipped them over to reveal a jack of
spades and an eight of hearts.

"*La Petite*," he said crisply, and the crowd stirred with
exhilaration. He had drawn the second best hand in baccarat. Only a nine could beat him.

The murmurs and whispers faded into silence. The Aga
Khan waited, unruffled and impassive. Zarakas turned over
his cards to reveal a king of hearts and a queen of spades,
both cards useless. A few murmurs of commiseration rose
from the spectators.

"It looks like the end for Zarakas," the director whispered to Nick. "The odds against his draw are overwhelming."

Watching the little Greek, for an instant Nick saw what
he was certain few in the crowd noticed, an involuntary
pulsing in his temple, a vein wriggling like a tiny, frantic
worm. The lapse was swift and slight and gone quickly,
but it revealed to Nick the tension Zarakas endured while,
on the surface, he appeared chiseled from marble.

Zarakas moved his slender fingers toward the shoe. He
dealt himself a third card. As it fell face up, a stunned gasp
burst from the watchers. Zarakas had drawn a nine of diamonds and had won.

He stared calmly across the table at the Aga Khan,
whose eyes seemed hooked to the red nine.

"*La Grande*," Zarakas said softly.

The spectators gave up any effort to contain their noisy
excitement and the director looked up to heaven.

"*Mon Dieu!*" he cried fervently. "*Magnifique!*"

The Aga Khan lurched his bulk away from the table.
Two attendants hurried to places on either side of him and

helped him rise slowly and ponderously from his chair. He stood there, a black-clad, shapeless behemoth with a Gargantuan head that concealed his neck.

"You escape my traps, Monsieur Zarakas, like a swift and cunning fox."

"You may catch me yet, Your Highness." Zarakas spoke with elaborate politeness while his dark eyes sparkled.

"Yes, yes," the Aga Khan said. "Even the craftiest fox cannot escape the good hunter forever. Perhaps next month, in Cannes or Deauville, I will try again."

"I am always at your disposal, Your Highness." Zarakas bowed slightly.

As the Aga Khan lumbered away from the table, escorted by his entourage, the crowd of well-wishers swarmed in to surround and congratulate Zarakas. After a few hectic moments he managed, smiling and nodding, to break free of them and hurried to escape. As he passed by Nick and the director, the director reached out to grasp the little Greek's shoulders, bending to kiss each of his cheeks in zealous felicitation.

"You honor our club, Monsieur Zarakas!" he cried.

"Thank you, André," Zarakas said, and smiled at Nick, revealing small, well-formed white teeth. He turned to move on.

"May I delay you just an instant longer," the director said, "and present Monsieur Dandolos from the United States of America. I roused him from his dinner to come and watch your magnificent play."

"You are wicked, André, disturbing the poor man's dinner." Zarakas reproved the director as he shook Nick's hand cordially. Nick was beguiled by his sparkling eyes, which seemed able to pierce another's thoughts.

"The game I watched confirms the exemplary things I

have heard about you since coming to Paris, Mr. Zarakas," Nick said.

"I have heard about you too, Mr. Dandolos," Zarakas said with a wink. "Nick the Greek, *non?*" He laughed heartily. "They only call me 'that goddamed Greek!'" He waved to the director. "I will take Mr. Dandolos to my suite," he said. "Please send us a maître de and a champagne steward and keep all visitors away." He looked uneasily at the crowd that seemed to be gathering to pursue him again and grasped Nick's arm. "Come, my young friend, let us flee before we are buried alive under the hot flesh of André's patrons!"

They ate and drank in the lavish suite of Zarakas on a tortoise-shell table inlaid with ivory and silver. The walls of the suite were decorated with murals, a multitude of tiny, winged cherubs ascending among fleecy, billowing clouds. Through the open windows of the terrace, the soft strains of a chamber ensemble floated across the summer night.

Zarakas breathed a contented sigh.

"How good to eat and drink when the suspense has passed," he said. "Nothing matches the excitement and tension of the game . . . but, afterwards, food, drink, love."

"You seem to have more excitement in your life than most gamblers ever achieve," Nick said.

"That is not always true," Zarakas said. "I learned years ago that there is a deadly monotony in most games of chance, particularly those where luck, not skill, is the predominant factor."

"It's hard to imagine monotony in a game such as you played tonight."

"That is certainly true!" Zarakas cried. "But, we are old

antagonists, the Aga Khan and I. He is a serious, dangerous foe with unlimited reserves of money." He raised his glass and sipped his champagne. "With lesser men, ordinary millionaires, I goad and taunt them so they become angry and play badly." He released an exuberant peal of laughter. "But playing with the Aga Khan is different. The money is secondary to the challenge of the confrontation.

"I've found dice the quickest way to win or lose," Nick said. "Poker, the most satisfying. You seem to prefer baccarat."

"I have played all the games of chance," Zarakas said. "Baccarat has intrigued me since I discovered years ago that few players like to bank the game because they felt it was risky. After studying the game, I determined this fact was untrue. There is a small margin of profit for the bank, only 1 per cent, but enough if the stakes are big enough. So I began to bank baccarat. I travel to the various casinos at Cannes and Biarritz, London and Paris. I announce, '*Tout va!*' the sky is the limit, and the gamblers are frantic to try and break me. It has been terrifyingly close at times, like the game tonight, but they have not yet succeeded!"

He laughed again, delighted with himself, and Nick felt drawn to the nimble and charming man. As they spoke of things other than gambling for the next hour, he was also astonished at the range of Zarakas' mind, moving penetratingly across the fields of history, philosophy, and politics. He was startled to learn, finally, that Zarakas worked as an agent for one of the largest munitions firms in the world. He referred to himself as Prime Minister of Munitions for the Balkans.

"During the war, I sold munitions to one and all," he said. "To the English and to the French, to the Greeks and to the Turks, to the Germans and to the Russians, before, of course, their untimely collapse into Bolshevism and chaos. I would have preferred to sell only to my own country, but that would not have been sporting." He looked amiably at Nick. "Does that shock you?"

"Yes, it does," Nick said. "What about your principles?"

"My dear friend," Zarakas said. "You are a gambler and should understand the ambiguity of destiny. War is simply the extension of gambling into the arena of international politics. If I did not service this fundamental human drive, others would profit instead."

"Gambling is one thing. Playing God is another."

"But that is exactly what any monarch does!" Zarakas cried. "And only an accident of birth prevented my being born a king. I would have made a marvelous, arrogant, and benevolent king. Louis XIV could well have been Zarakas XIV. They compared him to the sun. At Versailles, his courtiers turned their backs on the church altar and knelt to their monarch instead. When his mistresses quarreled, poets compared their wrangling to the battle of goddesses fighting over the affections of Zeus! So, you see, it is quite legitimate for a human being to play God."

"I see you are quite right about admitting that you are arrogant and . . . unprincipled," Nick said.

"I agree!" Zarakas cried gaily. "In addition, I am a man who pursues pleasure and excitement as relentlessly as Alexander the Great and Julius Caesar pursued war!"

Suddenly Nick felt the hiss and bubble of the champagne whirling in his head. He pushed back his chair and rose from the table to walk unsteadily out on the terrace. He stood in the darkness, the warm night air carrying the fragrance of the gardens, listening to the sadness of the chamber strings.

Zarakas came out to the terrace. For a few moments both of them were silent. When Zarakas finally spoke, his tone was quieter, his ebullience more restrained.

"They speak of you in the casinos, my friend," Zarakas said gently. "Women admire you, men envy you. They say your melancholy demeanor conceals a tragic love affair." He hesitated, as if fearing Nick might take offense. "Forgive me," he went on. "I do not make light of love, but, from the vantage point of my years I now understand it is an affliction from which one can recover completely. One need only understand the absurdity of feeling that one woman alone exists for a man in the whole world."

He spoke with such conviction that Nick had to smile.

"Have you been in love?" he asked.

"Hundreds of times!" Zarakas said. "With lovely and exquisite women all over the world! But, as the snake-bite victim finds survival in a serum made from the venom of other snakes, I find my antidote to love in other women." He put his hand consolingly on Nick's shoulder. "Would you believe that on two occasions when I was a young man I decided to commit suicide for love? Fortunately, I refrained from doing so both times. I gave up drowning myself because the water temperature was beastly cold and I rejected poison because of a congenital digestive weakness as regards any medication."

Nick laughed heartily and Zarakas joined him.

"Bravo!" Zarakas cried when they both paused for breath. "After a battle cry, laughter is the most therapeutic of sounds the human animal can utter!" He paused. "I have just made a resolution. I assume the responsibility of helping to heal your present debilitating ailment. And I will commence treatment tonight!"

"You have some snake-bite serum handy?"

"Do not jest, Nicholas, please," Zarakas said gravely. "I am now engaged in a serious endeavor. My treatment will begin with two exquisite girls I want you to meet. They are the 'Darling Sisters,' marvelous singers who are now the toast of Paris." He pulled a watch from his vest pocket and moved into the doorway to read the face in the light from the room. "Their performance should be finishing shortly," he said. "We must hurry to the theater!"

In the nearly two months Nick had been traveling since leaving the United States, Marina filled his thoughts. His body felt drained, his heart poured out like wax, and he had no desire for any other girl. He shook his head slowly.

"I don't think I am ready for adventures yet," he said quietly.

"But I insist!" Zarakas said. Then, seeing Nick's face set in unyielding objection, he altered his attack.

"They tell me you are quite a gambler, Nicholas," he said, his voice arched and teasing. "Very well, we will settle this matter as good gamblers should. We will cut the cards once. If I beat you, you come willingly with me. If you beat me, you go quietly to your solitary bed. Would you deny your new friend so uncomplicated a wager?"

"All right, all right," Nick said. In the presence of the buoyant and magnetic Zarakas, he saw his somberness in a less imposing frame. "Even if I go, I make no promises."

"Splendid!" Zarakas said. He went to an antique side table and from a drawer drew out a deck of cards.

"Do you wish to shuffle?" he asked Nick with a grin.

Nick shook his head. Zarakas fanned the cards out on the table. He motioned to Nick to go first.

Nick drew a card and flipped over the jack of diamonds. Zarakas drew his card and threw down the queen of hearts. He crossed himself hastily.

"Even Zeus could not draw against me tonight!" he said
fervently.

"All right, I'm ready," Nick said. "Prime Minister of
Munitions for the Balkans, let's go."

They descended to the courtyard of the club and entered Zarakas' limousine. They drove through the streets
of Paris, the air scented with jasmine from the gardens, the
boulevards teeming with men and women, sounds of music
and gaiety from the cafés.

The chauffeur let them out at the stage door of the theater, into the midst of a bevy of old rakes and young dandies, waiting for the dancers of the chorus. Zarakas towed
Nick briskly through them and knocked boldly at the
locked door. The stern-faced doorman who opened it
prepared to refuse them admission until he recognized
Zarakas. He bowed with deference and quickly allowed
them to enter.

They passed beneath a maze of ropes and pullies, walking by curtained dressing alcoves noisy with the chatter of
young women. A clown with great flapping shoes stamped
by them almost causing Nick to collide with a musician
carrying a cello.

Zarakas paused before a dressing room whose door was
decorated with a pair of crimson roses. He knocked vigorously.

"Who is it?" a girl's voice, melodious as a song, called
from inside the room.

"Thanasi and a handsome young friend!" Zarakas cried.

"Just a moment, Thanasi!" the girl called. There were
whispers from the room and a squeal of laughter. Zarakas,
his cheeks flushed with animation, motioned toward the

door. "Wait until you see them," he whispered to Nick. "They are models from a *Degas* painting."

"You can come in now, Thanasi!"

Zarakas motioned for Nick to precede him and opened the door. Nick stepped into the dressing room and looked in astonishment at two lovely, totally naked women. They stood poised in a parody of a *Follies* tableau, one hand modestly concealing the nipple of one breast, the other folded demurely over the soft down of their pubes.

Zarakas stepped inside and closed the door and then saw the girls. He let loose a delighted explosion of mirth.

Against the colorful backdrop of slippers, ribbons, and silken costumes gleaming with sequins, the girls added the stunning ornament of their nakedness. Their hair was golden, their flesh white and flawless as the surface of poured cream, their breasts, high and firm, the nipples pink, shimmering buds.

"What did I tell you?" Zarakas cried to Nick, and ran to embrace the girls. "Have you ever seen such lovely little animals? This one is Jacqueline and this one, Ilona. Look at those thighs, those breasts! Look at everything shining and bursting with life! If you had won, you would not have met these beautiful little beasts!"

While Nick felt his cheeks flushed, Zarakas hugged the girls, who kissed him with endearing little caresses. Then, with a final, voluptuous swing of their buttocks, they scampered behind screens to dress, leaving Nick with a shaken sense of having been overpowered by their festive young nakedness.

That night was exhilarating for Nick. They went to Weber's and then to Maxim's on the Rue Royale, and,

finally, to a café in Montmarte. They drank champagne
and danced, laughed and flirted. In each of the cafés, other
men looked at Nick and Zarakas with envy.

Nick felt his body sparking alive, the months of weariness and melancholy stripped away like a threadbare old
coat. He was drunk and did not care because he understood his intoxication did not come from champagne alone
but was provoked by bright eyes, red lips, sweet laughter,
and the gilded recollection of naked, seminal bodies.

The sisters lived in separate apartments and shortly before dawn Nick went home with Jacqueline, leaving Ilona
with Zarakas. Nick had hired a carriage and he and Jacqueline sat in a gentle embrace as the carriage creaked slowly
under a row of graceful chestnut trees. Through their foliage he caught the rollicking sparkle of stars.

When the carriage stopped before a brownstone, he
tried to descend with dignity and stumbled, laughing
sheepishly as he caught his balance. He paid and dismissed
the carriage and walked up a flight of marble stairs into a
sitting room where a sleepy-eyed little maid, wakened by
the bell took Jacqueline's wrap. They walked on to enter a
spacious bedroom with candles flickering magic light
across tapestries depicting figures embraced in acts of love.
There were tinted mirrors on the ceiling, producing multi-
ple reflections of their bodies as they undressed. They
made love, finally, in a bed with a huge carved headboard
of mahogany, under a canopy of deep pink and rose dam-
ask.

He woke later in the morning, a wooly coating across
his tongue. For a moment, feeling a warm, naked body be-

side him, he reached out urgently for Marina. Jacqueline stirred awake.

"I didn't mean to wake you," he said softly.

She snuggled closer to him and spoke with her voice partially muffled by the pillow.

"You called me Marina several times," she pouted sleepily. "I'm Jacqueline, my darling, not Marina." Almost at once she was asleep again.

He lay quietly beside her, listening to the daylight sounds from the street below. He felt a strangeness in that moment, a mournful aftermath to the abandon and pleasure of the night. He felt somehow he had betrayed Marina again.

But the pangs of his guilt and remorse were subdued in the following three weeks. He was fascinated by the grace and loveliness of Jacqueline and caught up in the hedonistic joy of the world in which she lived. When Zarakas suggested Nick move on with him to Cannes, Nick told him he'd rather remain in Paris with her.

"Move on, Nicky!" Zarakas cried. "Move on while the first marvelous radiance of love still exists! Stay longer and one or both of you might become possessive. You may come to love each other more deeply but you will also court unhappiness. She cannot belong to one man. Her beauty is destined to ornament the lives of many men." Zarakas nodded sagely. "And I tell you something, Nicky, even your farewell, if you leave now, will be a matchless moment. You will both weep and embrace one last time. She will swear there is no other man in the world she will ever love as she might have come to love you. You will believe her. Love anticipated is always immeasurably greater than love achieved!"

"What a devil you are, Thanasi," Nick sighed. "We walk with our heads among the stars and you remind us that our feet remain mired in clay. Your damn wisdoms are as hard to digest as peach stones."

So they moved on. After a tearful and tender farewell with Jacqueline, much as Zarakas had predicted, Nick left with him for Cannes.

Nick knew that he had seen only the smallest portion of Paris. Beyond the sumptuous hotels and elegant casinos loomed the Paris of workers, soldiers, and shopkeepers still recovering from the ravages of war. Now and then, driving through a dark district to a party, he had caught a disturbing glimpse of that shabbiness and poverty. But with Zarakas as a guide, they touched only the summits of affluence and luxury. From the wealth of the casinos in Paris, they moved to the opulence of the casinos of Cannes, great palaces lit by massive chandeliers and separated from the world by the mints of Midas.

In a single evening, playing roulette at Nick's table, was an Indian maharaja, a deposed French duke, an exiled Belgian prince, a banished Prussian Junker, and a member of the Rothschild family. In the anterooms of the casinos Nick saw women more ravishing than Jacqueline, holding to the arms of aged millionaires or wealthy Americans in yachting jackets with escutcheons and crested coats of arms they had bought.

When he was not playing roulette, Nick ran the bank at baccarat with Zarakas. They lost two million francs the first night he played and won five million francs the second night. One weekend they began a game that lasted thirty-two hours against a sultan from Morocco. When the contest ended, they were ten million francs ahead. But they

lost almost that much three nights later in a game with a
Persian Shah.

Like Babylon, Nick thought in the fleeting passage of
those glittering days and nights, like Babylon or perhaps
Sodom and Gomorrah, a spangled succession of revels and
raptures. And, for a while, he enjoyed the luxury, savored
the pleasure, basked in the admiration of those men and
women who came to regard him as a gambler with nerve
and skill equal to that of Zarakas.

He thought from time to time of Marina. He told
Zarakas about her, told him, as well, of the events of his
life, the games in Chicago, even of his debt to the Gennas.
As a swift counteractant for any pensiveness or distress
these recollections could produce, Zarakas introduced him
to a Croatian princess, a tall, magnificently endowed girl
with titian hair and languorous brown eyes. She wore
black gowns from which her arms and throat sprang like
blossoms. Her name, she told Nick, was the Princess
Celenza and he did not learn until their fourth night
together that she was the daughter of a pork butcher
from Manchester. But in the way she moved and spoke, she
was sovereign and regal and Nick, validating the illusion,
accorded her the respect one showed a princess.

Following the princess from Manchester, he formed a
brief liaison with a dark Syrian girl who gleamed with the
beauty of an Old Testament psalm. Afterward, there was a
Swedish gymnast, a golden-haired and supple-bodied Ama-
zon whose indefatigable energy, he sadly discovered, was
not synchronous with the long hours he spent at the gambling tables.

Sometimes, in the afternoons when the sun was bright
and alluring, as a neutralizer to the cloistered life within

the bedrooms and casinos, Nick and Zarakas went down to the beach. The expanse of white, fine sand was dappled with colorful parasols and elegant cabanas. Zarakas, an ankle-length silk cape over his bathing attire, made a ceremony of his descent into the ocean. He was preceded by an attendant who removed any odd-sized stones from his path. Behind him came a second attendant holding a parasol over Zarakas' head to protect him from the sun. On his way, like a monarch, looking right and left, he offered gratuitous acknowledgment to the bathers who applauded his passage. By the time he reached the water's edge, everyone on the beach was watching him. One attendant tested the temperature of the water and the other removed the cape from Zarakas' shoulders. For one glorious moment, like Neptune embodied, Zarakas stood poised at the water's edge in his striking yellow-and-black-striped swimming suit. Then, as Nick splashed into the water that washed in toward the beach, Zarakas extended one foot. He dipped his toes gingerly into the shallows. With a shiver of distaste he retreated, the swift dip completing his bathing. The attendant placed the cape once more around Zarakas' shoulders. Slowly and solemnly he walked back up the beach to one of the most luxurious of the cabanas, a colorful, high-domed tent that would have pleased a Bedouin chieftain. He sat at a table beneath an upraised parasol, drinking absinthe and receiving occasional visitors.

On one afternoon, during the golden days of late September, Nick emerged from the water, drying himself on the way to the cabana. When he reached the tent, Zarakas handed him a cablegram. Nick opened it in a whirl of hope and fear, wondering if Korakas and Joey had found Marina.

PRINCIPAL DUE ON DEBT. URGENT
YOU RETURN AT ONCE.

KORAKAS

"So it has come," Zarakas said, after Nick had given him the cable to read. "Debts, like death, cannot be escaped." He paused anxiously. "Of course, you will not go?"

"I will go back."

"But this is not merely a debt!" Zarakas exclaimed. "This is a confounded mystery! You may be returning to your own destruction!"

"I have to go back."

"Why?" Zarakas cried. "Because of some outmoded ethic? Because you feel an obligation and responsibility? Forget those absurd standards of the bourgeoisie!"

"I must return, Thanasi," Nick said. "I would put my friends in danger if I didn't go back. Korakas, Lambri, even old Nestor might pay for my forfeit. Genna warned me about that and I believe him."

"Are their lives more important than your survival?" Zarakas asked indignantly. "If the decision were left to them, I'm sure they would want you to remain here and gladly take their chances." His cheeks trembled in unusual agitation. "All life is chance and hazard, Nicky. One's primary responsibility must be to survive."

"I can't live by that rule," Nick said quietly.

For a moment both men were silent. A group of children ran by their tent, squealing and kicking a beach ball, their voices fading as they ran up the beach. Nick slipped

into his robe and tied the cord. Zarakas watched him and
then spoke with a poignance in his voice.

"Nicky, please don't go," Zarakas said. "I have a marvelous plan I have been devising for years, waiting only for
the war to end and to find the right associates. A dear
friend of mine, an Armenian millionaire named Couyoumdjian, and I wish to form a gambling syndicate. We will put
up a hundred million francs and bank baccarat at Cannes,
Deauville, Biarritz, wherever there are casinos that draw
monarchs and millionaires." He tugged entreatingly at the
sleeve of Nick's robe. "I have written Couyoumdjian about
having you join us. He will be delighted, I know! Can you
imagine what the games will be like? Kings and sultans will
rush to wipe us out. We will play for immense and unmatched stakes!"

"Thanasi . . ." Nick began. Zarakas waved him hurriedly to silence.

"There will be other excitements and pleasures beside
gambling," he went on. "You have tasted a few. Stay with
me and learn to savor them. It will not be a monotonous
existence, I promise you that! The dreadful war is over and
people hunger for joy, license, abandon. We are on the
verge of a wild, bacchanalian decade that will dwarf
Elizabethan England and Periclean Greece!"

Once again, he refused to allow Nick to interrupt him.

"A thrilling time!" he cried. "A magnificent time filled
with triumphs and excitements as we gamble and love!"

He ended, breathless and trembling. While Nick
watched him for a moment in silence, a naked pleading entered his voice. "Nicky, I have come to regard you as a
son. Don't leave me now."

As if suddenly embarrassed by his emotion, Zarakas

looked down at his knees, frowning and struggling to regain his composure.

"This is your life, Thanasi," Nick said gently. "This excitement and splendor belong to you. If the cable had not come today, I might have stayed awhile longer, but I could not go on indefinitely. Can you honestly see me permanently installed at the court in Versailles? This period has been a fantasy from which I knew one day I would have to wake up."

Zarakas shook his head slowly in stern disapproval.

"Weren't you the person who told me in Paris when I wanted to remain with Jacqueline that one must move on while the radiance still exists?" Nick said. "I will never forget you, my dear friend, or the days and nights we have spent together. So let me go now and we will make our farewell this evening an event to remember. We will bank baccarat once more together, and drink champagne, and say our farewells as it is written in our life that we must part."

Zarakas sighed.

"How quickly you learn to use my own words to skewer me," he said plaintively. "Go, then go! You are an ungrateful wretch and I will not miss you or even shed a single tear as you depart! I no longer wish you to stay!"

His effort at anger trailed away and a melancholy swept his cheeks. "We could have walked the earth together like kings," he said softly.

"You are a king, Thanasi," Nick said. "A true king in this kingdom, while I am an impostor. And a true king walks with loneliness. You told me that too."

He started up the beach toward the hotel to cable Korakas that he was booking passage at once for America.

Walking across the sun-drenched sand, he paused and looked back. Zarakas had risen to stand in the doorway of the cabana, staring after him. The great, domed tent dwarfed his small, forlorn figure. Nick felt a tug of affection and remorse and raised his hand to wave. After a moment, Zarakas, in a frail flutter of his fingers, waved back.

CHAPTER 11

When the French liner on which Nick had sailed from
Europe to America docked in the port of New York, a
gloomy fog obscured the harbor and the city. He disem-
barked down the gangplank with the other passengers, and
saw them slipping off like wraiths into the mist. They assembled again in the cavernous hall that housed the cus-
toms.

After Nick had been checked and cleared by the official
who examined his luggage, he took a taxi from the port to
the railroad station. Before boarding a Pullman car for
Chicago, he wired Korakas the time of his projected arrival.

During the period of his journey he took his meals in the
seclusion of his drawing room. He tried to read but his
concentration wavered and he spent hours staring out the
window at the landscape of small towns and farms. The
houses evoked for him an image of families sitting around
dinner tables in the evening, a placidity and steadfastness
of existence he envied in those moments. At night in his

bed, tense and unsleeping, he raised his shades so he could watch the silhouette of trees and barns flashing against a horizon of lighter sky. When the first glow of dawn illuminated the trees and hills, weariness overcame him and he slept.

The porter wakened him on the morning of the second day to tell him they would be arriving in Chicago in an hour. He washed and dressed. When the train entered the terminal and pulled slowly, shuddering and steaming, to a stop, he joined the passengers in the narrow corridor. Stepping down to the platform, he found Korakas and Joey waiting for him. They embraced warmly, and with affection and gratefulness for the reunion, he understood how much he had missed them.

"You look great, Nick!" Joey said. "Even more prosperous and elegant than when you left! Isn't that right, Korakas?"

"Sure! Sure!" Korakas forced his enthusiasm. "That must come from cleaning up on them dukes and counts you played over there!"

"You're both shameless liars," Nick said. "When I shaved this morning, I thought I looked embalmed."

"Nick, what's all this business with Genna about?" Joey asked in a low voice as the three of them walked through the station.

"A debt that has to be paid," Nick said.

"What can you owe him, Nick?" Korakas asked. "You never had no dealings with that devil."

Nick waved their queries aside, unwilling to involve them further. For a few moments the three of them walked in an uneasy silence. They emerged from the terminal into a loading area where men and women climbed into taxis and cars while several policemen directed the traffic. Nick started toward the taxi stand.

"Joey learned to drive and bought a car while you were gone, Nick," Korakas said. "Wait till you see it."

"That's fine, Joey."

"I got things to do," Joey said. "And I was getting ready for your return. Wait here and I'll bring it up."

Nick waited with Korakas in silence. The overcast day sharpened his depression.

Joey drove up in a gleaming sedan and got out proudly to show it to Nick. They stored his luggage and Nick got into the front seat beside Joey. Korakas climbed into the back and hunched forward, speaking close to Nick's ear.

"A bad time for you to be coming back, Nick," Korakas said. "The gang war has been bloodier in these past weeks than any time since the killing began. I guess the hoodlums feel the presidential elections next month act like a smoke screen." He shook his head grimly. "But I tell you everyone on Halsted Street worries about getting caught in some crossfire or ambush. A week ago, Spike O'Donnell's boys bombed a speakeasy a block from the No-worry Club. I was in the kitchen and when I heard the explosion, I jumped behind the stove. The place was a watering hole for some of Genna's gunsels and the bomb killed two of them. But they also got a bartender. His face was badly cut by broken glass, and a poor devil of a waiter had his hand blown off."

"What about the police?" Nick asked. "What about the newspapers?"

"You know how this city operates," Korakas said somberly. "The mobsters got so many cops and city officials on their payrolls, they do what they want. People feel the war

may end only when either Angelo Genna or Spike O'Donnell get knocked off. They're the head of their families and
they hate each other the most."

"Where am I supposed to meet Genna?"

" 'Bloody' Angelo must be hiding in a hole so deep, only
a snake could find him," Korakas said nervously. "We just
got orders to take you straight from the station to a garage
over on Blue Island. We're supposed to leave you there,
but Joey and me decided we're staying with you."

"To hell with them!" Joey said. "We're sticking with
you."

They drove along a street of dingy labor exchanges,
signs for dishwashers and laborers plastered in the grimy
windows. Before each exchange a little ragged band of men
clustered, some sitting on the sidewalks with their backs
braced against the stores, passing around a bottle wrapped
in an old brown bag.

"Did you hear what we said, Nick?" Korakas asked.

"Maybe we shouldn't even go to the garage," Joey said.
"I got some good buddies who could find a safe place for
you to hide out. We can guard you and hope the bastards kill each other."

"There's nothing either of you can do now," Nick said.
"Just drop me at the garage where they told you to take
me and go back to wait at the club."

They drove a few more blocks in silence, Joey twisting
his head nervously several times to look at Korakas. Once,
his attention distracted, he did not see another automobile
crossing his path at an intersection. Nick cried a warning
and Joey braked desperately. Nick grabbed the dashboard
to keep from butting his head against the windshield.

"I'm sorry, Nick!" Joey cried.

"In God's name, Joey!" Nick said sharply. "Keep driving like this and we won't have to worry about Genna. What's the matter with both of you? He hasn't brought me back across the ocean to kill me here! Let's wait and see what happens before you go to pieces."

Joey started the car again and drove cautiously for another block.

"There's something else besides Genna, Nick." Korakas spoke in a low, shaken voice. "Joey and me weren't even sure we should tell you now. You got enough on your mind . . ."

"Tell me what?"

Korakas hesitated and Nick waved him urgently to speak.

"Marina is back."

For a moment, his senses scattered, Nick sat motionless. He had dreamed for so long of her return. In the last weeks, haunted by the debt to Genna, he recalled the time spent with Marina, as if it belonged to a past as distant as childhood. Now, the stunning news swept him with jubilation.

"How long has she been back? Why didn't you wire me?"

"She's only been back about a week," Korakas said. "There wasn't time to let you know before you'd left."

"Has she asked for me?"

"I saw her at her uncle's store yesterday," Joey said. "She asked me about you then. I told her you were on the way home."

"Drive to the store now!"

"Maybe that isn't wise, Nick," Korakas said uneasily. "Genna's hoodlums could be trailing us to see if we go right to the garage . . ."

"To hell with them!" Nick said. "I've come across the world for Genna so let him wait another goddam hour now!"

Joey turned the car at the corner and started driving back to the Rantoulis' grocery. With his desire to see Marina becoming more compelling every moment, Nick wondered how she would feel about him now. What should he say to her?

As they approached the Athens Wholesale Grocery, Korakas stared out the rear window.

"Wait in the car with Joey around the corner, please, Nick," he pleaded. "Let me make sure she's there before you go in."

Nick haltered his impatience and nodded. Joey parked around the corner from the grocery and Korakas got out of the car. His head bent under the gray thunderheads of the sky, he walked in a quick and awkward stride around the corner.

Joey reached across to clasp Nick's arm in reassurance.

"I got a feeling things are going to be okay, Nick," he said gently. "Things are going to work out. You'll see."

Korakas reappeared as a burst of thunder rumbled through the sky. He looked up startled and then broke into a run. When he opened the car door and tumbled inside, he carried in the first sprinkle of rain.

"She's not there," Korakas said, and paused to get his breath. "She's gone . . . to the Greek church."

Nick motioned to Joey, who started the motor and moved the car into the traffic. They traveled the few blocks to the church in silence. When Joey pulled up in front of the worn stone steps, Nick left the car. He entered the shadowed narthex of the church, inhaling the scents of incense and piety, making his cross and murmuring a brief prayer before the icons. Beyond the narthex he saw the deserted nave of the church, the sanctuary vacant and dark, except for the small votive candles burning before the paintings of the saints.

He followed the corridor leading to the church offices. A rim of light shone beneath one of the doors and muffled voices carried through the wooden panels. He hesitated a minute before knocking. The door was opened by the old parish priest, Father Ladas, clad in a cassock that hung from his throat to his ankles. Nick stared past him for a glimpse of Marina but did not see her. There was only a stocky, dark-haired man seated in a chair beside the desk.

"Excuse me, Father Ladas," Nick said. "I am looking for Marina Lefkas."

"She is busy just now . . ." The priest peered into the shadows that obscured Nick.

"I am Nick Dandolos, Father, you know, the cousin of Elias and Lambri Korakas. I don't have much time now . . . could you please ask Marina to step out here?"

He walked away from the office, back to the narthex, struggling to calm his emotions.

"Nick?"

He turned at the sound of her soft, remembered voice. In the sanctity of the candles, her face glistened like a medieval icon of a madonna. That vision muted his rebuke.

"My God, Marina, you're so beautiful . . ."

She moved her hand in a fitful gesture to her breast.

"I tried for months to find you," he said sharply, repenting his initial lapse. "You left without a note or a word. Why did you run away?"

"I was afraid to listen to you again," she said, "I wouldn't have had the courage to leave."

"You were free to do as you wished," he said, "but you should have talked to me first."

"I know that, Nick," she said. She moved closer to him, her cheeks wavering in the candlelight. "What I did was cowardly and I am sorry."

"All right, what was done is done now," he said. "Let the past rest. I understand . . ."

"Do you understand, Nick?" she asked. "Do you really understand that I left because I loved you?"

A bitterness pinched his flesh.

"If you loved me, Marina, what took you so long to come back?"

"I wanted to come back many times," she said. She looked up toward the narrow windows in the dome of the narthex, the glass darkened under the overcast sky. "Days without you were hard and lonely, and the nights . . . the nights were endless."

He felt the distance between them warmed and linked.

"I missed you too," he said quietly. "For weeks I searched and asked and hoped to find you. Finally, I couldn't bear waiting any longer and I left too."

In that moment he had a sudden, tender recall of her naked body, lithe and lovely in his arms. With a tingling in his fingers he moved closer to her, reached out to touch her cheek.

"Marina . . ."

"Nick, listen." She spoke quickly. "Before you say anything about us . . . Nick, I'm going to be married . . . that's why we're here in church."

Her words shocked him, stung him with a feeling he had been betrayed. Yet, they confirmed a truth he had feared from the moment she had left him, that he had lost her forever. He tried to speak flippantly.

"Obviously not to me," he said.

"I met Peter in Boston, where I went to live," she said quietly. "When I was grieving and trying to patch my life together, he helped me."

"So you reward him by marrying him."

"I love him too."

He felt a dryness in his mouth, his tongue and throat parched.

"I cannot say that it's the same as it was with us," she said softly. "My love now is less than you and I shared, perhaps, but safer and more comforting."

He remembered the first night he had spent with Jacqueline in Paris, wondering if Marina had touched her lover and called his name as he had called hers.

"I haven't been sleeping alone either," he said. He was ashamed the moment he hurled those rancorous words at her.

"Oh, Nick!" She seemed to be fighting tears. "Let's not be cruel and bitter! Help me now! We both know it was hopeless, round and round like a carousel, a ring of lost pledges and broken promises."

"Marina, our lives were at stake!" he cried.

"If I felt any hope for us, I would have come back to you."

"You should have given us one more chance!"

"My mother sickened and died on chances like that."

As if in remorse then, she reached up slowly to touch his cheek. Her fingers burned his flesh.

"Goddam you, Marina!" he said hoarsely, his anger unleashed. "Goddam you! We might have worked things out!"

"I could not live as you need to live!"

"We could have tried!"

"We would have destroyed each other!"

"That's a coward's excuse, Marina!"

"It's the truth! As real for me as your games were for you!"

His anger fled as quickly as it had broken. He stared past her head at the candles flickering before the icons. He felt his own heart melting.

"Marina?"

The shadow of a man fell across the entrance to the narthex. Nick did not want to meet him, did not want to see any more of him than he had glimpsed in the office.

"I hope to God you find happiness, Marina," he said. "I wish that for you from deep in my heart."

He walked unsteadily toward the door. Marina called his name once. He wondered if the man she was going to marry heard the low, wild sadness in her farewell. He opened the door and hurried down the steps to the car.

They drove the city streets toward the garage, rain streaking the car windows, and the wheels slapping loudly on the water-slick pavements. Joey drove grimly, looking straight ahead. Korakas kept a sympathetic silence.

Nick's thoughts tangled with questions. Should he have tried to convince her she was wrong? Did he understand, that she was really right, her decision as true for her as his decision had been for him? He stared silently out the window, all his speculations prodigal and futile. He waited, resigned now for whatever lay ahead.

When they arrived before the garage, a large, shabby building with metal grills imprisoning the painted windows, Joey slowed down. Korakas spoke in a tense whisper.

"They said to use the entrance off the alley."

Joey drove forward a short distance and swung the car into the alley, stopping before a closed overhead door. Someone had been waiting for them, and the door slid open. They drove into a gloomy interior, deserted except for the hulks of a few wrecked cars.

"Jesus Christ," Korakas muttered. "Like a graveyard."

Joey gave him a reproving look and swung open his door to climb out. He peered warily into the shadows as Nick emerged from the opposite side. Korakas got out as well, and pleaded again in a whisper for Nick to let them remain.

"Go back to the club and wait," Nick said. "I'll be in touch with you both as soon as I can."

For a moment longer both of them stood watching him, and then Joey got back into the car. Korakas joined him. Joey started the motor and drove forward to turn around a column and start back to the door. As the car passed Nick his last view of them was the pale, anxious face of Korakas staring at him through the window. When the car left the garage, entering the alley, the door closed again.

In the murky, ominous silence, Nick fought an impulse to run after the car. At that instant two men startled him by emerging suddenly from the deeper shadows of the garage. Both were dressed in dark suits and felt hats, their faces so cold and sullen, they might have been twins. Neither man spoke but one of them motioned Nick to follow.

He walked with them down a metal staircase to a lower level. One of the men pulled a strip of black cloth from his pocket.

"What's that for?" Nick asked.

"We got to blindfold you for a while," the man said.

In the first moment of darkness, as the blindfold covered his eyes, he drew on the image of Marina as she had looked in the church. He tried to retain that warm vision.

As one man led him forward by the arm, he shuffled awkwardly and, once, stumbled.

"Easy," the man holding his arm said. "Step up now."

Nick raised his foot and fumbled until he found a step.

"Keep your head down," the man said.

Nick sensed he was entering the enclosure of a truck. The man tugged him down to a bench and sat beside him. Nick heard the doors bang closed and a few moments later, the motor started. The truck vibrated beneath him and began to move.

They ascended a ramp and a door opened, the squeal of metal sliding along a track. They bumped into the street, joining the noise of traffic.

"Where are we going?" he asked. The man beside him did not answer.

He did not know how long they drove, time unsettled for him by the darkness. After a while the clamor of traffic grew quieter as if they might have entered a residential area.

The truck stopped. The man beside him moved away. The doors opened and he heard the mumble of voices and someone entered the truck again. Smelling the strong odor of cigars and some raw, indefinable menace, Nick knew it was Angelo Genna.

"I got no time to waste, so listen carefully," Genna said, his voice shriller than Nick remembered. "The boys will drive you to a farmhouse some miles from here. Someone will join you there tonight. Play poker with him."

"You didn't call me back across the ocean just to play a game of cards," Nick said.

"Listen and don't ask questions! Play cards like I tell you and keep your mouth shut about me or how you got there!"

"I've got to know what's going on!"

"You'll know what I tell you!" Genna said harshly. "I'm calling in your marker and after you've played this game, we'll be square! Don't try a double cross or we'll bury Korakas and his wife together in the river! Understand?"

As he heard Genna leaving the truck, Nick made a final plea.

"Tell me what this is all about, please?"

Genna did not answer and left the truck. The other man entered and sat beside him again. As the doors slammed shut, Nick fumbled for the blindfold. The man pushed his hand away.

"Just relax," the man said. "We're going to take a drive now."

Fear blurred Nick's sense of time and he wasn't sure how long they drove. There were periods of silence except when a car passed them going the opposite way. Several times they rumbled over railroad tracks. The scent of fields and trees seeped into the truck.

"Where are we now?" he asked once. The man did not answer.

The truck turned off the paved road and lurched and bumped over a rutted path. The man beside Nick supported his arm to keep him from falling. When the truck stopped, and the motor was turned off, the man untied Nick's blindfold. The doors were opened and daylight burst with a brightness that stung his eyes. When he climbed down from the truck, he saw they were parked before an old, unpainted frame farmhouse and large shabby barn. Both buildings were isolated in acres of fields. A grove of trees, their foliage burnished with the browns and yellows of autumn, stood some distance away.

One of the men handed an attaché case to Nick.

"Some money, sealed decks, and a toothbrush," the man said gravely. He motioned Nick to follow him up the path to the farmhouse. A tall, thin man in coveralls waited on the porch, a small, gray-haired woman in a print dress standing in the doorway behind him.

"This is Mr. and Mrs. Ritter," the man said. "And this is Mr. Ferguson. You were expecting him."

"We sure were." Mr. Ritter shook hands cordially with Nick. His wife greeted him warmly as well.

"You must be tired, Mr. Ferguson," she said. "My husband will show you your room so you can rest, if you like. Supper will be ready in about an hour."

Genna's man turned to leave and Nick called after him.

"Will you be coming back to get me?"

"Someone will get you," the man said with a brittle laugh.

He lay across the bed in a second-floor bedroom of the farmhouse, staring at the twilight reflecting through the sheer curtains like dark water. In the stillness of the country he heard the warble and chirp of birds. For a while he considered methods of escape but understood the futility of flight.

When Mrs. Ritter knocked at his door to announce supper, although he was not hungry he went down to discover what he could from them. He learned they were caretakers for an absentee landlord who held the farm in a trust. There wasn't a phone in the house and the nearest town was fifteen miles away. Beyond that information, Nick found the Ritters gracious, farm-rooted people who, he was quickly convinced, knew no more than he knew. They had been told only to expect Nick and another man, who would be joining him to play cards.

After supper, the October evening carrying a chill into the house, Mr. Ritter built a fire. Nick sat before the stone hearth watching the flames curl and crackle around the logs when he heard the rumble of a car stopping before the farmhouse. Through the hallway, Nick saw Mr. Ritter open the door and admit a group of perhaps half a dozen men. They dispersed swiftly, inspecting the rooms, several of them going up the stairs to the second floor. One of the men, somber-faced, with his hand in the pocket of his suit-coat, came into the parlor.

"You carrying a rod?" he asked Nick.

Nick shook his head.

"I got to frisk you anyway," the man said. Nick stood up and raised his arms. While the man checked him over deftly, he heard the tramp of the men searching the rooms upstairs. One called down from the landing.

"Patty, the house is clean."

The man with Nick went back to the door. As the men took up positions at the windows, another man came into the house. He walked into the parlor with authority and crossed to the fireplace where Nick stood. He was of slen-der, but wiry build, dressed in a dark suit, dark shirt, and yellow tie. He shook Nick's hand with vigor. Under his thatch of reddish hair, Nick saw his bright, cunning eyes. There was something familiar about his face, a vague asso-ciation with pictures seen in newspapers.

"Nick the Greek," the man said, excitement flushing his cheeks. He gestured to the men in the parlor. "Here he is, Nick the Greek, in the flesh." He shook his head and grinned. "This is the guy who cut the balls off Loukanas and who dropped a cool million bucks to Rosenberg in New York." He winked at Nick. "I know all about you, all right, and I been wanting to play you, one on one, for a long time. Patty here doesn't want me to tell you my name but maybe after I beat you, you'll guess it. I got some rep-utation as a poker player myself. Now, let's play."

Nick and the red-haired leader sat across from one an-other at the dining room table, several lamps beaming down upon the cards. The lieutenant, Patty, sat in a chair in the corner. The Ritters had gone to bed but Nick could hear the men in adjoining rooms, calling in low voices to others on guard outside.

His opponent was a bold gambler, with a canny skill at the cards. Under normal conditions Nick felt he could have beaten him. But the mystery around the game, the undeniably important man pitted against him, and the shadow of Genna prevented him from concentrating. Nor could he help those moments when he thought of Marina. Knowing she was lost to him forever further weakened his spirit.

They played till midnight. When Patty brought them coffee from the kitchen, Nick had lost about eight thousand dollars. Patty bent and whispered in his chief's ear.

"Yeh, pretty soon," the red-haired man said impatiently. "I think I got him on the run now."

In the next two hours, Nick won back most of that money, almost without any special effort. After losing a pot of several thousand dollars to Nick on a bluff that Nick called, the leader turned on his lieutenant with a snarl.

"How the hell can I play with you breathing down my neck! You squat there like a goddam vulture! Get the hell out of the room!"

Patty stalked out in silent indignation.

Nick grew weary, the tension surrounding the game more exhausting than gambling. He began betting recklessly, remaining in pots even when he suspected he was beaten. By just before dawn his opponent was almost fifteen thousand dollars ahead. Patty had slipped back into

the room, poised nervously in the shadows. When the red-
haired man paused once to rise from his chair and stretch,
Patty found the courage to approach him again.

"Jesus Christ, boss, you'd be crazy to stick around any
longer! It'll be daylight in a little while! Let's get the hell
away, please!"

The red-haired man looked down at his winnings and
then stared across the table at Nick. Finally, he made up
his mind, picking up the thick wad of bills and stuffing
them into his pockets.

"I guess the game's over," he smirked at Nick. "No
offense, Nick, but I expected to find you tougher. Won't
be the first time a guy's reputation is bigger than he really
is, eh, Patty?" Patty laughed nervously in agreement. He
started eagerly from the room and then turned back to
look at his boss, who had not left the table. For a suspenseful moment, no one spoke.

"Boss . . . please . . ."

The red-haired man spoke to Nick with a curl to his
lips.

"Now you want to know who beat you?"

"Jesus Christ, boss!" Patty pleaded. "You swore you
wouldn't!"

"To hell with it!" the red-haired man cried. "What
harm can it do now? The goddam pleasure is gone if he
doesn't know who beat him." He waited a moment with
the glee of a child about to spring some staggering surprise.
"When they ask who beat you, Nick," he said, "tell them
Spike 'Four Deuces' O'Donnell . . . O'Donnell from the
southwest side was the man." He laughed in loud and raucous triumph and left the room.

Nick knew then that he had been used as bait to lure

Spike O'Donnell from his hiding place. For a rattled moment, the men climbing into the car to leave, Nick started out to stop them. But he was afraid they would kill him when they discovered the ruse. Even if they let him live and managed to escape the ambush, an enraged Genna might carry out his threat to kill Lambri and Korakas. So he let O'Donnell and his men drive away knowing that somewhere on the road leading from the farm to Chicago, Genna's gunmen would be waiting for them.

As the first glow of dawn lightened the sky, Mrs. Ritter came downstairs and brewed a pot of coffee. Nick drank a cup and then went up to his bedroom. He did not undress but lay wearily across the bed, hearing the birds that chirped in the branches of the tree outside his window. As the sun rose, light streaming through the curtains, he turned on his stomach and pressed his face into the pillow.

Later that afternoon, a man in a pickup drove down the road to the farmhouse. He had been sent, he said, to take Mr. Ferguson to the train in a nearby city. Nick told the Ritters good-by and climbed into the cab beside the driver, a leathery-cheeked, unshaven handy man who chewed plug tobacco and spit buoyantly out the window.

The pickup bumped and rattled over the rutted track, and turned onto a paved road with a sign reading, GARY —15 MILES. The driver spit again.

"Hear about the massa-cree?"

Nick looked down and shook his head.

"Some big gangster from Chee-ca-go," the man grinned. "Him and a car full of his boys got ambushed just 'tother side of Gary. Must of been a real mob waiting for them, blocking the road. Used pistols and shotguns, tore their car apart, and killed every last one. Heard on the wireless there was 'nough blood on the road to float a boat. Think I'll go have a look after I drop you at the train."

He blew a low whistle and spit again with gusto.

Nick stared out the window, chilled and silent. My debt is paid, he thought in remorse and despair, my debt is paid in blood.

CHAPTER 12

From the train station in Chicago, Nick took a taxi at once to the No-worry Club. He found Lambri, Korakas, and Joey waiting fearfully for word about him. They had heard about Spike O'Donnell's murder and without understanding how Nick might have been linked to that savage killing, they felt the call from Genna was more than coincidence.

In the apartment above the club, weary and grateful to be among his friends, Nick told them, finally, of the debt he owed Angelo Genna, and how the cablegram called in that obligation. He told them, as well, about the moment he discovered the identity of O'Donnell and knew an ambush was planned.

"I had the chance to warn those men then," Nick said grimly. "If I hadn't lacked the courage, I might have saved their lives."

"And lost your own," Korakas said with a shudder. "If you'd warned them, still figuring you set them up, O'Donnell would have killed you."

"Do you think they would have warned you?" Lambri asked. "You cannot treat such killers with the mercy and compassion you show human beings."

"What worries me now is what happens if word of that game gets around," Korakas said nervously. "Who else knew O'Donnell was coming to meet you? One of his brothers might decide you fingered him and come after you."

"Anybody who knows Nick understands he wouldn't finger anyone," Joey said.

"But they're mad dogs!" Korakas cried. "They kill first and ask questions afterwards!"

"The old man is right," Lambri said quietly. "I think, Niko, you should leave this city for a while. Go someplace and remain quiet until we see what happens here."

"I need to rest, not run."

"Go somewhere else and rest." Korakas joined his urgent plea to that of Lambri's. "We'll get your tickets wherever you want to go. But don't delay, Nick. The quicker you can go, the better."

Joey made a gesture of entreaty for him to agree.

"All right, I can leave," Nick said. "That might be safer for me and even less dangerous for all of you if I'm not around. I had been thinking about San Francisco. The truth is that nothing really holds me here now."

By their silence, he understood Korakas and Joey had told Lambri of his last meeting with Marina.

"The only person I still want to see is Nestor," Nick said. "I wrote him several times but he never answered. How is the old man?"

"I haven't seen him in about two weeks now," Korakas said. "We tried to keep an eye on him while you were gone, but you know how stubborn and independent the old ram has always been."

"Has he been gambling?"

"Only a few small, beggar games," Korakas said. "Loukanas and the other owners don't stake him for the big contests any more. They say since his eyesight keeps getting worse, he's no challenge to the suckers . . . I can go find him for you, Nick, and bring him here."

"I don't want to sit locked up here," Nick said. "Joey can drive me to the coffeehouse where Nestor drinks. We should find him there or in the loft."

"All right," Korakas said. "I'll get over to the Apollo and pick up what the street is saying about the killings."

"Don't show yourself around too much, Niko," Lambri said. "I will not rest until you get safely away from this cesspool."

Nick and Joey drove from the No-worry Club toward the Minerva. On Halsted Street the crowds on the sidewalks seemed larger than usual, men pushing in and out of the casinos. At the corner of Harrison, a newsman hawked his papers with the bold, black headlines announcing Spike O'Donnell's murder. Joey looked uneasily at the pedestrians they passed.

"I feel like we're sitting on a keg of explosives," he muttered.

The waiter at the Minerva told them he hadn't seen Nestor in about a week. They drove from there to the loft. Twilight had passed into evening when Joey parked before the old building. He started from the car and Nick caught his arm.

"Nick, maybe someone figures you'll look the old man up," Joey said. "You better wait here."

"I'll go up," Nick said. "I don't think anyone even knew where the old man lived."

Entering the lower hall of the building, Nick started up the stairs. As he walked from one landing to another, he remembered the months he had spent in the chilled, drafty loft with Nestor tutoring and drilling him in the skills of gambling. That period seemed a lifetime away.

He knocked at the loft door and waited. When there wasn't any answer, he knocked more loudly and tried the knob but the door was locked. He returned to the first floor, to the landlady's flat. She answered his knock, looking exactly as he remembered her, a stringy-haired virago with her mouth carved in a snarl.

"He don't live here no more." She answered Nick's question brusquely.

"Do you know where he's gone?"

"I don't know and don't care! His rent always late, and him mostly drunk, stumbling and vomiting on the stairs. He belonged in a gutter, not a decent Christian house!"

"You are a kind, Christian woman all right," Nick said. "I hope you get your proper reward someday."

Her bony jaw clamped on a curse and she slammed the door. Nick turned to leave, wondering anxiously where he might look for Nestor, when the door on the opposite side of the landing opened. A stocky man in an undershirt stepped into the hallway.

"I heard the bitch," the man said. "You looking for the old player?"

"Yes. Do you know where he is?"

"He's in that beat-up Paradise Hotel on Franklin," the man said. "I moved a table, a few chairs, and a cot into a room over there for him. Fourth floor in the rear and be

careful. If the old whores don't get you, you can fall over
them rotten railings on the stairs."

The Paradise Hotel was a notorious tenement, filthy as a
cow shed, occupied mainly by derelicts and aging harlots.
Entering the hallway of the building, Nick and Joey
inhaled the stench of garbage, cheap wine, and mud from
the yard. At each landing, from the long dark halls
that concealed the rooms they heard laughs and shrieks and
the discordant strains of music. On the third floor, her
misery hidden behind one of the doors, a woman screamed
in a cry that echoed down the stairs.

"We'll get Nestor out of here tonight," Nick said
grimly.

The fourth floor was quieter, the landing lit only by a
flutter of light from the hallway below. In one of the
rooms, a needle, stuck in the groove of a record, repeated a
short, grating scratch.

Making their way slowly to a door at the end of the corridor, Nick knocked on the wooden panel. After a moment
the door was opened by a grubby-looking man smelling of
sweat and wine.

"What ya want?"

"Is Nestor here?" Nick said.

"He's busy now."

Nick brushed by the man and Joey followed him into
the gloomy, airless room. The only light came from a
kerosene lamp on a small table where two men huddled
over cards and some crumpled dollar bills and coins.

"Where is he?" Nick asked sharply.

One man gestured idly toward an alcove, a narrow addition to the room that contained a solitary window. As

Nick walked toward it, he made out the faint lines of a cot and the lump of a figure.

"C'mon, Len, deal!" one of the men at the table cried. "I can't get even just sitting here!"

Bending over the cot, Nick pulled aside a tattered quilt to expose the white hair and craggy face of Nestor. Hollowed and webbed as his countenance had been, some new and wretched disfiguration had been added, his cheeks moist and ashen.

Nick stroked the old man's temple and forehead, feeling the flesh damp and hot beneath his fingers. "He's sick," he said to Joey, who had come to stand beside him. Nick turned toward the men at the table. "How long has he been like this?" he asked angrily.

"He's just sleeping off a drunk," one man said.

"See if you can get the old bastard up, will ya?" another man spoke. "He owes me twenty bucks."

Joey moved swiftly to the table.

"Get the hell out of here, you grubby shits!" he cried.

The startled men pushed back their chairs, collected their money hurriedly, and started toward the door. One man hung behind. "What about my twenty bucks?" he whined.

Joey pulled some bills from his pocket and peeled one off. He gave it to the man and added a shove. "You got your dough! Now clear out!"

The men left the room quickly and Joey closed the door. Their grumbling, cursing voices receded down the corridor to the stairs.

"Go back to the club, Joey," Nick said. "Have Korakas find a doctor and bring him here as soon as you can."

Joey returned with Korakas and the doctor in less than an hour. He examined Nestor, pushing aside the shred of undershirt, using a stethoscope on his bony, almost fleshless body. After a few moments he stood and stared down at the old man in silence. He put his instruments back in his bag and snapped the lock.

"He's dying," the doctor said. "He should have been dead hours ago."

"Can't you help him, Doctor?" Nick pleaded. "Give him some treatment or medication?"

"His pulse is so faint now, I can hardly hear it," the doctor said. "I think he's suffered a stroke. He might regain consciousness or he may never wake up. He could last ten minutes or a few hours."

"Can we get him into a hospital?" Joey asked.

"He wouldn't last until you got there," the doctor said. "Nothing you can do now but wait with him." He moved toward the door.

After the doctor had gone, Korakas spoke in a low, remorseful voice.

"We should have looked after him better," he said. "I didn't even know he had moved into this snakepit."

"He was stubborn and proud and lived the way he wanted to live." Nick looked sadly at Nestor. "I'll wait here with him now."

"Do you want us to stay?" Joey asked. Nick shook his head.

"Then I'll drive Korakas back to the club and come back to wait in the car downstairs, Nick," Joey said. "I'll be there whenever you come down."

Korakas stood beside the cot for a final moment.

"In his prime, he was the greatest gambler of all," he said quietly. "I remember after he'd won a fortune in some big game, fifty men pressing to buy him a drink and fifty lovely women longing for his touch and his kiss." His voice faltered. "Look what's left of the poor devil's glory now."

Nick sat beside Nestor through the evening and into the night. From time to time, doubting the old gambler knew he was there, he gently pressed his hand or whispered words of reassurance. Each hour altered the dying man's face, power and blood draining stealthily away, the flesh of his cheeks growing yellow and dry. His mouth hung open, the pale, pink leaf of his tongue visible as he sucked in tight, shallow breaths.

Once during the darkest, quietest hours of the night, when the noises of revelry from the other floors was muted, in a nearby room a baby wailed a fretful cry. Three, four times the strange, startling cry rose and fell and then was abruptly silenced as if the infant had been given its mother's breast.

The baby's cries drew Nestor back from some remote borderland. He stirred and raised one hand a few inches from the quilt, flexing his long, gaunt fingers.

"Raise the fours," the old man whispered. "Raise the fours."

"I'm here." Nick leaned close to Nestor's trembling lips. "Old friend, it's Nick."

"Call the kings." Nestor's voice rose. "He's bluffing."

"I'm here, Nestor." Nick clasped his arm. "I'm with you now."

"He won't meet the raise!" Nestor said hoarsely. "Mother of Christ, he'll break!"

Caught in the fevered vision of old games, he thrashed and gasped. Nick held him as firmly as he could, feeling the old gambler's wild, straining heart. As quickly as the spell came, his frenzy passed. Suddenly exhausted, he grew quiet, and turned his head slightly to stare at the window. A glint of moonlight shone around the perimeter of the shade.

Nestor trembled. "Who's there?" he whispered.

"Your friends!" Nick spoke loudly, close to the old man's ear. "Your friends come to cheer you. A hundred of them in the hall. Can you hear them, Nestor?"

As if he were listening for the murmur of phantom voices, Nestor labored to rise. For a moment his head appeared to float weightless off his pillow, until his inert body pulled it down. His cheeks and lips tensed, and a short, sharp breath burst from his mouth. Then his freed spirit flew like an arrow toward the window to vanish into the moonlight.

Nick gently raised his friend's limp hand, pressing the flesh. He cried as he kissed the old gambler's fingers in a final farewell.

The moonlight seeped into dawn. As the light of the day slipped into the room, a mist became visible in the gloomy corners. Around the alcove where he sat beside Nestor's body, the brawl of the day began. Doors slammed, people tramped up and down the stairs, women shrieked to one another from the landings.

He left the room once to walk down to the street and tell Joey, waiting in his car, that Nestor had died. He returned to the room, unwilling to leave the old man alone.

In those hours he thought of the ways his life had been linked to the old gambler, his destiny directed by their months together. He remembered things Nestor had told him, drawing upon experiences that his age had encrusted like a great reef of coral. A few times, swept by sadness, longing to believe the old gambler might simply be asleep, Nick touched him. When he felt the stony coldness of his cheek, he had to accept that his friend and mentor was gone forever.

Later in the morning, as news of the death of Nestor carried along the street, Loukanas, Prince Pierre, and Big Gorgio climbed the four flights of stairs to the old gambler's room.

They stood uneasily at the foot of the cot, looking anxiously from the corpse around the squalid room as if they feared infection from disease or poverty. For several moments no one spoke, the only sound the labored wheezing of Loukanas, struggling to regain his breath after the arduous climb.

"He don't look too bad." Big Gorgio stared impassively at the body of Nestor.

"A terrible thing," Prince Pierre said gravely. "I saw the dear man just a week ago and asked him if he needed anything."

Loukanas finally managed to catch his breath.

"Nick." His voice shook slightly. "Could we speak to you for just a minute?" He appealed to him to move to an area of the room away from the cot. Nick joined the three of them near the door.

"I think I speak for all of us, Nick," Loukanas said somberly, "when I express our sincere and heartfelt regrets. We know you were close as a son to our dear friend."

Nick did not speak. Loukanas blinked nervously and continued.

"A great man has passed on," Loukanas said. "We must not allow his death to go unnoticed, but make certain that proper respect and homage are paid. Now . . . we have agreed, Nick, and we hope you will not have any objection if we give the revered sportsman we loved and respected a funeral worthy of his fame in life. The mayor has promised he would attend and we'll personally contact the most influential aldermen, judges, attorneys, union leaders, the important entertainers . . . all will join us in this final, magnificent tribute."

"A big funeral for the old man won't hurt us either," Big Gorgio said gruffly. "They'll be burying Spike O'Donnell the next few days, with plenty of publicity. This funeral will remind the goddam Sicilians and the bloody, black Irish who we Greeks are."

He faltered and then frowned as Loukanas glared at him and Prince Pierre gave him a stern, censuring look.

"The advantages to us are not important!" Loukanas said impatiently. "The tribute to Nestor is all that matters!"

"That's what I meant," Big Gorgio muttered.

"Now, as a beginning," Loukanas went on quickly, "we have taken the liberty of arranging for the finest funeral home on the south side to pick up the body." He looked with repugnance around the room and spoke earnestly to Nick. "We should get him out of this cesspool as soon as we can, before the newspapers send reporters and photographers around. Don't you agree?"

Nick did not answer but walked back to the cot to look for the last time at the withered figure lying so straight and still. The ridges and gullies of the old gambler's face seemed to have been cast into a mask of fired clay and stone. Nick scarcely recognized his friend.

He walked from the cot to a table to collect a few of
Nestor's possessions he wanted to take. There was a deck
of linen cards, some tintypes of the old gambler as a cocky,
grinning young man, and a faded silk scarf Nick had seen
him wearing at the tables. He started for the door, pausing
beside the owners.

"Pay him your tribute," Nick said. "It makes little
difference to him now, but go ahead."

"Splendid, Nick!" Loukanas cried. "We will make all
the arrangements so you need not be concerned about a
thing, but we want you in the first carriage with the mayor
. . . all of us agree that place of honor belongs to you."

Nick shook his head. "I will be leaving the city," he said.
"Make your plans without me."

Three days later, on the same afternoon Nick was to
leave for San Francisco, the street prepared for Nestor's
funeral.

In the Korakas apartment, Nick had finished packing his
suitcases. Lambri dressed to attend the services at the
church, while Korakas, already attired in a wrinkled black
suit, white shirt, and dark tie, sat stiffly and uncomfortably
on the couch.

Joey entered the apartment, coming through the kitchen
and hall to join Nick and Korakas in the parlor.

"I had to park the auto in the alley," he said. "Halsted
Street is all blocked off for the funeral procession. They're
assembling on Jackson and should be passing out in front
on their way to church in just a few minutes."

Korakas walked to the window and raised the pane of
glass. A scent of fading, cooling autumn carried into the
room. Nick and Joey joined him and the three of them

looked down on the crowds that lined the curbs of Halsted Street, pressing against the wooden barricades that had been erected by the police. A pair of mounted policemen clattered by, tails and manes of their horses tossing like banners, waving their sticks at stragglers who had not yet vacated the street. After they passed, from the vicinity of Jackson Boulevard, sounded the rumble of drums.

Korakas leaned out the window to stare down the street and then drew back inside. "Here they come," he said.

A platoon of drummers appeared, bodies moving in slow, formal gait, their drums draped in black bunting, their sticks rising and falling in measured, mournful beats. The drumbeats grew louder as the drummers marched beneath the window and then diminished in volume as they passed on.

After the drummers came a retinue of young girls, dressed like nymphs in flowing white gowns, garlands of flowers in their hair. From a small, ribboned basket each girl held, she scattered petals of white and red blossoms in her wake.

A short distance behind the last rank of nymphs rolled a caisson drawn by four coal-black horses, driven by an attendant in black, formal livery. Plumes rose like unicorn's horns from the foreheads of the horses above their harness and trappings, which flashed and glittered in the afternoon light. On the surface of the caisson, draped in black silk cloth with a valance of spun gold lace, was a great bronze casket. An American flag was draped at the head while a Greek flag mantled the foot. The horses' hoofs rapped and thumped upon the street, the wheels of the caisson swayed and creaked, the bunting and valance shimmering in ceremonial pomp.

Korakas made his cross. "Rest in peace, old friend," he
said softly.

Rest in peace, Nick echoed silently. He closed his eyes
and envisioned the leonine head of Nestor sealed now in
the resplendent casket of bronze, the last hand folded, the
last game played.

After the caisson bearing the casket came the first in a
cavalcade of open carriages. The lead one held the bushy-
haired, flamboyant mayor of the city along with Loukanas
and Prince Pierre, both men dressed elegantly in formal attire, with diamonds shining on their fingers and at their
cuffs. They nodded gravely, first to the left and then to the
right, displaying their sorrow-burdened faces to the silent,
watchful crowds. Each carriage that followed the first one
held a procession of eminent mourners.

"Aldermen, judges, and city officials," Korakas said
morosely. "Not an honest, true-souled man among them."

After the carriages came the wagons filled with flowers,
a mass of wreaths and sprays and baskets. There were
marigolds and mums, gladioli and roses, red, yellow, pink,
and white efflorescence on which banners carried messages
in letters of block and script, REST IN PEACE . . . GO
WITH GOD . . . FAREWELL, DEAR FRIEND.

Before the last of the flower-laden wagons had passed,
the squeal of bouzoukia pierced the air. Several ranks of
players came into view, plucking the strings of their instruments in a wild and clamorous wail. Behind the players
tramped a throng made up of dealers, pit bosses, checkers
and cashiers, waitresses and bouncers, from the street's casinos and cafés. With them marched gaudy pimps sur-
rounded by their harlots holding colorful parasols, waving

gaily to customers along the street. As that company passed, the crowd broke around the barricades to join them. Some carried small Greek and American flags, while others held flasks from which they took frequent swigs.

Bringing up the rear of the funeral cavalcade were several scores of ragged children, shrieking and dancing as they set off strings of firecrackers that burst with little claps of thunder in their wake.

Korakas banged down the window in disgust.

"A damn circus," Joey said.

For a moment Nick was bitter at the way the venal owners had exploited the old gambler's death, and remorseful that he had not suspected what they planned. But he understood Nestor was beyond their hypocrisy.

"All the goddam pomp and pageantry won't do the owners any good," Korakas said. "They're little fish and sharks like the Gennas and Spike O'Donnell's brothers will swallow them, diamonds and all. Their days are numbered now . . ."

Preparing to leave the apartment, Nick knocked at the door of Lambri's bedroom. She opened the door, wearing a black dress, a small black hat perched on her graying head. Nick embraced her for a final time, warmed by their bond of love.

"God go with you, Niko."

"God belongs here with you," Nick said. "But keep me in your prayers."

He pulled a thick envelope from his pocket, which he handed to Lambri.

"I once promised you wouldn't have to remain on this wretched street forever," Nick said. "So take this money now and buy a house with grass and a garden where you can plant and grow flowers."

"Niko!" she protested. "You don't have to give me . . ."

"Hush!" he said. "Money is not important for me now. I want you to do what I say and in that way I may have a place to come home to someday."

"There will always be a place for you with me, Niko," she said. She accepted the envelope and turned away to dab at her eyes.

Korakas and Joey waited for Nick in the kitchen. Struggling against his tears and as if he were fearful of breaking down, Korakas scowled and struck Nick's arm with his fist.

"Don't forget your old friends, Nick," he said in a husky voice.

"You won't ever be coming back here to stay," Joey said sadly. "I know you won't come back."

"I told you when I settled someplace, I'd send for you," Nick said gently. "Meanwhile, you can do something else besides worry about me. I told you I wanted you to go on in school. You see about that now."

"Maybe I can take a few classes with Joey too!" Korakas cried. "Then, when you send for him, I'll be ready as well! We'll join you, Nick, in the great games you're going to play! The Three Musketeers will be together again!"

Nick smiled and nodded. He and Joey picked up his suitcases and left the apartment. They walked down the stairs and passed through the quiet, deserted kitchen of the No-worry Club. As they emerged into the alley, the wail

of the bouzoukia trailed faintly back to them over the
roofs of the buildings.

The train traveled slowly through the outskirts of the
city, passing a stretch of ramshackle houses, run-down
sheds, the fences with missing or broken pickets. A solitary
tree, stripped of all but a few withered leaves, stood like a
gaunt sentinel against the smoke-gray sky. Clinging to an
upper branch of the tree, a child waved at the train.

Nick waved back, though he doubted the child could
see him. Afterward, he left his compartment, walking
along the corridor to the parlor car. The wheels rumbling
and rocking beneath him recalled the mournful drums that
had marked the funeral.

He entered the parlor car, which was occupied by a few
women and several men sitting around a small table. He
walked to an armchair at the rear of the car and sat down.

Through the observation window he saw that the coun-
tryside had altered into an expanse of fields broken only by
the looming frame of a silo, a barn, and a grove of autumn
trees. For a while he watched the land rushing by and
then, as if a shade were suddenly lowered, the earth turned
in a swift, fall of night. Darkness swept through the window, consuming the frail lights of the car, and settled with
a chill into his body. He thought of winter, death, and the
eternity of the grave.

Someone touched his shoulder and he shivered. When he
looked up he saw a well-dressed commercial traveler standing beside his chair.

"I beg your pardon, sir," the man said. "My friends and
I were going to play a little poker to pass the time until

dinner. We'd be pleased to have you join us if stakes of a quarter and a half dollar aren't too steep."

Nick started to refuse and then changed his mind.

They played several rounds of stud. The spark of the game and the company of the players slowly banished Nick's gloom. He heard their voices and laughter, was conscious of his voice joining their chatter and their mirth. In that moment, with some sharpened clarity of vision, he grasped the significance of his journey. Behind him were his love and his friend, both lost to him forever. Behind him was the debt to Genna, requited by the murder of O'Donnell and his men. Behind him were staunch friends, bitter struggles, fair victories, and sad defeats.

Ahead of him were unexplored cities and exotic lands, challenging contests, and exhilarating games. Ahead of him, heart willing, were glowing, redemptive loves. He would try to weave the fiber of the life he had lived into his future, implementing and understanding what still lay before him. All men eventually make the final journey Nestor has now made, he thought, but before that time there is life to be wagered and played.

"Half dollar raise to you, friend," one of the players said.

"Your half dollar and a half dollar more, friend," Nick smiled.

He won the hand and the next player shuffled the cards to deal.

Nick
the
Greek

Books by Harry Mark Petrakis

NOVELS

Lion at My Heart
The Odyssey of Kostas Volakis
A Dream of Kings
In the Land of Morning
The Hour of the Bell
Nick the Greek
Days of Vengeance
Ghost of the Sun

SHORT STORIES

Pericles on 31st Street
The Waves of Night
A Petrakis Reader
Collected Stories

MEMOIRS AND ESSAYS

Stelmark
Reflections: A Writer's Life-A Writer's Work
Tales of the Heart

BIOGRAPHIES

The Founder's Touch
Henry Crown: The Life and Times of the Colonel